With Finding Love in  displays a real talent for on-your-luck romances, and this one doesn't disappoint. A great, well-written book!
 --Amy Matayo, award-winning author of *The End of the World* and *Sway*

Soul-satisfying romance, laugh-aloud humor, and characters so real they visited me in my dreams. Finding Love in Big Sky is my favorite book of the year.
-- Heather Woodhaven, author of *The Secret Life of Book Club*

Finding Love in Big Sky feels like my favorite holiday movies: Perfect casting, delightful witty banter, and a story deep enough to leave me emotional in the end. Purely delightful!
--Christina Coryell, author of *The Camdyn Series*

Praise for *Finding Love in Sun Valley, Idaho*

Once I started reading, I didn't want to stop. I thoroughly enjoyed each page of this book and am excited to find a new author to follow!
--Tracey Bateman, Christy award-winning author

Finding Love in Sun Valley, Idaho swept me off my feet! I fell in love with Tracen and Emily in this unique romance.
--Christina Berry Tarabochia, Carol award-winning author

Finding Love in Big Sky, Montana

Resort to Love Series

Finding Love in Sun Valley, Idaho
Finding Love in Big Sky, Montana
Finding Love in Park City, Utah

Finding Love in Big Sky, Montana

Book two in the Resort to Love Series

By
Angela Ruth Strong

Finding Love in Big Sky, Montana
Published by Mountain Brook Ink
White Salmon, WA U.S.A.

All rights reserved. Except for brief excerpts for review purposes, no part of this book may be reproduced or used in any form without written permission from the publisher.

The website addresses shown in this book are not intended in any way to be or imply an endorsement on the part of Mountain Brook Ink, nor do we vouch for their content.

This story is a work of fiction. All characters and events are the product of the author's imagination. Any resemblance to any person, living or dead, is coincidental.

Scripture quotations are taken from the King James Version of the Bible. Public domain.
ISBN 978-1-943959-10-5
© 2016 Angela Ruth Strong

The Team: Miralee Ferrell, Nikki Wright, Cindy Jackson, **Kristen Ventress**
Cover Design: Indie Cover Design, Lynnette Bonner Designer

Mountain Brook Ink is an inspirational publisher offering fiction you can believe in.
Printed in the United States of America

First Edition 2016

1 2 3 4 5 6 7 8 9 10

To Charla, a gift from heaven

When they saw the star, they rejoiced exceedingly with great joy. -- Matthew 2:10

ACKNOWLEDGEMENTS

God—I had worse writer's block with this story than with any other story, but now it could very well be my favorite. God gets all the glory for that.

Jim—Writers probably don't make the best housewives. But I'm enough for him anyway. Now that's a love story.

My Kiddos—The month I finished this novel, I actually warned them I wouldn't be making sense when I spoke because I was in fiction land. My daughter responded, "Fun!" And it was, thanks to them.

My mom—It's a joke among writers that you should never think your book is good just because your mom likes it. But most writers don't have my mom. She was my first editor and my biggest cheerleader.

My dad—In my next book, I'll finally give the main character a good dad. He'll call to check on her all the time and brag about her everywhere he goes just like my dad does for me.

Miralee—I never would have written this story if she hadn't offered a three-book contract. I've learned a lot, and now I have a new mentor/friend.

Kristin—Her gracious editing and words of wisdom made this story better and encouraged me not to give up on getting that last line perfect.

Heather—I always love sharing my stories with my critique partner because she is so understanding and encouraging.

Corinne—All I know about horses I learned from a day at her farm. This book would have been an embarrassment if not for my trip to Willows Edge.

Leslie and Rosie—These women inspired the characters of Dot and Annabel. I should bring them along to book-signings so you can all get their autographs, as well. Such joy is contagious.

Safe Place Ministries—A safe place for Christian women healing from abuse. And where I go for godly counsel when God allows trials in my life to grow me the same way I do to my characters.

CHAPTER ONE

PAISLEY SHERIDAN PINNED HER LAST HELP wanted flyer to the bulletin board between an advertisement for Breakfast with Santa and free ski passes to Military Appreciation Day. Maybe next year she'd have time for holiday fun, but this year she had work to do, and she needed to hire someone to help her do it.

She stepped back and took a deep breath. Was she really ready for this? Did she have what it took to reopen Grandpa's old ranch? Only one way to find out.

Hopefully she'd get a response to the flyers she'd hung all over town. For now she'd reward her efforts with a sugar-free cream cheese croissant and warm up with a cappuccino. She'd purposefully made The Coffee Cottage her final stop, as Dot and Annabel were sure to want to play "twenty questions."

"Let's see it." Dot clapped her hands and stepped from behind the counter to get a better look at the advertisement. Though the woman was close to Grandpa Johan's age when he died, she had more energy than Paisley.

Her best friend Annabel followed, pink cowboy boots clacking. "It's very lovely. How many people are you hiring?"

Paisley scrunched her nose. She only had the money for a single employee until the bank loan came through. If that wasn't enough, maybe she could recruit an intern. "One person at the moment. I need someone to help me host birthday parties and guide sleigh rides while I get ready for the building expansion in the spring."

Dot squealed. "That sounds like so much fun. Hire me."

Paisley couldn't help smiling at the memory of Dot trying to put a saddle on backwards the one time she'd visited the ranch. "You already have a job."

"Oh, yeah."

Annabel smacked her business partner's shoulder before turning to face Paisley. "So what are you building?"

Talking about her plans made them much more real. This was really happening. "Four cabins and a chapel-slash-cafeteria. And I'll be opening up the pond for ice skating in December to draw tourists and get publicity. Grandpa had it all planned but never got around to it."

Annabel's fake red hair brushed her shoulders as she nodded seriously. "I love skating rinks. Did you know I used to figure skate?"

Paisley laughed. Enthusiasm for life was contagious. "I had no idea, Annabel, but I can picture it." The woman would have been a beauty when she was younger. And out of the pair of store owners, she was the one with the tenacity to compete seriously. Dot was more the performer.

"Oh, you don't have to picture it. I've got photographs." Annabel trotted out through the back door, presumably to the upstairs apartment she shared with Dot.

Paisley glanced at her watch. "Can I get a cream cheese croissant while I wait to see Annabel's pictures?" She enjoyed the socializing as much as she enjoyed the fresh pastries filling the air with their sweet scent, but her day demanded she enjoy them at the same time.

"Yes, yes, in a moment." Dot reached up to grab the brim of the knit newsboy hat she wore over spiky silver hair. "But first . . . I have a picture of my own to show you." She whipped off the cap and spun to reveal where she'd shaved the back part of her head to have a cross tattooed on her skull.

Paisley blinked in shock, thanking God that Dot was facing the other direction and couldn't see her reaction.

Dot pivoted around.

Paisley forced the corners of her lips to turn up in a smile. She had to say something. But what?

"I got a tattoo!"

That much was obvious, though the reason behind such an act was not. "Why did you put it on your head?"

Dot shrugged. "I figured if I didn't like it, I could grow my hair over it and nobody would ever have to look at it again."

"Of course."

"Earl used to make fun of me because I was afraid to get tattoos. Well, he has no room to talk now."

Paisley's toes curled in her boots at the thought of the pain that surely came with needles to the scalp. Dot really went to extremes to get over an ex. Paisley wasn't that bad, was she? Moving to a different state and reopening the ranch as a retreat center and kids' camp was something she'd have loved to do anyway. And it wasn't going to bring her pain. Only healing. "Didn't that hurt?" she asked.

"Sweetie, I wanted to kick the tattoo artist in his face."

Paisley choked on her spit at the image. "You didn't, did you?"

"I couldn't. He was behind me."

"That's a relief." Paisley pulled a scarred, wooden chair out from a nearby table to take a seat. She didn't want to be standing for any more outrageous news.

The skin around Dot's eyes crinkled into a familiar pattern as she grinned. "Snake is a marvelous man actually. I can't believe he doesn't own a Harley. Anyway, he's going to let me be his apprentice."

Sitting wasn't enough. Paisley also needed to clean out her ears. Because she couldn't have heard that correctly. "You're going to . . . you're going to become a tattoo artist?"

"Yessiree. It will have to be a side job. Good thing I didn't take your horse ranch position."

Paisley stared. "Good thing."

"But before I start at the tattoo parlor, Snake has me taking art classes first."

Saved by the clack of Annabel's boots. "We are both taking art classes. Invite her to the Christmas art show this weekend, Dot."

"You have to come see our art sometime this weekend."

That was better than having Dot want to practice tattoo design on her body. "Sure. I'd love to."

Dot clapped again before scampering behind the counter to retrieve Paisley's order. Then both women leaned over her shoulders as Annabel shared the newspaper clippings. According to photo captions, the woman had been an Olympic hopeful in the 60s. Who'd have thought?

The bell tinkled above the front door, and cold air rushed in to announce the entry of a group of skiers. Dot and Annabel scurried back to work, leaving Paisley to eat her croissant and read the articles in peace. Except she didn't. She watched the older women laugh and joke and charm their customers. They were single like her, but they weren't alone. They had each other.

Paisley might have a purpose, but she didn't have anybody to share it with. Not even family, as Mom had died years ago, and she'd been glad to leave her dad in Sun Valley.

That's what she wanted for Christmas. A friend who not only cared about her big ideas, but pursued them alongside her. A friend who made her a better person. A friend who took her mind off the ache of emptiness that came with her cancelled wedding.

JOSHUA LAKE'S WHOLE BODY ached with exhaustion. He blinked awake and tightened his grip on the steering wheel. How long had he been driving now? The sun had recently come up to reflect off the snow and blind him, proving he'd successfully pulled his first all-nighter since college. Though he doubted anyone would call him a success.

He glanced at the dashboard clock. Ten in the morning. That meant he'd been behind the wheel for almost twenty-four hours. Practically a whole day. Worst day of his life.

Josh shifted his weight from one numb butt cheek to the other then arched his back to stretch his sore spine. He pressed the window lever in hopes of reviving himself with crisp mountain air. He was used to the icy wind, but the sweet earthy scent of pine trees stung his nostrils. He definitely wasn't in Chicago anymore.

According to the GPS screen on his dashboard, he had another five hours until he reached Tracen's house in Sun Valley, Idaho. Which was worse? Driving five more hours or facing his brothers with their questions of why he'd had to drive in the first place?

He'd always been the prosperous brother. First the cocky bull-rider. Then the big city businessman. Yet now he didn't have enough money to spend the night in a cheap hotel—not that there were going to be any cheap hotels in the next town of Big Sky. Most gorgeous ski resort he'd ever visited. Back when he could afford it.

Dare he pull his brand new Mercedes to the side of the road and recline the seat for a little shut-eye, huddled underneath his goose down parka? Or should he muscle through with the radio blaring and caffeine pumping in his veins?

He cranked up the volume to yet another station playing holiday music, to inspire himself to sing along. But all the cheerful songs started sounding the same after a while. Where was Elvis's rendition of Blue Christmas when he needed it?

He squared his jaw as he rounded a bend. The Coffee Cottage. As close to an oasis as he could get in this frozen landscape.

The small brown coffee shop looked more like a house than a business with its bright red trim and steep, blue metal roof peeking out from a blanket of snow. White twinkle lights and a wicker reindeer on the steps gave it a girly feel, but surely the owners could sell him a manly cup of black coffee. He glanced at the coins in his center console. That's all he'd be able to afford anyway.

He slowed to pull off the road and park then scooped the change into his pocket and unfolded his limbs from the front seat. Too bad he'd traded in his Lexus for this new lease. Now he couldn't even sell the car to get a little cash. He was that pathetic.

Snow crunched under his feet. He'd forgotten what silence sounded like. It made him itch with apprehension.

The bell over the bright red door jingled as he entered, slicing through the quiet like an alarm clock. If only it could wake him from this nightmare.

"Joshua Lake."

Someone recognized him? His nightmare was getting worse.

That voice. That tone. Where had he heard it before? And why was he hearing it in Big Sky?

He scanned the room. Two grandmothers dressed like high schoolers twittered and gabbed from behind the counter. One glanced his way for a moment before focusing back on the group of men laughing at their antics. There. With her elbows propped on a nearby table, her ambereyes focused on him. Where had he seen those freckles before?

Sheridan Ranch. Paisley Sheridan. She'd been a little behind him in school—in Sam's class, if he remembered correctly—and seemed to avoid him when he'd worked with her dad. He'd gotten the impression it was because she was disgusted with all the girls he dated as a teenager, but he was a changed man now.

Not that Paisley's opinion mattered. Or it shouldn't matter. So why did he cringe at the idea of admitting to her he was broke and alone at Christmas?

He didn't actually have to admit he was broke, did he? He'd turn on his charm and keep the conversation focused on her. He'd make her like him. Then maybe he'd like himself a little better.

"Paisley Sheridan. What are you doing here? Aren't you supposed to be on the top of a Christmas tree this time of year?"

PAISLEY FOUGHT THE URGE to roll her eyes. He was calling her an angel? Figured. Most girls from high school would have blushed and giggled at such a line, but that had never been their relationship. And ten years later, Josh should know not to expect anything else from her. "What are you doing here? Aren't you supposed to be giving Mary a ride to Bethlehem?"

One corner of his mouth curved up as he sauntered her way. His eyes narrowed in scrutiny. "Are you calling me a—"

"Yes."

"Same old Paisley."

"Same old Josh."

A warm current zipped through her body. Like that day when she was eight and she'd touched an electric fence even though Dad told her not to. This was worse.

Of all the times for Josh to show up in her life, it had to be right after she swore off men. She'd wanted a friend, but not one whose kiss made her feel as if her blood sugar dipped too low.

Of course, there was no reason they ever had to see each other again. He was probably only in town for the holidays. Maybe even on his honeymoon. After all, he'd been engaged the last time she'd spoken with his brother. Goodness, she shouldn't be thinking about kissing him at all.

There wasn't any mistletoe around, was there? She did a quick scan of the doorways to make sure she was safe. For the moment. Though she retrieved a tube of lip gloss from her pocket because her lips felt dry all of a sudden.

"Seriously, what are you doing here? Vacation?" he pressed. "You must be doing well for yourself."

Not yet. But she was living in a spot where others vacation. That was pretty good, right? She'd tell herself it was. She glazed the makeup wand over her lips then rubbed them together. "I inherited my grandpa's ranch."

He planted one palm on the back of the chair across from her and leaned onto it as if he needed it to hold him up. "What an opportunity."

Dot appeared. "It is. Paisley's turning the ranch into a retreat center and camp. It's going to be great. I'd go work for her myself if I wasn't already training to become a tattoo artist."

Paisley stuck her lip gloss back in her pocket. She might not have to talk to Josh after all. Dot could do it for her. Paisley would sit back and enjoy the entertainment of Josh's expressions as he struggled with how to respond to the shop owner.

His eyes widened. And they looked a little bloodshot for some reason. "What an opportunity," he said again. Was he okay?

Dot clapped her hands. "Oh, Joshua, you have to see my tattoo." She whirled and removed her hat all in one motion.

Paisley dragged her eyes from Josh to frown up at Dot. How did they know each other? "You know him?"

Had Josh been coming to the shop regularly? Had he moved to Big Sky? That meant there would be the chance of running into him repeatedly. She might have to start starving her sweet tooth to keep that from happening.

"I do now." Dot sat her hat back on her head. "I heard you call him by name when he entered, and I'm sure we are going to be the best of friends." She looked over her shoulder at the man in question. "You like tattoos and coffee, right Joshua?"

There was that half smirk again. His gaze dipped to Paisley for a second. "Love them. How much for a cup of black coffee?"

"First cup is always free for Paisley's friends," Annabel called from behind the counter as she poured him a steaming mug.

Paisley pressed her lips together to keep from arguing that he wasn't her friend. She didn't need the older women to admonish her for being such a Grinch. And she didn't want to answer any questions about what kind of relationship she used to have with Josh. Especially in front of him.

Josh stuck a hand in his pocket and coins clinked. Somehow paying for coffee with change didn't match the image she had of "the same old Josh." And where was that fiancée of his? Back in Chicago? Had he left her there for a reason? Paisley should have gotten a look at his ring finger before his hand disappeared from view.

"That's really nice of you, ma'am. Could I possibly get the coffee to go? I've been driving all night, and I have five more hours until I reach Sun Valley."

"What?" Dot took the words right out of Paisley's mouth. Though Paisley wouldn't have had quite the volume or dramatic flair.

Paying for coffee with change was one thing, but driving cross-country? According to Josh's little brother Sam, Josh always flew first class. And besides, driving straight through from Chicago by himself wasn't safe. "That's not safe."

"I know." Josh shifted his weight. He looked out the window then at Paisley. "The last pass was closed, otherwise I'd be there by now."

Paisley tilted her head. Something was off.

Annabel clomped over and held out the paper cup he'd requested. "Aren't you exhausted? You should really get some sleep."

All three women watched as he took a sip. He didn't seem as comfortable with the female attention as Paisley remembered.

He cleared his throat. "I'll sleep when I get there. I doubt there are any hotel rooms open here as it's ski season and all."

"Not true." Dot turned from Josh to Annabel. "That's not true, is it? Didn't Hazel say there was a cancellation at her bed and breakfast this morning?"

Annabel nodded. "Yes, I believe she did. I'll go call her right now and—"

"Wait." Josh scrunched his eyebrows together and rubbed a couple fingers to his temple. No wedding band.

Not that it mattered. Maybe he lost the ring. Or he was going to get a ring tattoo. Dot could help with that. The sooner the better because . . .

She shook her head to remind herself it didn't matter.

He opened his eyes to meet Paisley's scrutiny honestly, without the normal flash of arrogance. "I can't pay to stay here. I'm broke."

Her chin didn't completely drop, but her lips parted a little. Josh had been voted most likely to succeed in high school, and she'd never doubted it for a minute. He looked rich in his shiny boots, designer jeans, and thick sweater. Even his messy hair appeared professionally styled. How could he possibly be broke, not to mention single?

His gaze flicked to the floor then up to meet hers. "It's a long story, but let's just say two days ago I was ordering thousand dollar bottles of wine, and now I can barely afford coffee."

That would be quite a story. But it was none of her business. He'd be fine for a few more hours on the road. Then Sam could take care of him. Sam—the former soldier and firefighter—was good at rescuing people.

"Oh, sweetie." Dot enveloped one of his big hands between hers. "I was in the same place when I arrived five years ago. But God provides. And I believe He brought you to us for a reason."

Josh's jaw shifted side to side. He looked Paisley's way. He probably wasn't used to charity.

She lifted her eyebrows in response. How silly of her to think Dot would actually let him go. Dot liked being a part of everyone's business. She wasn't only a coffee shop owner and tattoo artist in training, Dot was a rescue hero in her own right.

"You'll never believe this, but. . . ." Dot turned sideways to motion toward Paisley. Uh-oh. "Paisley has a whole bunk house at her ranch.

Nobody is using it right now. In fact, if you need money, she could hire you."

Paisley took back her former sentiment. Dot ruined lives.

CHAPTER TWO

JOSH IMAGINED A COLD, LOG ROOM filled with bunkbeds. Under normal circumstances the image wouldn't be considered inviting. But after a full day of sitting behind a steering wheel . . .

The vision faded, forcing him to focus on Paisley's horrified expression. Really? Why did she find the idea so repulsive? He wasn't a stranger. He wasn't rude or uncivilized. People usually liked having him around. Until lately.

Fine. He wouldn't go where he wasn't wanted. This was the kind of reaction he'd left Chicago to avoid. "No, I couldn't impose."

Dot shoved Paisley out of her seat. "No imposition," said the older woman.

Paisley's eyes grew round as she helplessly stumbled toward him. It would have been cute if he didn't feel like a burden forced upon her—if he wasn't getting set up for more rejection. He held up his free hand to catch her upper arm and steady her.

She froze as soon as he made contact. Her mouth opened and closed a couple times, and though nothing came out, her message was loud and clear. The one person who could provide him a chance to get some much-needed sleep was snubbing him.

He dropped his hand. "I'm sure you're busy. I'll be fine with my coffee."

Yeah. Give her an excuse to get rid of him and console her for feeling bad about it at the same time. But it was better than hearing the words come from her mouth.

How had his life come to this? He was supposed to be the guy who took the risks. The guy people couldn't say no to. The guy women adored.

She looked up into his eyes. That wasn't adoration. That was pity. And it stung like Chicago wind. He'd be better off blowing the place.

Her eyes shifted to something past him. Her face softened. Her shiny lips pressed together as if trying to hide a smile, but a dimple flashed anyway.

Josh twisted his neck to follow her gaze.

The red-headed woman behind him froze with her head tilted and her hands tucked under one cheek, pantomiming sleeping. Her eyes blinked when she realized she'd been caught. She straightened and cleared her throat.

She'd been pleading his case, which was very sweet, but—

The woman with the head tattoo stepped forward. "You know what, Joshua? It doesn't appear Paisley is much of a friend to you, so we are going to have to charge you for your cup of coffee after all."

What? Was Paisley's dislike that contagious? Or had he truly become revolting all of a sudden? He'd best pay and make his escape.

Josh reached for his change once again. "How much?"

"A dollar twenty-five."

Paisley dropped her hands to her sides and stared at Dot, forehead wrinkling. Was she going to stand up for him now? Like a sibling who wanted to be the only one who picked on him? He'd had a couple brothers like that growing up. He could do without her false show of support.

Josh pulled the cool quarters from his pocket to count out the payment for the coffee.

"On second thought . . ." said Dot.

Josh kept counting. Thankfully, he had enough. He'd pay Dot whether she changed her mind again or not. He needed the coffee as much as he needed to get going.

"On second thought, the price of coffee beans is going up, and we need to raise our prices, as well. Two dollars."

The red-head gasped. "Dot."

Paisley held out her hands in disbelief. "What are you doing, Dot? He needs the caffeine to keep him awake for the drive home."

Dot shrugged. "If you were his friend, we'd give him the coffee for free, but then again, if you were his friend, he wouldn't need the coffee because you'd let him rest in your bunk house."

Coercion?

Paisley covered her face with both hands.

Any other day, Josh could sweet talk his way through such absurdity. But whether it was due to his lack of sleep or a lack of funds, the old lady had him outwitted. He'd have to ask for help.

"Paisley?" He swallowed over the lump of embarrassment in his throat. "Can I borrow seventy-five cents?" He'd pay her back. With interest. Heck, he'd buy her the whole coffee shop if she wanted. Once he got his job reinstated.

Paisley dropped her hand and gave him an incredulous smile. As if they were on the same team now—both being played like a game of Pinochle. "You don't need the coffee, Josh."

He searched her eyes. No more pity. No more resentment. Not quite friendship, but still an offer to work together. *If* that's what she was offering. He wouldn't assume anything. "I do if I'm going to drive—"

She rolled her eyes, but her smile stayed intact. "You're not going to drive home until you get some sleep. Come on. You can bunk at the ranch."

Dot raised her fists in victory.

Annabel laughed. "Dot, I never knew you were so clever."

"Me neither," Dot agreed.

Josh tightened his grip on the warm cup, not quite ready to accept her deal. He tilted his head toward the giggling shop owners and addressed Paisley. "You're going to let them win?"

Paisley pulled mittens out of her coat pockets. "I'm going to let them think they won."

Dot spun from her celebration with the red-head. "We *did* win."

Paisley headed toward the front door. "What they don't realize is that I'm winning by getting out of here and avoiding any more of their meddling. Even in my barn stalls, I have *less horse apples* to deal with." She looked at him but yelled the words back, loud enough for the women to hear.

Dot and the red-head laughed even louder.

It was nice they could laugh about it. Nice for them, but not for him. He was the joke.

Paisley obviously didn't want to have anything to do with him, but she was going to house him to make the old busybodies happy. He'd accept her grudging agreement because it was his best option. But he wouldn't leave indebted to her.

He was Joshua Lake, for goodness sake. And that should mean something. It used to.

If she needed help mucking out stalls or hauling hay, he could do it. It had been a while since he'd worked on a ranch, but he was older and more experienced now, so manual labor would be like child's play. Plus, it would keep him busy. There wasn't much he hated more than not having a goal to work toward.

No, he wasn't going to be a burden. He was going to be a bargain. By the time he left Paisley's ranch, she'd be begging him to stay.

PAISLEY COULD HANDLE ONE day. She would have preferred to avoid having Josh at the ranch, but this wasn't about her. He clearly needed the sleep. Which meant she wouldn't even have to interact with him at all, right? And she'd get Dot and Annabel off her back.

Those two—Dot especially—were more conniving than she'd realized. And as they were most likely trying to play matchmaker with her and Josh, she'd do better to get him away from their meddlesome behavior.

She reached for the doorknob to lead the man outside to safety.

His hand darted in front of her to grab the knob first. He pulled the door wide and stepped aside with one of those dashing grins that could have landed him a part in a toothpaste commercial. She preferred to think of it as a little too slick.

Dot and Annabel giggled. "What a gentleman," Dot called. But she didn't know Josh like Paisley did.

He did seem a little different, though. Maybe his recent poverty had humbled him.

She shot him a small smile to thank him for holding the door as she stepped through it. The smile froze on her face. Parked in front of her was a brand new silver Mercedes sports coupe. She didn't know whether to laugh or cry.

The door thunked shut, and she registered Josh's warmth at her back, but she continued to stare in shock. A laugh bubbled out like a hiccup. "What is *that*?"

Josh eased to her side on the tiny landing and ran a hand over his mouth. "My new car."

At least he sounded sheepish. How could he drive something so ostentatious and be broke at the same time? She'd laugh again if she weren't sobered by the fact he was going to have to ride with her now. "You can't drive that to the ranch. It's down a long, bumpy, gravel road covered in snow."

His eyes darted toward the car and back. "I'm sure it'll be fine."

Fine? If he was as poor as he said he was, it wouldn't be long before he'd have to sell the thing, and it wouldn't sell very well with scratches or dings from loose pebbles. And that was if it even made it all the way there.

She closed her eyes. *God, I'm really trying here. But he's trying me more.*

The car engine revved to life, drawing Paisley back to reality. She opened her eyes to find Josh had started the Mercedes by pushing a button on his remote. Did he really think he was going to follow her down the back roads in a luxury vehicle?

She lifted an eyebrow in challenge. "I'll let Dot and Annabel know you're leaving your car here while you grab your stuff. Then I'll meet you at my truck."

He tilted his head. "No, I don't want to—"

The bell interrupted him as she pushed the coffee shop door open again. She spoke over her shoulder. "It's a bit of a drive out to the ranch. I'm saving you gas money. Plus, you can sleep on the way."

He sighed and pressed a button on the remote to pop his trunk.

Later she'd find some special way to "thank" the coffee shop ladies for forcing her to take care of the man. For now, she just had to let them know they'd be babysitting his vehicle.

Dot stood on a chair at the far wall, hanging a strand of white twinkle lights as Annabel unraveled them for her. "Leave something here?"

Funny question. "I need to, actually. You don't mind letting Josh park his fancy little Mercedes out front overnight, do you?"

Both faces turned her way.

Dot climbed down from the chair, dropping the lights at Annabel's feet. "Joshua drives a fancy little Mercedes?"

"Ohhh . . ." Annabel gently laid down the rest of the strand.

They both rushed to the window.

"It's beautiful," Annabel whispered.

Paisley watched from behind the women as Josh swung a leather duffle bag over his shoulder, slammed the trunk, and waved. She ducked in hopes he hadn't seen her and mistakenly gotten the impression she was also admiring the vehicle. Because she wasn't admiring the car. Correction: She wasn't admiring anything at all.

With a huff, Paisley headed back outside to play chauffeur and innkeeper. That's all she was. Like the Good Samaritan. Though the Good Samaritan's heartrate probably didn't speed up when nearing the man in need.

She avoided eye contact and trekked through the snow toward the spot behind The Coffee Cottage where she'd parked her old truck out of the way. "Back here, city boy."

Josh crunched after her. Then the crunching stopped. "Whoa."

What? She glanced in his direction.

"You still drive Big Red?"

Josh knew about Big Red? Of course he did. It used to be her dad's truck. And it worked well for ranch life. When it wasn't breaking down. Fixing up the '77 Ford was always cheaper than replacing it. But someone like Josh probably couldn't relate to such a sentiment. Which might be why he'd gone bankrupt or whatever.

She brushed snow off the hood. "I thought about getting a Mercedes, but those don't haul hay as well."

His grin flashed. "I deserved that."

She looked down at her keys to hide her own smile, and not because she needed them to unlock Big Red's doors. Those were never locked. "Hop in."

The heavy door squeaked as Paisley hoisted herself into the driver's seat. The vinyl surface chilled her through her jeans, and the rip in the material tugged at a pocket. Not the interior Josh would be used to.

"Hey." Josh joined her on the bench seat and wrestled with the antiquated seatbelt until it loosened enough for him to buckle. "I'm sorry to put you in this position, but I really appreciate the place to stay."

She may not have wanted to spend the extra time with him, but she didn't have to be rude. "Don't worry about it." She turned the key. The engine sputtered and died. The perfect opportunity for Josh to hassle her about her vehicle in return. He stayed silent. Probably praying he wouldn't be stranded with her. She turned the key again.

The ignition cranked to life.

She relaxed into the squeaky springs.

Josh leaned his head back, as well . . . until she shifted into drive and stepped on the gas. Then the truck rocked over mounds of snow, knocking Josh sideways against the door.

He rubbed his scalp where his head had bumped glass. "You know, I'd like to pay you somehow. I'd work on Big Red if I was good with engines, but I'm not. So if there's anything else you need, let me know, okay?"

Paisley rolled past the coffee shop, ignoring the faces peering at them through the window. Wouldn't those old women love it if Josh stayed on to help her? Though that couldn't happen. And not only because the big businessman wouldn't want to stick around to feed animals and shovel poo. She'd graciously accept his empty gesture. "That's nice of you to offer, but I'm sure your family is anxiously awaiting your arrival."

Josh snorted.

Paisley turned onto the highway then slid her eyes sideways to covertly study Josh's expression. The man she expected him to be would have been much too smooth to make such a sound.

Josh rubbed his face. "I'm sorry. I'm apparently exhausted and can't handle a normal conversation."

She nodded. Since neither of them wanted to talk, she wouldn't talk.

He leaned into the corner between the door and seat, and within minutes, his head rocked to the side at an angle that couldn't in any way be comfortable. She scanned the floor for the blanket she carried with her in case Big Red broke down in the middle of nowhere. It must have been pushed under the seat. But if he pulled it out, he could use it to prop his head up.

She'd wait for a pause in Josh's rhythmic breathing to give the advice on getting comfortable. No pause. Not even when she bumped onto the gravel road. Wow, he was tired.

Guilt nibbled her gut at the realization she'd almost refused to let him stay. He could have fallen asleep at the wheel and totaled his Mercedes. Or worse.

What was wrong with her? Yeah, he'd snubbed her when they were teenagers. But that was a long time ago. His mistakes shouldn't change the kind of person she was. She liked helping people. And besides, it was Christmas.

She took a deep breath of resolve. She'd done the right thing. Dot and Annabel had also done the right thing.

It wouldn't be that bad. She'd house Josh the way the innkeeper housed Mary and Joseph when there was no room in the inn. Then he'd be on his way, and she'd get back to work on the ranch as if nothing had happened.

The red barn greeted her when she rounded a grove of evergreen trees. Memories of working in her childhood barn next to Josh invaded her thoughts. The way he spoke to the horses. The way he looked so regal and confident when riding. The way he rarely glanced her way.

She pulled up the driveway to the farmhouse and shifted into park. Now what? How did she wake the man in the passenger seat without making their circumstances more awkward?

She leaned back against the vinyl and glanced toward the top of the vehicle, though she was actually searching heaven for answers. No response from the Almighty, so she dropped her head to the side to survey Josh and analyze the situation.

Hazel eyes focused on her—not quite brown and not quite green. Usually they sparkled with mischief, daring others to keep up. But for some reason, most likely sleep deprivation, they watched her with hesitance, waiting for her to make the first move.

Her pulse throbbed in her neck.

Her first move would be to get Josh rested and back to The Coffee Cottage as quickly as possible. Maybe he could leave that same day after a nap. Otherwise she would get hurt again.

CHAPTER THREE

Josh yawned, stretched his aching neck side to side, and kicked out of the sleeping bag. The room was warmer now as Paisley apparently built a fire after he'd all but collapsed on a mattress. It crackled and popped and filled the room with the scent of burning cedar, bringing back memories from standing around the burn barrels at his parents' Christmas tree farm as a kid. The gas fireplace back in Chicago didn't compare.

Had he really gone that soft? Not only did he drive a car incapable of making it to Paisley's ranch, but he'd lie down and let her do the work needed to build the fire. No wonder she'd cringed at the idea of taking him in. He was going to have to split logs and shovel snow to keep from losing all her respect—if she had any left.

She certainly had *his* respect. He didn't know any other woman who could possibly run a whole ranch on her own. Of course, the place was incredible—the surrounding mountains as majestic as the barn was quaint. This would be the perfect place to spend Christmas if he wasn't broke and alone.

On that depressing note, Josh swung his feet to the floor. A look out the window at the dark sky told him he'd slept a lot longer than he'd planned. He pushed to his feet and fished in the pocket of his jacket hung over the side of the bunk. Smooth plastic met his fingers. He pulled his cell phone out and clicked on a button to view the screen.

Five o'clock in the evening. When was the last time he'd gone all day without looking at his phone? Would anyone even have missed him, or would his coworkers and former fiancée all have gone on with their lives as usual?

No text or emails. The realization of his insignificance registered as an itch underneath his ribs. He couldn't reach it to scratch, so he'd have to distract himself from the discomfort.

He'd tell himself it was the mark of a good leader that he'd trained his assistant well enough to take over for him when he was gone. But what about relationships? Was he nothing more than a moneymaker to Synergy Ad Agency? And what about Bree?

Unfortunately, he already knew the answer to that question.

His brothers might not say, "I told you so," but they had. Back when Bree had been too busy to travel with him to Tracen's wedding.

Josh sighed. He'd call Tracen now. If Paisley drove him back to town, he could be in Sun Valley by ten o'clock. She'd surely be thrilled with the thought of getting rid of him. He punched in the number and waited for it to connect.

A "dialing" icon appeared. It spun lazily. And it kept spinning.

Josh squinted. He checked the connection signal. No bars. So that's why he hadn't received any texts or emails.

He grabbed his expensive new boots. If he'd known he was going to be going home for the holidays, he would have spent all that money on a pair of boots that provided warmth rather than just looking sharp. Too late for that now. Unless there was a voicemail waiting for him with good news.

In a rush to borrow Paisley's landline, Josh scrambled out the door before stuffing his arms in his coat sleeves. Soft snowflakes floated down, stinging as they melted against his skin. He pulled the coat closed and yanked up his hood, but it fell back down as he ran. Later he could focus on the beauty and serenity of nature. Right now he had to reconnect with his life.

For all he knew, Marcus had already proven Josh hadn't leaked Computex's ad campaign to their competitors, even though it appeared that way when Digimax's commercial aired. If that were the case, Computex would have kept their agreement to sign with Synergy Ad Agency, and Josh would have a big fat deposit waiting in his bank account. He'd have to get back to work immediately. He'd catch the first flight to Chicago and leave his car to his little brother Sam. Nobody would be making fun of the Mercedes then.

He pounded up the stairs to the deck of the main lodge entrance, directly above the part of the building with a sign that read "Office." Through the wall of windows, he spotted Paisley in a kitchen alcove at the back of the great room, stirring something in a pot on the stove. She'd probably offer him dinner, but if Marcus had come through, he'd take her to Moonlight Tavern to celebrate—and to thank her for letting him stay in her bunkhouse. Maybe she would like him then.

He grinned as he knocked on the large, solid door. All he'd needed was a little sleep to put his life back into perspective.

The lock jiggled and the knob turned. The door swung open to bathe him in light, warmth, and the buttery scent of bread and salty smell of seafood.

Paisley didn't smile, though she didn't frown, either. He'd consider that an improvement. "I was beginning to think you would sleep all night," she said.

He gave her a confident smile because he was going to win her over yet. "Think about me a lot?"

She stepped back so he could enter but crossed her arms. "Ways to get rid of you."

"Well." He surveyed the vaulted room being held up by log beams. Huge place for a single woman. "If you let me use your phone, then that could possibly be arranged."

She closed the door and pointed toward an iron and stone end table before returning to the stove.

Not bothering to shrug out of his jacket despite the heat, Josh dialed his own phone number on the corded phone that had to be left over from when Paisley's grandpa owned the place. When he didn't answer the cell phone, it clicked over to voicemail. Josh pushed in his passcode to retrieve messages.

A recording greeted him. His heart thrummed in his chest. *Please God, let there be a message from Marcus.*

"You have zero new messages."

Zero? Not even an "I'm trying to clear this up, Josh"? Heck, he'd even take an "I miss you, and I want to get back together" from Bree. He wouldn't actually take Bree back, but it would be nice to be missed.

He slouched into the leather cushions. Maybe he *should* have slept all night.

"Clam chowder?" Paisley appeared beside him holding a steaming bowl. She was nice when she felt pity for him. He preferred her feisty side.

As for the chowder? His stomach growled.

"Thank you." He took the bowl without looking into her eyes. Even though they hadn't been in the same graduating class, seeing her feel sorry for him made him feel like they were at a high school reunion and he was the bald, fat guy who'd once been football captain. He may not be bald and fat, but he was practically unemployed. How stupid of him to think he could impress her by taking her out for a steak dinner.

She retrieved a bowl for herself and lowered onto the couch across from him. "So, how long am I going to be stuck with you?"

Josh stirred the thick soup. When was the last time he'd eaten homemade chowder? Probably never. Nice of her to share her dinner.

Life could be worse, right? He could be stranded in his car in the snow. Or she could be treating him with kid gloves rather than challenging him with her sass.

"Not long. If you'll drive me back to the coffee shop, I can make it to Sun Valley before midnight."

She nodded. Took a bite.

He followed suit. The hearty mixture ignited his taste buds and warmed his insides. He might have to have seconds.

"Who were you calling?"

He looked up. He hadn't expected such a question, though he *had* implied he was calling someone who could possibly get him out of her hair.

Her gaze darted back down to her bowl but not before he caught the curious glint. He might as well give her an explanation. It was the least he could do, since he wouldn't be able to thank her financially for a while.

"I was hoping to have voicemail from the owner of the advertising company I work for." Should he call Marcus? He would after the weekend if he didn't hear anything. But as it was already 6:00 in Chicago, Marcus would have gone home for the day. "I made a pitch to a computer company. It would have been the biggest deal I'd ever gotten. The biggest deal anybody at Synergy had ever gotten. Television, radio, magazine, billboard. The works. They were going to sign yesterday."

She studied him with renewed interest. Maybe he could impress her after all.

"My commission would have been enough to retire on. And I . . . uh . . . celebrated a little prematurely. I took my whole team out on the town. Traded in my car. Booked a cruise for my honeymoon." Okay, not impressive at all.

Her eyes narrowed. "What happened?"

Was she asking about the job or the fiancée? Same answer. "A competitor's commercial aired with my very same campaign idea."

She let go of her spoon and clutched her bowl with both hands. "How?"

That was the twenty-million-dollar question. He shrugged. "I have no clue. They accused me of stealing the idea. But it was my idea. I don't know how it ended up with another agency. So I'm on leave without pay while they investigate."

PAISLEY RUBBED HER LIPS together. It was a lot of information to process. Now the car and fancy clothes made sense, as well as the lack of funds. He hadn't explained the fiancée situation, but that was none of her business. If she wanted to know, she'd check with Dot and Annabel who would probably get the information out of him when she took him back to the coffee shop to pick up his car. Or she could ask Sam. But no, she didn't want to know.

It was the advertising part that should interest her. How had she not remembered Josh worked in marketing? And he must have been pretty good at it.

She might not want him around, but she couldn't ignore the fact that she was in the middle of designing a logo for the new name of her ranch. And he owed her.

How could she tactfully suggest he give her advice as a consultant? She'd have to be subtle so she could maintain her distance. What were they talking about again?

Leave without pay . . . She connected a few more dots. "Which is why you are driving to stay with your brother in Sun Valley."

Josh blew his breath into his cheeks as if about to share something big. How much bigger could it get?

He met her gaze. His hazel eyes hid nothing, not even the hope of gaining her understanding. Again, not the expression she was used to from him.

She scooted away without meaning to. But that kind of openness threatened to cut through the cast she'd wrapped around her heart in order for it to heal.

Josh registered her movement. He looked down but then met her gaze again—this time as if expecting her to kick him out. "I would have stayed in Chicago if not for the fact my fiancée believed I'd stolen the ideas and didn't feel she could trust me anymore. We were supposed to elope and get married in the Bahamas over Christmas, so she'd sold her condo to move in with me."

Paisley sank back into the cushions. Josh wasn't only dumped, he was dumped unfairly. Yet, if she understood correctly, he'd left home so his ex had a roof over her head. "She's living in your place?"

Josh ran a hand over his mouth. "Yes."

Paisley stared. Who was this man?

"Pretty pathetic, huh?"

She blinked. More like heroic. Not that she would ever tell him so. But what had his fiancée been thinking? How could Paisley encourage him without telling him she thought his ex was missing out? Though, of course, the ex would probably get back together with Josh when his company absolved him of any wrongdoing. "I'm sure your company will get this all cleared up. In the meantime, you get to go to Sun Valley for Christmas."

Josh looked down at the bowl in his hands. "And I got to stay at a gorgeous Montana ranch and eat some good home cookin' on the way."

He didn't mention the joy of having her company, but that shouldn't be surprising. She hadn't shown him her most pleasant side. He knew she'd been trying to get rid of him. But now she needed him to stay a bit longer. And he'd given her just the opening to do so by mentioning her gorgeous Montana ranch.

"You want the tour?" She could lead him into the office where she'd hopefully left her logo design file open on the computer. If the computer was in sleep mode, she could offer to let him check email—in case his employer wrote, of course.

Josh stood and headed toward the kitchen area with his bowl. "I'd love a tour. And I'd love to hear what you're planning for this place. Such an amazing opportunity."

"I think you said that already." Paisley rushed to grab his bowl and beat him to the sink to let the dishes soak. She didn't want to waste his time cleaning up the kitchen when she could be using him as a pro bono advertising consultant.

Josh leaned one hand on the butcher block island. "What else did I say at the coffee shop? I was pretty sleep deprived at the time. It's all kind of a blur."

He'd called her an angel. Which had made her think he was his old flirtatious self when really he was healing from a broken heart, same as her. But they didn't need to discuss that subject anymore.

She motioned him forward and flipped a switch to illuminate the hallway wall sconces. "I think you told Dot you'd let her give you a tattoo."

Josh's lips curled up in amusement, which was almost more attractive than his "charming smile." He followed her to the doorway of the den and leaned on it, looking at her rather than Grandpa's wooden carvings and hunting trophies. "I did not."

"Yeah, you did. She invited you to her art show and you said, 'I'd actually rather have you give me a tattoo like yours.'" She left him looking after her as she descended the steps toward the office.

Footsteps thumped down the stairs after her. "You'd be willing to shave the back of my head for me, wouldn't you?"

Not a chance. She couldn't get close to him. But she didn't want him to know that. "Sure." She turned at the bottom of the stairs to give him her most innocent expression. See? She could be charming, too. It was almost as good a defense as being irritable.

He smirked down at her. "You want to design the tattoo, as well?"

Butterflies stirred in her belly. She needed to go back to being irritable. Charm could easily backfire on her, but it did give her the segue she needed. "I've never designed a tattoo before, but I'm working on a design logo for the ranch. Want to see?"

He lifted his eyebrows. "Even more than I want a tattoo on my head."

"That much, huh?" She turned away to keep him from becoming aware of her delight at his response. And to lead him around the center of the T-shaped desk.

"I can hardly contain myself." He followed. "Are you going to keep the horseshoe your dad used?"

"No." She rolled the leather chair out, took a seat, and clicked the mouse. "Horseshoes are used a lot. Plus, this place is going to be more of a retreat center and camp for kids. So I want a logo that has something to do with kids. And with God's love for them."

She clicked to minimize the screen with her website design and opened the file for her logo. The outline of a star with the silhouette of a horse inside had taken her days to produce. But she was proud of it. Maybe more than consultation, she wanted validation. She wanted a top ad executive to tell her she was on the right track. She looked expectantly over her shoulder.

Josh rested his square jaw on his fist as he studied her image. His eyes didn't sparkle the way she'd hoped they would. They squinted instead. "Star Horse Ranch?"

"No, Bright Star Ranch. Like the star the three wise men followed to find baby Jesus."

He nodded. "I like the name. It's memorable, and it conveys your purpose."

She slumped. "You don't like the logo?" But simply because he didn't like it, that didn't mean other people wouldn't. She didn't have to change it. She didn't want to change it. With the building expansion and the sleigh rides she'd already booked, she didn't have the time to spend another week perfecting something that was good enough.

Josh clicked his tongue. "It's not that I don't like it. It's that it doesn't fit the name. You need something simple and bright, while this is..."

"Dark."

"Yeah. And kind of..."

"Busy."

Was it better that she said it instead of him? Because that meant she was admitting she saw the problem as well. She should have argued, sent him away, and done her own thing. He didn't even work for an advertising agency anymore. What did he know?

He nodded to her seat. "May I?"

What could it hurt? She spun in the chair and stood so he could take her place.

He deleted the horse. He clicked on the icon to draw. "The best designs and ideas are the ones that are so perfect, whenever somebody sees them, they think, 'I should have been able to come up with that.' You don't want complicated. You want catchy. Memorable."

Okay, he made sense. She'd have to take his advice and run with it. Because he had to leave soon, and he couldn't possibly whip something together before—

"There. What do you think?"

Paisley blinked. It was so perfect she should have been able to come up with it.

"If I had more time I could play with the font, but this is a good place to start."

He was a genius. She wasn't going to mess with font. He'd nailed it. If she had the same kind of budget Computex had, she'd *so* hire him.

He grinned up at her. "I'm going to tell myself you're speechless." He twisted back to the computer, and his tone turned wry. "That's what I've been telling myself about everybody who doesn't want to talk to me right now. Less crushing to my ego."

"No, I really am... I'm..." She waved her arms around, looking for the right word, even though he couldn't see her from his position. "I'm speechless."

He clicked on the mouse to reopen her website design program. "Your logo should go right here." He added the design in. "Though I can give you feedback on your website, too, if you want."

She'd be stupid not to take it. But . . . She glanced at her watch.

It was after six already. If Josh didn't get going, he wouldn't make it to Sun Valley before midnight, and she couldn't let him pull another all-nighter.

She dropped her wrist and grimaced.

Josh's eyes flashed green in the dim light. He'd caught her checking the time. "What else are you going to do to promote the place?"

She hadn't thought that far ahead. The logo had been her first step. "Business cards. Flyers." What else was there? "Newspaper ad?"

Josh waited. Did he think she could afford more than that?

She twisted her lips to one side as she thought. "Ice skating?"

Josh's eyes bulged, but he blinked the expression away. "Very creative."

"*I* thought so."

Josh spun his chair all the way around to face her. "I've got a lot more ideas, Paisley. And I've got nothing else to do."

She stepped back. What was he suggesting?

"I know you were planning to hire a ranch hand, but I think you need a marketer even more. I'm the best, and I'll work for free. All you have to do is feed me, and let me stay in the bunk house."

Him? He wanted her to hire him?

They'd worked together before, and she'd been crushed when he'd left. But she was older now. And this could be the difference between her dream taking off and her dream never leaving the ground.

Warning sirens sounded their alarm in her head, in her heart. She blocked them out. Because this wasn't about her. It was about the lives she wanted to touch. About the change she wanted to make in the world.

She'd be stupid to look this Christmas gift horse in the mouth. Wasn't she thinking only moments ago that she'd hire him if she had the funds? Well, now she had the funds. "You're hired."

CHAPTER FOUR

"You're really going to leave me alone with the coffee shop owners?"

Paisley tried not to laugh at Josh's grimace as she turned Big Red into the Town Center parking lot where Gallatin River Gallery would be displaying locals' artwork in a Christmas Bazaar extravaganza. "What's wrong with Dot and Annabel?" she asked. "They like you better than anyone else in town."

Josh looked her direction, chin lowered, eyebrows raised in challenge. "You're the only other person in town who knows me."

"Yeah? Well then, this is a chance for you to meet more people." He wouldn't acknowledge her backhanded compliment. Every time she put Josh down, he'd try harder to charm her. It was actually kind of fun. "Rich people spend lots of money on art. They should be your kind of people."

He narrowed his eyes. "I wouldn't be complaining, except I thought you'd want to keep me away from your conniving friends and their matchmaking ways."

Paisley's knuckles cramped around the steering wheel. Why did he have to bring up the idea of matchmaking at all? She'd been doing so well pretending she didn't feel anything toward him. She'd keep pretending. "They're harmless, really."

Except for when Dot acted like she'd slipped on the ice to get the doctor over to the coffee shop to meet her niece. Now John and Whitney were planning a summer wedding. And then there was the time Annabel said she'd meet the children's church director at Riverhouse Grill to discuss curriculum, but what she'd really wanted to do was introduce the woman to their waiter. Seth and Marissa were expecting their baby any day.

Josh tilted his head. "There are a lot of words I'd use for Dot and Annabel, but harmless isn't one of them."

Paisley scrunched up her nose as she pulled up to the entrance. "You may be right. Keep an eye open for mistletoe, and if all else fails, ask Dot to design you a tattoo."

Josh reached for the door handle but tilted his head toward her. "Because having ink permanently embedded into my skin is better than kissing you?"

"Yes." Well, no, but it would be safer. Not that she was going to go into details. "Now get out. I'll join you after I meet with the loan officer at the bank."

"Got it." Josh opened the door, letting in a burst of frigid air. "I'd wish you luck, but I'm probably the one who's going to need it."

She waved him away, but couldn't keep from smiling. Maybe Dot and Annabel would set him up with someone else, and she wouldn't have to worry so much. Though he was hardly in a place for starting a new relationship. Unfortunately, she knew what that felt like.

At least she was in a good place now. She was a ranch owner. With big plans for the future.

Paisley took her foot off the brake to roll through the shopping center designed to look rustic with exposed wooden beams and stonework. White twinkle lights and a huge Christmas tree had also been added since Thanksgiving the week before.

She pulled up at the curb in front of the building with a flat, square façade similar to one from the Wild West. Shifting into park, she hoped she'd made it between parking lot lines since it was hard to tell with the layer of fresh snow. Heather, the teller, already knew her, but she wanted to make a good first impression on Mr. Allen Marshall.

She pulled off her boots to change into black heels that would dress up her jeans and sweater, then she double checked her folder with all the financial records for the ranch and her own taxes from the year before.

Grandpa had slowly been selling off the horses until the ranch was a lot smaller than it used to be when she was younger, but she still had all she needed for pony parties and sleigh rides. Plus, it gave her extra space she could rent out for others to board their horses.

Please, Lord, let your will be done. She'd put her confidence in Him and walk into the bank with a poise she didn't feel—especially when snow melted against her skin and dripped into her shoes. She even swayed a little as she pulled the front door open, but maybe no one noticed.

"Paisley," Heather greeted. "You're going to get frostbite. Aren't your toes freezing?"

So much for dressing up. Though honestly, Heather's dark eyeliner was as out of place in the mountain town as Paisley's heels. "A little bit."

"Oh, you're here to apply for a loan, aren't you?"

Paisley wobbled her way across the lobby to lean against the slick, marble counter and take the pressure off her feet. "Yes. I have an appointment."

"I was afraid of that." Heather tapped a pen against her lips. "Allen is out sick today. Pneumonia. I'm really hoping I don't get it, because I'm supposed to have a cookie exchange tomorrow afternoon. Wanna come?"

Paisley dropped her head toward the counter. If the loan officer had pneumonia, what did that mean for her timeline of getting approved?

"I'm sorry." Heather's hand rubbed the sleeve of her sweater. "I forgot. You have diabetes and can't have cookies, huh? How insensitive of me."

Paisley's head snapped up. She studied the girl in confusion. How did Heather know about her diabetes? Paisley didn't like to talk about it. Preferred to inject her insulin in private. "Where did you hear that?"

"Dot and Annabel. They are coming to my cookie exchange, and Annabel mentioned she'd been trying to make more sugar free items for people like you."

People like her. Paisley knew Annabel meant well, but that didn't make being categorized by a disease feel any better. She wouldn't respond to the label. "Thanks for the invite, but I have a party at the ranch tomorrow. Pastor Taylor's daughter is turning four, so I'm hosting her Frozen party."

"Frozen? Like the Disney movie?"

"Yep." Paisley had been thrilled to find out the film featured the same kind of Fjord horses Grandpa shipped over from Norway. Adding the package option to her birthday party selection had brought in quite a bit of business.

Heather burst into a song from the musical.

Paisley might as well "let it go." She'd leave her application for Mr. Marshall to consider when he returned to work, and she'd head over to the art gallery to stop Dot and Annabel from revealing any more private information about her. Especially to Josh.

JOSH CROSSED HIS ARMS and pretended to study the sketch of mountains under the track lighting at the art gallery as he waited for Paisley's return. Dot's art wasn't bad, but he was still having trouble focusing on it after the information she'd shared. "So, Paisley was engaged before she moved here? What happened?"

Dot leaned forward, between him and the framed piece. Apparently gossip took precedence over her exhibit. "Nobody knows . . ." she whispered dramatically.

Annabel stood on his other side, wringing her hands. "It's not our business, Dot. I'm sure Paisley realized he wasn't the man for her, and that's that."

Josh shifted his jaw side to side. Was the new ranch owner mourning a broken heart? Was that why she'd been so cranky with him? Could she simply be angry at men?

Who was the guy? Maybe Josh knew him. "Was her fiancé from Sun Valley?" he asked.

"Yes." Dot nodded, her grey spikes threatening to poke him. "Yessiree."

"What was his name?" If Dot didn't know, maybe his brother Sam would.

"I think it was . . . Chris."

"No, it wasn't," Annabel countered.

"Oh, that's right. Henry."

"How do you go from Chris to Henry?"

Dot threw her arms wide. "I'm pretty sure it's one of those."

Annabel pushed Dot aside. "She doesn't know what she's talking about, Joshua. Now come look at my picture of a horse. I was thinking about giving it to Paisley for Christmas."

Annabel led the way to another display wall. Her horse looked like something out of a Disney cartoon.

"That's really cute," he said. "Paisley will love it."

Annabel beamed. "You think so?"

Dot huffed. "I told you the same thing, Annabel. Why don't you listen to me?"

"Maybe I will when you get your facts right. You don't even know the name of Paisley's former fiancé."

The chime over the door rang. Paisley stood inside it, a grim expression on her face. "His name is Nick. As in St. Nick who's going to put you two ladies on the naughty list for spreading rumors."

Josh covered his mouth to hide a smile. They'd been caught. And Paisley couldn't have handled it better.

Annabel stepped in front of her drawing to shield Paisley's future Christmas gift from sight.

"Now, Paisley." Dot distracted her as if on cue. The shop owners made quite the team. "We weren't spreading rumors. Rumors are untrue. You really were engaged to a fella from Sun Valley."

Paisley lowered her chin to give the woman another chance to fess up. "And what did you say his name was?"

"Uh . . ." Dot froze for a moment then jerked her arms to point at the sketch she'd drawn. "Look what I made."

Paisley shot Josh a warning look before following Dot to the frame on the wall. Her message came across loud and clear. He'd better keep his nose out of her affairs. But the funny thing was he hadn't really cared much about her affairs until she sent him that look. Now he was curious as to what she had to hide.

He'd been completely open with her. He'd confessed the most embarrassing of situations. And honestly, how could her broken engagement be any worse than his?

Annabel patted his arm. "Paisley is a treasure. She's just been through a lot."

Nice of the older woman to defend her, but what had Paisley gone through? Her fiancé left. Her grandpa died. That would be overwhelming, but the timing worked out well. She'd gotten to make a fresh start in a new town.

Josh liked to believe God was good like that. Two wrongs didn't make a right, but God could put them together in a way that brought redemption. Josh hoped it would be his turn for redemption soon.

He covered Annabel's frail hand on his arm. "I'm glad she has you." And hopefully she got her loan, too.

He walked Annabel across the room so they could join in the admiration of Dot's mountains.

Dot sighed. "Thanks, guys. But the image was better in my imagination. I'm not sure I'm cut out for art after all. I guess I'll stick to coffee for now."

Josh smiled over the woman's spiky hair at Paisley. She pressed her shiny lips together to hide her grin.

Dot looked from Josh to Paisley. "Oh, my. You look happy. You got your loan, didn't you? Maybe I should come work for you after all."

Paisley shook her head. But she didn't seem too emotional about it. "The loan officer has pneumonia. I should hear back soon."

That wasn't necessarily bad news.

"Allen is sick? I should take him some soup." Annabel nibbled a fingernail and stared off into space.

Well, it was bad news for Allen. But only a minor setback for Paisley.

Dot clapped. "I'm sure your loan will go through. Annabel and I got approved for our business loan. Hey, do you guys want to head back to The Coffee Cottage with us? I'm tired of this place. I think it'll be busier tomorrow—on a Saturday."

Paisley hugged the woman. "I'd love to, but there's work to do on the ranch. Thanks for inviting us to your exhibit."

Dot turned to hug Josh. Annabel followed. Then the two women stepped back and looped their arms around each other as if waiting for some form of entertainment.

Josh paused. He glanced at the doorway he was about to head toward with Paisley. There. Above the frame. A tiny green sprig of something held up by a slim red bow. Pretty sneaky.

Josh wouldn't point it out. No need to create any more embarrassment. The older women meant well, but they didn't know how vehemently Paisley would hate having Josh kiss her. She'd made that clear in the truck earlier.

Personally, Josh wouldn't have minded a distraction from his blue Christmas. But as he hoped to keep working with her for a while until everything was fixed back home, he'd keep the spark of attraction to himself.

He stepped to the side and swept one arm in front of him. "After you, Miss Sheridan."

Paisley breezed through, completely oblivious to Dot's exclamation of "Shuckaroonies."

CHAPTER FIVE

Josh dragged the logo to the final page of Paisley's website and hit publish, before rolling the desk chair over to the window and watching her lead a group of overeager preschoolers in taking turns riding around a small arena. The new website would help promote birthday parties and sleigh rides. And it wasn't like he had anything better to do.

Was that why Dot and Annabel gossiped so much? Because there was nothing better to do in such a small town? Though they hadn't been much help on getting background information on Paisley's fiancé.

Sam would know. Their graduating class had been close, and Sam had mentioned he kept in touch with her. Josh pulled out his cell phone and waved it around the room to find a signal. Nothing. He picked up the cordless landline.

Sam answered on the second ring. "Hi, Paze."

Josh frowned at the recognition in his little brother's voice. Josh hadn't realized they were *that* close. But girls had always liked Sam. And after serving in the military and volunteering to fight wildfires over the summer, the baby of the family was more of a man than Josh at the moment. Of course, since Josh had been recently dumped by his fiancée and suspended from his job, that really wasn't saying much.

"Hey, Sam. This is Josh."

"Dude. Good to hear from you. Tracen told me you're doing some promotional work for Paisley's new ranch. I love that girl."

Love? Josh eyed the phone as if a bad connection had garbled the words. If Sammy loved anything, it was his freedom.

"I went to the shooting range with her when I returned from Afghanistan, and man, she could have been a sniper."

Oh . . . Josh's heart settled back down in his chest. Not that it had anything to get worked up about in the first place. Paisley deserved a good guy, and she couldn't do any better than Sam. But he still felt relief in knowing Sam's affection was that of a foxhole buddy.

"Yeah?" Josh kept the sentence short so as not to reveal any misplaced emotion.

"Yeah." Sam quieted like he was listening for the words Josh hadn't spoken. "I bet Bree didn't know how to handle a gun."

Josh sank deeper into the leather chair. He didn't need a lecture about what an idiot he'd been. Yes, Bree was a mistake, but it wasn't fair of Sam to judge her for not being a sharpshooter. Chicago had some of the strictest gun laws in the nation. And from what he'd learned about city girls, most of them didn't hunt. "I didn't call to talk about my ex, bro."

He could almost hear Sam's smile. "You want to talk about Paisley some more?"

Sam was onto him. Josh scratched at the unfamiliar growth of stubble on his jaw. He couldn't ask his questions now. But maybe if he mentioned helping Paisley on the ranch, Sam would reference the man who should have been helping her. "I wanted to let you know I might not make it home for Christmas. It depends on what Paisley needs here."

"Huh."

Not exactly the wealth of information Josh had hoped for.

"What's she doing right now?" Sam asked.

Josh looked back down the hill toward the barn to watch Paisley place a plastic crown on top of a little girl's head. It must have been a princess party. Josh had been to a princess party before. When his niece Daisy turned four. He'd worn a suit of armor and clashed swords with the little knights in attendance. Seemed like forever ago. "She's leading a group of kids around and around on ponies."

"Cool . . ." Sam paused. "And what are you doing?"

"Well, I'm finishing up the website."

"Holy buckets. Don't you have anything better to do than play on the computer?"

Josh missed the days when he could take Sam in a wrestling match. "Like listening to my little brother make fun of me?"

"If you don't want me to make fun of you, don't be stupid." What a waste of a phone call. "Thanks for the advice, man."

Sam chuckled. "If you want advice, I can do better. Get your butt outside, and be the ranch hand you used to be."

Josh hung up the phone and stood. Whether he wanted to admit it or not, Sam was right. Paisley wouldn't open up to Josh unless they were working together. If only he hadn't grown so soft sitting behind a desk at work. Sure, he ran on a treadmill every evening, but that wasn't the same as bailing hay or hauling tack. "I'm gonna be sore tomorrow."

PAISLEY LIFTED THE BIRTHDAY girl off Sundance, Grandpa's favorite dun.

"No. I wanna wide more. I Pwincess Anna."

Paisley smiled at the princess's speech impediment. She loved that kids enjoyed her ranch so much and how her Frozen parties had been such a big hit. Though being so frozen that she was having trouble feeling her toes inside her thermal socks and boots might be taking the theme a little too far.

Didn't kids ever get cold? Probably not since Natalie's mom, Cindy, had insisted she wear snow pants under her ballet tutu.

"We've got a castle cake inside the barn for you, sweetheart. Don't you want to blow out your candles and open presents?"

Princess Natalie smiled to reveal a gap where her top two teeth used to be. "I get a pony for a pwesant?"

Paisley pasted on a smile and looked with bug eyes over the little girl's head to silently beg Pastor Taylor and his wife for help.

Josh's confident gaze met hers. What was he doing there?

"Is this the birthday princess?" he asked in a theatrical voice.

Of course. He was there to put on a show like he always did. If it distracted Natalie from the pony rides, Paisley would be grateful.

"Why, yes." It couldn't hurt to play along with his performance. "This is Princess Anna. Her royal subjects are awaiting her presence so they may celebrate her fourth year of life."

Josh bent down on one knee. "Fair maiden. I have traveled a great distance to meet thee. May I have the honor of escorting you to the festivities?"

Natalie giggled and bopped him on the chest with the snowflake at the end of her light-up wand. "You silly."

Paisley shook her head. First Dot and Annabel, and now Natalie. Sir Josh charmed females of all ages.

Josh sent Paisley a sly smile. But it was because they were coconspirators. That's all. No reason for her toes to tingle back to life. She curled them against the sensation and turned to lead Sundance to the grooming stall.

Josh had Natalie taken care of, but who had Josh taken care of? He was supposed to be inside working on her website, not in her barn playing with kids as if he knew that was the secret for melting her heart. And she'd thought seeing him with horses in high school had been bad.

Why did he want to even be around her at all? She'd been all prickly and rude ever since he'd gotten there. Didn't he have enough troubles of his own without having to worry about the survival of an old ranch?

She pulled off Sundance's saddle and brushed him. His muzzle turned toward her, and warm air puffed from his nostrils. She took off one of her mittens and held her hand in front of his nose to enjoy the heat.

"You did good today, Sundance." Dad had never liked the Fjords. Some were as short as ponies, but they weren't allowed to compete in the same contests since they were thicker and stronger. And Dad was all about competing. But the Fjords were perfect for these parties and for pulling sleighs, which kept Grandpa's ranch going after he got sick. And it could keep her going, too.

She glanced over her shoulder toward the party/tack room. That's where she should be headed. It was usually her favorite part of an event. Because then she was done working and could just enjoy the laughter and sweet innocence that came with youth. The soft hands. The honest eyes. The funny questions.

But today she'd have to let Josh enjoy it for her. And enjoying it he was. Through the window she could see a couple of little silhouettes swiping at him with plastic swords. He spun and ducked out of the way. If she didn't know better, she would have assumed he didn't have a care in the world. How did he make life look so easy?

Maybe his life *was* easy. She turned her back on the scene and led Sundance to his stall, but her thoughts stayed on the man who was adored everywhere he went. Sure, he'd been accused of stealing advertising ideas and lost his fiancée, but he'd bounce back. He was talented enough to land a multi-million-dollar deal in the first place, so he could do it again. And he'd never lacked for female admirers. He'd be snatched up as soon as word spread that he was on the market again. But if neither of those things worked out, he'd still have his family.

With four brothers and lots of nieces and nephews, he probably knew more about kids than she did. He'd want to have a big family of his own, no doubt.

"He doesn't need us." She smoothed the horse's hair away from his eyes. "We'll have to try to forget all about him."

Hay rustled behind her.

Paisley froze.

"Who do you have to forget about?"

Oh dear. He'd know she was talking about him. Because there were no other men in her life. Grandpa was gone, not forgotten. And Dad—but she wanted to forget her childhood with him. And then Nick of course, but . . . Nick.

"You know I was engaged." She wasn't going to answer his question with a lie. She was simply going to change the subject. "I decided to move to the ranch when our engagement was called off. So I'm forgetting the past and moving on here." She peeked up to find Josh crossing his arms over the gate. That meant he was settling in for a longer conversation. But at least he didn't know he was harder to forget about than Nick.

Josh tilted his head. "Sam never mentioned you were engaged."

Yeah, like Josh asked Sam for updates on her relationship status after he moved to Chicago. "Nick Riley from high school. He became a vet and helped out at Dad's ranch quite a bit."

"Riley?" Josh's jaw shifted side to side.

Did he have bad memories of Nick, or did he not like the idea of her being married? Nah. That was ridiculous. She'd pretty much been the only girl Josh hadn't ever asked out. Which wouldn't have been so bad if he hadn't kissed her at his senior masquerade prom.

She looked away in case her eyes might display her memories like a movie screen. "You probably don't remember him. He was pretty quiet."

Josh had turned quiet himself. She glanced up.

Mistake. Because though Josh wasn't reading her thoughts, he was studying her intently. "Did he break your heart? Is that why you've been so irritable?"

The heat from his gaze dissipated the moment he reminded her of her attitude. She pulled her hat lower over her face. "The stress of taking over the ranch would be enough to make anyone irritable."

Josh held up his hands as if to defend himself. "Hey, I'm here to help."

Sure, he was here for the moment. But that wouldn't last long. As soon as he got his job back, he'd be gone. Which was okay. Because they were both adults now. Maybe it was time she started acting like one. "I know. Thanks for your assistance with the 'pwincess.'"

His stare softened. It roamed her face.

The tingle in her toes traveled up into her belly. If she couldn't be irritable and push him away, she'd have to do the leaving herself. She closed the gate on the horse stall to head into the party.

His hand caught her arm. His skin might as well have been sandpaper, and her arm might as well have been bare with the way his touch rubbed her raw. It was definitely uncomfortable knowing he had the power to smooth her rough edges.

"I want to do more, Paisley."

She inhaled the fresh scent of straw mixed with the mossy scent of Josh's cologne. What was he talking about? She couldn't let her imagination hunt for an answer. Because it might run away with her.

"More?"

"Yeah." He let her go, but his eyes held on.

She couldn't look away. She couldn't step back. Why couldn't he have treated her this way in high school when working at Dad's ranch? Now it was too late for anything to come of it.

"Since your loan isn't going through right away, and I have nowhere else to be, I could step in as the ranch hand you planned to hire."

By "more" he wanted to be her ranch hand. Until he had a better opportunity anyway.

Her shoulders dropped slightly with the weight of the idea.

On the one side, he wasn't trying to get closer to her. He was trying to help get her closer to her new dream. This was like an answer to a prayer for a friend to share her excitement.

Except, on the other side, their relationship was a lot different than Dot and Annabel's. If she took him up on his suggestion, she would be working with him. Which would make it harder to let go of her old dreams.

She'd have to take what she could get. Since she couldn't have both. Could she?

She shifted her gaze past him to survey Butch and Cassidy, Sundance's brother and sister. "You haven't worked with horses for a long time, Josh. Would you feel comfortable leading trail rides or sleigh rides by yourself?"

Josh's brow dipped as if he were incredulous. "You don't know me at all, do you Paisley Sheridan?"

Did she? "I know you chose to move to Chicago. What else is there to know?"

Josh pulled a carrot from his back pocket and held it over the gate for Sundance to reach up and nip. "You should know I once had dreams, too."

What did Josh dream for that he hadn't achieved? "Like . . ." she prompted.

"Well." A small smile played on his lips as he looked down at her pony. "The very first thing I ever asked Santa for was a horse."

Was he opening up or was he trying to prove himself capable of the job she was informally interviewing him for? If he wanted to talk about horses, she'd talk about horses.

"Did you go to a pony birthday party? Is that what made you want one?" She wouldn't be surprised if Natalie asked Santa for a horse when she didn't get one for her birthday.

His eyes darted her way in good humor. "No, I liked playing cowboys and Indians."

"Of course." Maybe she would have played cowboys and Indians if she'd had a brother. "Did Santa come through?"

Josh turned toward her, one elbow resting on the stall door. "You know, I thought he did. I woke up Christmas morning and ran to the window, and there on our lawn stood the most beautiful horse I'd ever seen. Chestnut. With black legs and a black mane."

What a gift. Except Josh hadn't said Santa came through. He said he'd "thought" Santa had come through. "The horse wasn't for you?"

Josh shook his head slowly. "I ran out the front door yelling that Santa had brought me my horse to the utter shock of both my parents. And then *I* was shocked when that gorgeous horse ran away."

Paisley wrinkled her brow. That didn't make any sense. "He ran away?"

"Wild horse. Must have come down from the preserve in Challis."

"Oh no." Paisley covered her mouth. She'd actually gotten a horse for Christmas when she was little. Named him Ranger after her hero, The Lone Ranger. Whenever Dad was yelling at Mom, she'd go out to the barn and hide in his stall. What would life have been like if Ranger had never been hers? If getting him as a gift had turned out to be a cruel joke?

Josh shrugged. "My parents tried to make it better with a new bike, but I was so mad at Santa. Made me hate working at our Christmas tree farm as a kid because families would come to get trees, and I'd hear them talking about Santa, and I wanted to go tell the other children it was all a big lie."

Paisley licked her lips to keep from smiling. The horse thing was sad, but Josh's anger toward a man who didn't exist was kind of humorous.

"I see that smile," he teased. Maybe he was good at marketing because he could read people so well.

At least she didn't have to hide her amusement. She grinned but tried to remain sensitive. "I'm sure it was . . ." She pictured a miniature version of Josh glaring daggers at the man in the red suit at the Sun Valley shopping center. A chuckle escaped. ". . . tough."

"It was," big Josh defended little Josh. Which made her laugh even more. "And I never forgot about that horse. That's why I was drawn to the Independence Day Rodeo where I met your dad and why I accepted his offer for a job rather than work for my parents in high school."

Her joy deflated. Because Dad hadn't needed a ranch hand when he had her. But he'd preferred working with Josh. The same way he would have preferred her mom giving birth to a son. "Hmm," she said because she didn't know what else to say.

"So." Josh narrowed his eyes, probably wondering why she'd stopped laughing. "I wasn't born on a ranch the way you were, and I don't live on a ranch now, but I've always loved horses."

And he liked her dad. Everybody liked her dad. Nobody knew what he was really like. Nobody knew she would never be enough for him.

"Paisley?" Josh's eyes searched for a response.

Her initial instinct was to erase all emotion from her expression to hide the pain, but Josh wasn't looking at her with pity. His face reflected a similar longing for approval. As if he was afraid *he* wasn't enough.

Is that why Josh tried so hard to charm? Why he wanted to prove himself as a ranch hand? Why he'd told her that story?

He'd always walked around with such confidence. Like he owned the world. She hadn't thought his job suspension really affected him beyond the monetary.

"Do you want me to stay?" He broke the silence though it came back even thicker.

Did she want him to stay? So badly that he'd better go.

Had he moved closer? Or had she? They both had a hand on the gate now, facing each other. She wished she had her lip gloss with her because her lips felt dry again.

The question hung in the air. Why did he have to phrase it that way? It couldn't be about what she wanted. It had to be about what she needed. A ranch hand and a marketer. And a friend.

Perhaps they weren't so different after all.

"I need the help." What was wrong with her voice? Why had it gone all whispery?

His gaze dipped to her lips for a moment. Or did she imagine it? Or he could simply be wondering why she was whispering.

"I know," he said.

What did that mean? It could mean so many things. It could mean nothing.

She blinked and swallowed and willed her traitorous heart to slow its gallop.

"I won't let you down," he said. Again with the multiple meanings. Did he really care about her or was he trying to sell himself the way he sold computer parts for multimillion dollar companies?

The din of the party in the background interrupted her trance. The door opened and children spilled out.

"My pony," Natalie shouted, charging toward them.

"Wait, Nat. We need to clean the chocolate from your face." Cindy followed.

"There he is," shouted one boy, pointing at Josh.

A second boy drew his fake sword from a plastic sheath.

Back to work. Paisley brushed her hands together. She would have to put all thoughts of Josh on hold. She was probably better off this way. To truly think rationally, she couldn't be standing close enough for him to—

A tiny body bumped into her legs.

Paisley stepped forward to balance herself. Another tiny body blocked her sure footing. Wobbling on one leg, she reached for the gate. A plastic sword swiped randomly, knocking her hand away.

The earth teetered. Paisley swung her arms in an attempt to find something stable to grip. Nothing. She gritted her teeth for the landing.

Hopefully she wouldn't fall on top of any children. That wouldn't make for a good business review.

Josh's warm body leaned into hers. A solid arm wrapped around her back and held her in place. The scruff of facial hair rubbed against her temple.

She caught her breath. Because it would have been safer to *literally* fall head over heels.

Her pulse thrummed louder in her ears. The heat in her chest radiated to her limbs. She'd felt this way once before. It was so real, Josh had to feel it this time.

She searched for his eyes. They would tell her everything.

Josh's head bent forward. He ducked toward the ground and came back up with Natalie hooked in the crook of his elbow. The little girl had no idea how lucky she was.

"Oh, how cute." Natalie's mom, Cindy, stopped in front of them. "I didn't get the chocolate off her face, but this will actually make for a cuter picture." She pulled a cell phone from her purse.

Josh smiled for the camera. Paisley pinched her lips into a similar position.

"Hold on. I'm going to angle to the side to get Sundance in the picture, as well." Cindy tapped on her phone screen then stood up proudly. "I'll post this on Facebook and tell everyone how great you two are with birthday parties, Paisley." She lowered the camera and smiled. "Are you coming to church tomorrow, Josh? Because I should warn you that everyone will think you're a couple."

Josh turned his grin toward Paisley. His eyes flashed with delight at the warning. But it wasn't entertaining to her. Because there was no chance they'd ever end up together.

She lifted her chin. "Cindy, you can tell them he's my ranch hand."

"Woot-woot." Josh let her go to press a palm overhead and raise the roof. "I got the job."

Paisley shivered in the sudden chill and dodged tiny bodies as she made her way to the party room to start cleanup. If Josh was dancing over her "hiring" him, then that must have been all he'd been after with his sales pitch. And she'd been a fool to suspect anything more.

CHAPTER SIX

After Cindy's warning, Paisley dreaded going to church with Josh. But it wasn't like the guy was going to sleep in. He'd been the one who'd suggested she take her problems to God in the first place—back in high school when he caught her talking to Ranger after one of Dad's blowups. It had been before he kissed her. When she'd thought he was the one who walked on water. But whether she'd liked him then or not, she'd liked the idea of being able to talk to someone who might actually make a difference. So she'd started going to church.

But now she had to go with him as if they were a couple. Hopefully Cindy would quiet all the wagging tongues with the explanation of their employer/employee relationship.

Paisley stole a glance at Josh as she pulled into the parking lot of Big Sky Chapel. He didn't look like a ranch hand. With his slick, bright blue jacket and shiny boots, he looked like a business man on a ski vacation.

Josh didn't notice her looking at him, because he was too busy taking in the building with its stained glass steeple above the log frame set on the resort golf course. "This is gorgeous. I go to church in an elementary school gymnasium," he said.

Another reason she could never live in a big city. She rolled Big Red between two other trucks and shifted into park. "It *is* gorgeous. Lots of people get married here."

He smiled across at her. "Maybe you'll get married here someday."

Not in her plans, but he probably thought she was heartbroken from having her engagement called off, and he was trying to cheer her up. "Come on," she said. "We need to tell everyone you're my ranch hand so they don't start planning *our* wedding."

Josh chuckled and escorted her inside. He wasn't helping her avoid gossip with the way he held the door open and got her a coffee.

But she didn't have to worry for long because Dot and Annabel whisked him away and made all the introductions for her.

He sank into the wooden pew next to her as the worship band took the stage. "I'm going to have trouble hearing a word of today's sermon with that view," he whispered.

She didn't blame him. Behind the stage, three logs framed a triangle-shaped window looking out at the frosty mountain tops and an expanse of bright blue sky. But Pastor Taylor always had a way of making his messages relevant to wherever was happening in her life. Once the music ended and the first advent candle had been lit, she waited for him to bring Christmas alive for her in some new way.

"This is the time of year pastors talk about Mary and Joseph and the shepherds and angels and magi . . . but what I am most fascinated with is the star."

Stars. Definitely relevant as she'd named her ranch after one.

"I once went to a planetarium where they explained the whole science behind such a phenomenon. But it was a little over my head since I'm not much of a science guy. I'm more of a history guy. And I want to know the history behind how the magi knew to look for a star."

Paisley had never stopped to consider the question before. It had always been one of those Bible stories you heard when you were little and took for granted without asking questions. Kind of like the original Star Wars trilogy.

"We know the magi had come from the east. And we know that the magi were recognized for science and insight, which was often mistaken for magic in those times. This puts them in the same area and the same group that Daniel would have been in when Israel was captured by Babylon as well as the same area and group as Balaam — the guy who'd once been hired to curse Israel, but he couldn't do it and ended up blessing Israel instead."

Oh . . . Paisleys lips parted in awe as she connected the dots. Balaam spoke the truth about the Jews to another nation, and then Daniel taught what it meant. The idea made sense.

"I want to look at three passages that could have given the magi the knowledge they needed to seek out Jesus and then what that means for us. First, how did the magi even know about a star? When was a star mentioned in the Bible?"

Paisley knew there were prophecies, but she'd never really studied them. She let people like Pastor Taylor do that.

"Balaam prophesied, 'A Star shall come out of Jacob.'"

Wow. That was to the point.

"Second, is time frame. Had generations of magi been watching the sky for a star? Or had they known exactly when to look for it?"

Paisley sat up straighter. If the magi had known when to look for a star, how had the Jewish people missed it?

Pastor Taylor read from Daniel 9. It didn't reference the kind of calendar she was used to, but it definitely set the time frame for "the Anointed One."

"This link with Daniel and Balaam is as apparent in what the magi knew as with what they didn't know. They had to go to Herod to find out what Micah prophesied later on." Pastor Taylor paused to make sure everyone was listening. "He'd said the Ruler of Israel would come out of Bethlehem."

Paisley knew about Bethlehem thousands of years after the birth, but the Israelites had known about it before. Which made it even more amazing to think the Israelites had missed his birth. Strangers from a distant land presented to them what had been right in front of them the whole time.

Pastor Taylor closed his Bible. "It's a beautiful story, isn't it? But what can we learn from it?"

Paisley tilted her head in thought. This wasn't the usual Christmas sermon about God's love and giving gifts. It wasn't simply a history lesson, either.

Pastor Taylor leaned over his pulpit. "We can learn God has a plan to restore your life. He knows the how, the when, and the where, exactly like he knew about Jesus's birth. And he wants to reveal it to you. But if you don't seek God's direction, you could easily miss it."

Paisley shifted uncomfortably. What would it look like to have her life restored? Maybe it was inheriting the ranch. Maybe it was creating a family through the people whose lives her ranch would touch. Because that was the only way she'd ever have more family.

God wasn't going to bring Grandpa or Mom back from the dead. He wasn't going to heal her diabetes. Yeah, it had to be her ranch. Her Bright Star.

"When you find God's direction, it doesn't only bless you. It blesses others, as well." Pastor Taylor motioned for the worship team to take the stage again. "The magi did find Jesus. They brought Him gifts that we will talk about more next week. Today I want to end with one of my favorite Christmas verses about how the gifts of the magi touched Jesus's mother. In Luke 2:19, it says, 'Mary treasured up all these things in her heart.'"

Christmas wasn't about gifts. It was about treasure. Paisley smiled at the memory of Grandpa Johan calling her *min skatt*—my treasure in Norwegian. He'd always made her feel precious. He'd be proud of what she was doing with the ranch.

The band performed a song about the Christmas star, leaving Paisley relaxed and thankful. She had a blessing from heaven, and she wanted to share it with others. Even if that other was Josh.

The congregation began to break up, and Josh turned her way. "Great message."

"It was." She might as well practice what she'd learned. "Wanna go for a trail ride after lunch?"

IT HAD TO BE a test. Why else would Paisley have invited him to go riding with her when she usually tried to avoid him? She'd hired him as her ranch hand, and she wanted to make sure he was up for the work.

He was. Or he hoped he was. It had been a while.

Josh followed her out to the barn. He was dressed more for skiing than horseback riding, but at least he'd be warm.

Paisley nodded toward a gold gelding with black markings. His mane had been clipped short so that it stood up on end. "You take Butch," she said then led a lighter tan mare to the grooming stall and saddled her. "This is Cassidy."

Josh followed her lead, taking the tack she pointed to. "Butch, Cassidy, and Sundance?" he asked. Sundance had been the smaller horse Paisley had led the party girl around on the day before.

Paisley unhooked her bridle from the wall and slid it over Cassidy's muzzle. "Notice a theme?"

The process came back like he was climbing on a bike. It felt challenging yet soothing at the same time. And Butch was much easier to work with than the bucking broncos Josh used to ride. "I'm thinking your grandpa was a fan of Western movies."

Paisley caressed Cassidy's neck before walking her out to the middle of the alleyway and mounting. "Yep. *Butch Cassidy and the Sundance Kid* was his favorite movie. He sold Kid before he died."

Josh tested the stirrup then swung a leg over Butch's rump. His leg muscles resisted both the weight and the flexibility required for the maneuver, but sitting in a saddle again was almost a relief. Like he'd been holding his breath and hadn't realized it. He could breathe again. He needed to do this more often. "Speaking of Robert Redford movies, did you know our family is going to the Sundance Film Festival next month? My sister-in-law Emily Van Arsdale has a film being shown."

Paisley headed for the barn door. She smiled back at him. "I heard about Emily from Sam. Is it weird being related to a superstar?"

Josh squeezed Butch's sides with his legs. Butch moved forward on cue. Josh relaxed, loosening his death grip on both the reins in his left hand and saddle horn in his right. They emerged into the bright sunshine and stomped through the snow. "Emily doesn't act like a superstar. Though it was pretty funny the way Tracen told us they were dating. We'd all been discussing her like you would a normal celebrity, then she walked into the room."

Paisley chuckled. "Sundance should be fun. You'll be surrounded by all kinds of celebrities without even knowing it."

If he had the money by then to go. His family would be willing to let him stay with them for free, but he hated the idea of not carrying his own weight. "Yeah."

Paisley pointed to a grove of trees on a hill. "I like to ride up that way so I can look out over the ranch. It's also a really pretty place to ride at night if you like star gazing."

Josh tugged the reins to get Butch to turn. "I'll follow you."

Despite the freezing temperatures, the sun warmed his face. If he was going to be broke and unemployed, this was the place to do it. He closed his eyes to soak in the rest of the experience. The crunch of snow. The rhythm of the horse's movements beneath him. The earthy scent of animal and pine needles. The ring of a phone.

His eyes snapped open. His phone was ringing? That meant . . .

"Oh, sorry." Paisley halted at the edge of the grove. "This is the spot where I always get cell coverage. Let me check and see who's calling." She dug into her pocket.

Shoot. Her phone had been ringing, not his. Not that he even had a ringer. He'd programmed the jingle from his last commercial campaign to play instead. But if his phone had coverage here, maybe he should call Marcus and give the man the phone number to Paisley's ranch. That way Josh would be able to find out immediately when his job was reinstated.

He dug into his own pocket as Paisley frowned at her screen. "It's my dad."

"You can get it." Josh dismounted, ignoring how stiff his legs felt already. "If we have coverage, I'm going to make a call, too."

Paisley shoved the device back in her pocket. "I'll talk to him later. He probably wants to know about the loan, and there's no news yet." She swung a leg off Cassidy to join him in the snow. "But go ahead and make your call. Now is a good time to tighten our cinches anyway."

Right. Tighten cinches. Josh took a few steps into the trees for privacy. Just in case Marcus had bad news. He didn't want Paisley to overhear. He didn't want to feel her disdain. He yanked off a glove and dialed.

Well, he'd worried for nothing. Marcus didn't answer. Probably avoiding his calls. Or maybe just avoiding work because it was Sunday. The voicemail beeped for Josh to leave a message. Josh sighed. But this was what he'd expected, wasn't it?

"Hey, Marcus. I want to let you know I'm staying in a place without good cell service, so if you need to get hold of me for any reason, you can call the office phone for Bright Star Ranch. Just google Bright Star Ranch. I designed the site myself, so . . ." Yeah, like that would impress his boss. Josh could design websites in his sleep. "Hope to talk to you soon. 'Bye."

He rubbed his face and made his way back to Paisley. He didn't feel like riding much anymore. And the rock that had formed in the pit of his stomach would surely make him harder for Butch to carry. "Where now?" he asked out of duty.

Paisley smiled up the hill and rubbed Cassidy's neck. "Let's take these horses for a run."

She was in her happy place. He wouldn't ruin it for her. Plus, a little exercise might help him shake the depression. He shoved the cell phone back in his pocket and grabbed the saddle horn to climb up.

She looked over her shoulder, eyes flashing in pleasure, and one side of his mouth curved up at her contagious joy. Did he ever get that much pleasure from anything at work?

Josh didn't have time to consider it because the girl already had Cassidy breaking into a run. He squeezed his knees together once. Twice. And then the wind was blasting him in the face, snow was flying behind them, and his body rocked to the sound of Butch's hooves.

All right. This was good therapy. Anytime he was frustrated with not hearing from Marcus, he should climb on Butch and leave his troubles behind.

His right foot slipped. He jerked sideways. He gripped the horn to regain his balance. But the horn wasn't where it was supposed to be. The horn was shifting toward Butch's right flank.

The saddle rotated around Butch's belly. Because he hadn't checked the cinch like Paisley told him to.

Butch continued to chase Cassidy, but Josh needed him to stop if he was going to get off safely. He reached up from the horn to grab the reins with both hands and yank. He may have ridden bucking broncos before, but that had always been with a saddle firmly in place.

The saddle rotated farther under the weight of his right foot. His body flung to the side. The reins flopped out of his reach.

"Paisley!" He shouted her name in case he ended up flying sideways into a tree and getting knocked unconscious. In case she needed to find him and give him CPR.

Butch took off toward the trees as if spooked by his shouting.

He got a brief glimpse of Paisley turning around and galloping his way, but then all he could see was snow. The ground rushed up to catch him with all the softness of a prize fighter's punch. He grunted at the impact, but he didn't stay there for long. Butch continued on his path with Josh's designer boot caught in the stirrup.

Snow scraped underneath him, inside his waistband, up his shirt, over his face. He flopped over the ground, not sure if he was shaking his foot loose from the stirrup or if the stirrup was shaking him.

Something sharper than snow jabbed at him, caught hold, ripped at his clothing. A tree limb? But it was gone before he got a look.

Tree trunks raced his way. Josh curled his body forward to prevent his head from colliding. But something got his shoulder.

How long could this go on?

Another horse charged past. Paisley. She grabbed Butch's reins, and the ground bounced slower underneath him.

He slid to a stop, his leg still hanging from the saddle. His vision stopped spinning, and he could see Butch's rear legs only inches from his face. He was lucky he hadn't been trampled.

Josh stared up at the peaceful sky and gulped air. The horse's hooves may have stopped pounding, but his heartbeat continued to stampede. He took stock of his body parts to register the pain. A few areas throbbed, but nothing screamed broken bones.

He gritted his teeth and rolled up to his elbows to find Paisley unhooking him from the stirrup. What was worse—hurting himself or humiliating himself?

His foot dropped free.

She knelt beside him, amber eyes scanning him up and down. "What do you need?" she asked.

His job back. His condo back. His ego to heal from that bruising.

All he had left was his charm. It would have to get him by. "I need a Band-Aid. Because I think I just fell for you."

CHAPTER SEVEN

AS MANGLED AS JOSH'S RIBS FELT, he was afraid to look at his side. He pressed against the pain in hopes of stopping blood flow as he watched Paisley rip off a wad of paper towels in the kitchen on her way to retrieving a first aid kit.

I know what I'm doing, he'd said. *I won't let you down*, he'd said.

Gah, even if he didn't have to make a trip to the emergency room, she should send him packing.

The stabbing sensation in his torso paused long enough for the throbbing in his shoulder to pierce his consciousness. And then a burning in his knee.

At least the fall hadn't been worse. Not checking his cinch after riding for a few minutes could have resulted in a more severe accident. Which would have negatively affected Paisley's ranch insurance.

He gritted his teeth at the idea of being a safety hazard. Maybe he should try to walk it off. If he moved slowly, he could make it down to the bunkhouse. Then he could moan and groan without anyone being aware of what a pansy he'd turned into. "You got that Band-Aid for me?"

Paisley snorted and dragged a stool over for him to sit on. "You need more than a Band-Aid."

No bones were sticking out of his body. She'd been able to stop Butch before his head hit a tree, so he didn't have to worry about a concussion. And the bleeding would surely stop eventually. "I know you need to go feed the horses, so I'll take the first aid kit down to—"

"Sit." Paisley pointed at the stool.

Could she be any more demanding? He didn't have the energy to fight. "You're the boss." But sitting was easier said than done. Josh arched backwards to catch his weight with his right hand and lower himself with control. The muscles all along the left side of his body screamed in protest.

"Here." She reached for his throat to unzip his jacket then moved behind him to pull it down his arms.

Something white fluffed from it and floated towards the floor. Feathers. Oh man, the thing was shredded. So much for all the money he'd spent on buying name brand apparel. How would he even work outside now?

"You can borrow Grandpa's field coat. Grandpa always said there's no such thing as bad weather; only bad clothes."

If his jaw didn't hurt from grinding his teeth together so hard, he might have laughed. He'd thought falling off a horse would be humbling enough, but God apparently had more for him.

"Thanks." He looked down at the tear in his oxford shirt. Blood colored the spot bright red. He reached for the top button.

Paisley's hand stilled his. "Just . . . uh . . . lift up the side."

Josh's gaze slid her way. Would it bother her if he was shirtless? He'd been joking about falling for her earlier, but now it didn't seem so funny. "Okay." He gathered the material at his waist and tugged.

The large scrape didn't look as bad as it felt. The bleeding had pretty much stopped. Though lifting the shirt to see his side made the burn in his shoulder increase in temperature. He cringed and dropped his arm back down.

"What?"

He didn't want to admit it hurt to lift his arm. So he just pointed to his shoulder. If she checked it out and didn't think it was anything to worry about, he'd fight through the pain to hold his arm up without complaint.

Her gaze jerked to meet his as if she thought he might be messing with her. "Let me see."

But she didn't have to worry. The scorching fire shooting down his arm pushed all thoughts of her proximity away. He pinched his eyes closed and unfastened the top two buttons.

Her cool hands slid the shirt sideways over his shoulder until it snagged on a large splinter of wood embedded in his skin. The internal tug bit deeper than his flesh.

"That's a doozy." She wrinkled her nose in concentration as she worked her fingers down the remaining buttons to pull the shirt open before pressing the paper towels to his side. "Hold this."

He reached across his torso to clamp it in place. The pressure eased the ache, but light streaks of color oozed through. Was he getting light headed or was that her powdery, fresh scent playing tricks with his mind?

Ridiculous because she'd turned clinical, focusing on the chunk of wood in his shoulder. The larger section came out when she tugged at it with her fingernails, but the smaller splinters required tweezers.

Her breath warmed his skin as she worked, and he had to remind himself that she was probably thinking condescending thoughts about him, considering how he'd gotten into the situation in the first place. "I can't believe I was such an idiot."

She didn't look up. "It's my fault."

Ouch. He was so incompetent she didn't think he should even be held responsible for his own actions. "That doesn't help, Paisley."

She shrugged a shoulder then squatted back on her heels to remove the paper towel. The blood had started to clot, and when she wiped the excess away, all that remained was the thin beginnings of a scab. "It might not even scar."

She didn't even think he was man enough to get a scar? "It better scar."

She lifted both eyebrows. "You want it to scar?"

Was it because all his brothers had scars? And stories to go with them? Leaving the rodeo to become a big city boy had kept him safe from getting hurt. Well, externally anyway. Inside he was still bleeding from the sting of rejection. "A scar is proof that I'm stronger than whatever tried to hurt me."

Her dimples flashed as she reached for an antiseptic spray.

She really shouldn't smile when she was so close to him. "What?" he asked.

She squirted a cold liquid over his side then on his shoulder. Her lips pressed together smugly before her gaze darted his way. "I'm sorry." She stood above him and covered her mouth. "But Butch has never hurt anybody before."

Oh man. She was laughing at him. But he probably did create quite a scene as his saddle slipped sideways. It was the kind of stuff YouTube was made of. At least she'd waited until she knew he wasn't seriously injured before mocking him. "You're lucky you've got a cute smile," he said.

She blinked, and her smile disappeared for a moment before lighting up her face once again. "You're lucky I didn't get your fall on video."

Yeah. Because his brothers would never let him live that down. "I never thought you one for blackmail."

"Ha." She leaned against the counter, fingers curling around the edge. "Like you have any money to pay."

"Too true." Though her reminder didn't eat at him the way he would have expected. In Chicago, he'd grown accustomed to buying whatever he wanted whenever he felt like it. Maybe he didn't need as much here. Life was simpler. Slower. More fulfilling.

More fulfilling? Whoa. That's not what he meant. He loved his job. He loved the success he normally experienced. Ranch life wasn't fulfilling. It was like medicine. He only needed it to help him recover. Just because the mountains were beautiful and the horses reminded him of his childhood, and because when the woman in front of him looked him in the eye he forgot everything else . . .

He had to get back to the bunk house before he did something that would make it even harder for him to return to Chicago. Josh leaned forward to stand. His stiff left knee protested, and he dropped back onto the stool.

Looking at Paisley had erased the pain long enough for him to forget he'd been dragged up a hill by a horse. The throbbing in his side intensified enough to keep him from making that mistake again. Maybe if he stayed still for a moment the angry wounds would calm down again.

Paisley stooped over to examine his knee. "Oh, I didn't even notice this." She spread the rip in his jeans wider to dab the blood with gauze then squirt it with antiseptic.

Josh grimaced as her touch deepened the stabbing sensation. Punishment for thinking he wanted to be closer to her.

"Your pants are soaked from melted snow. Aren't you cold?"

Now that she mentioned it. "I guess so." He'd have to lay them over the fire down at the bunkhouse. Or throw them out along with his jacket. Soft, expensive jeans were a joke on the ranch. He needed something more durable.

She rose to stand. "I'll get you some of Grandpa's clothes to change into, then you can warm up by the fire while I broil us some steaks."

Grandpa's clothes? They would be durable at least. And steak? His mouth watered. "Sounds good."

This wasn't about being with Paisley. It was about nourishing his body and letting it rest. Though he couldn't think of a better way to do it.

PAISLEY COULDN'T MEET JOSH'S eyes as she emerged from the hallway a few minutes later. She didn't want him to guess she was holding back laughter, because then he would never put on the outfit she'd pulled from Grandpa's old dresser. "I left the clothes in the bathroom for you to change into."

He hadn't moved from his spot on the stool. Hopefully he could get up and dress okay.

"Do you need help?" She turned to busy herself with cooking so she could face the fridge and hide her smile.

He grunted.

She glanced over her shoulder to make sure he'd been able to stand. He leaned against the counter, but at least he was on his feet.

She turned toward the fridge again to retrieve the steaks, but she had to tense her shoulders to keep them from shaking in mirth.

"I'm okay." Josh finally answered. "Are you?"

He read her too well.

"Of course." She grabbed a knife from the butcher block and sliced the tape off the white paper packaging. "I'll probably have dinner done before you get out here again. So go."

His fancy boots clacked unevenly on the hardwood as he limped away.

Paisley spun the dial to turn on the old oven then bit her lip in anticipation. Couldn't Josh limp faster? She crept closer to the hallway to overhear his first reaction.

The bathroom light clicked on. The door whooshed shut. Something thunked to the floor. Another thunk. Probably his shoes as he undressed.

Wait for it . . .

"Pais-ley."

Her giggle bubbled out.

"I haven't worn overalls since preschool."

How perfect. "That's all Grandpa had," she called back. Though Josh wouldn't believe her if she didn't stop laughing.

She hadn't planned to pick out such a hillbilly outfit, but Grandpa only wore overalls through the last decade of life—ever since he had his colon removed and he had to wear an ostomy bag. At least Grandpa was tall, and Josh wouldn't be stuck in overalls that didn't reach his ankles.

She ground fresh pepper over the top of the ribeye and slid the pan under the heat element. No matter how upset Josh might be at her, the scent of sizzling meat was sure to improve his mood. Along with a sweet potato and salad. But even if Josh was not amused at all by his new attire, she'd still find great joy in his return.

If anybody had ever told her in high school Joshua Lake would reappear in her life ten years later, broke and wearing overalls, she never would have believed them. Even if they had told her three days ago that the smooth-talking, hair-gelling, Mercedes-driving business man who'd shown up at the Coffee Cottage would volunteer as her ranch hand, she would have taken that bet. But here he was.

The door snapped open, and the padding of his uneven gait drew her around the corner of the kitchen into the hallway for a first glimpse of the new Josh. She couldn't keep from laughing, though somehow the ensemble made him seem even more lovable.

He held out his arms wide so she could get a better look. His shiny boots hung from one hand, and his designer jeans and business shirt hung over the other arm. He spun on his good leg to model the backside of the overalls and the buffalo checked shirt for her. Then he pivoted around again. "Because falling off a horse wasn't embarrassing enough for me today?"

Her heart softened. Dressing like Grandpa Johan couldn't be easy for a guy who was used to looking like a GQ model. Especially on top of losing his job and fiancée. But he seemed to be taking it well.

"You're adorable." The words came out before she could consider how they might sound to his ears.

"Oh yeah?" He wiggled his eyebrows. "I didn't realize you went for the Pa Ingalls type."

"Well now you know." She didn't. She went for dashing rogues, which was why she'd made sure to keep so much distance between them. It wasn't fair that the scruff on his face enhanced his masculinity. She cleared her throat. "Go ahead and sit at the island. I'll get your laundry going in the wash."

She was cooking and cleaning for him? This was getting a little too cozy. Though Grandpa would have done the exact same thing were he still around to run the ranch.

She stepped forward and reached for Josh's clothing.

He pulled it back so that she was now standing in front of him for no reason. "Nah. It's garbage. I'll just keep the boots."

"Okay then." She'd still take his clothes and toss them for him since she was right there within reach. She scooped the clothing from his arms.

As she tugged, one strap of his overalls slipped toward her.

"Ah . . ." Josh grunted.

His shoulder. The one that had the twig sticking from it. She hadn't considered how the overalls might rub against a wound. Maybe overalls weren't that funny after all.

"Oh no." She flung the clothing on top of her garbage next to the fridge then reached to adjust his strap. The splinters had been on the outside part, so if she brought the strap in . . . She situated the strip of denim by tucking it underneath the collar of Grandpa's flannel shirt. If that didn't work, she could always run down to the bunkhouse to get one of his extravagant pairs of jeans. As cute as he was in the overalls, she didn't want him to have to suffer throughout the awesome meal she'd prepared.

"Do you want me to . . ." She looked up to find his eyes only a few inches away. And they seemed way too satisfied with her being that close.

All of a sudden she could feel his heat and smell his musk mixed with the scent of mothballs from Grandpa's clothing. Her blood flooded through her veins like a tidal wave. She'd been this close to him once before. She knew what came next. He was going to ask to kiss her.

She had to speak first. Because if he asked, she might mean to say no but accidentally say yes. Like she had before. "What are you doing?" she demanded.

His eyes flicked up from her lips. The heat of his gaze warmed her toes. "I'm trying not to think about kissing you."

Warning bells rang in her head even as her heart danced to the tune. Time to back away. "Try harder."

She tossed her hair as she turned, digging her fingernails into her palms to hide her nervous energy. She flipped the steaks, mixed the salad, dug through her purse on the counter for her lip gloss. Sweet relief.

Josh had made it back to the stool. He watched her every movement. But she had nowhere else to go.

"Why?" he asked.

Oh man. Her snide comment was supposed to have made him back off. If he still wanted to talk about kissing her, she'd have to treat the question with contempt. "Why don't I want you to think about kissing me?"

He rested his chin on a fist and narrowed his eyes. Could he see right through her? Because it felt like it. "Why don't you want me to kiss you?" he simplified.

Hadn't he learned the first time? Well, if he was going to ask so bluntly, she'd have to be just as direct. She tucked her lip gloss in her pocket and stepped forward to face him across the island, dropping down to her elbows to stare at him in return. "Do you want the top reason or the whole list?"

One side of his lips curved up. "You wrote a whole list of reasons why you shouldn't kiss me?"

That made it sound like she'd spent a lot of time thinking about kissing. Which she hadn't. Not for some time now. "I didn't have to write a list. You came with it. Kind of like a warning label."

Josh nodded thoughtfully. "What kind of warnings?"

How did he not know? "You're on the rebound."

"So are you."

She wasn't. Not at all. But that wasn't a story she wanted to explain. "Well then you should stay away from me, too."

Josh's mouth twisted to one side in contemplation. "Or . . ."

She chuckled at his persistence. Rather than get carried away with emotion, they were having a logical debate about the pros and cons of kissing. She could win this one. And if not, there was still an island between them. Plus, he was injured. The only way he could kiss her was if she let him. Which would never happen again.

"There is no 'or.'"

"*Or* we get over our exes together."

The buzzer interrupted that tempting idea. Problem was, she had more trouble getting over Josh than anyone. She grabbed a couple of hot pads to pull the mouth-watering main course from the oven. After arranging the steaks on Grandpa's brown, pinecone-embossed plates, she slid one dish across the butcher block to Josh while staying safely on the other side. She'd stand while she ate.

She looked Josh in the eye and gave a small shake of her head. "Aren't you going to get back together with your fiancée?"

Josh reached for the salad between them. "No. Bree was a mistake. I got engaged because I was tired of looking for the perfect girl, and she made it really easy for me to settle."

Paisley frowned. He was looking for the perfect girl? Was that why he dated so much in high school? Obviously she hadn't been perfect enough for him. At least he hadn't strung her along and proposed before breaking her heart.

She grabbed a potato to slice while it was still hot enough to melt the butter she stuffed inside. "But you're going back to Chicago."

Josh shrugged then reached for a potato of his own. "For sure."

There it was. He planned to get his job back. But in the meantime he felt like a nobody. Kissing her was only a way to make himself feel wanted again.

He was hurting. Which could lead him to hurt others. It made her want to protect herself all the more. But it also made her feel sorry for him. Could she love him platonically like she loved his brother Sam?

She reached across the counter and grasped his warm hands.

His gaze jumped to hers. Surprised. Aware. Hopeful.

The Bible said to put their hope in the Lord. "Shall we pray you get your job back?"

His eyes softened for a moment before flashing to life. "You need God's help to get rid of me, huh?"

"Pretty much."

CHAPTER EIGHT

Josh had offered to ride with her into town. He'd said he should know what kind of design the architects were planning so he could use it for promotional purposes. She would have let him if she didn't also have a diabetes checkup. But she couldn't tell him that. She didn't like to remind anyone of her weakness and give them the chance to pity her . . . or worse, scorn her. So she asked him to shovel the snow off the pond in preparation for the ice skating rink instead. Even though he was still sore from his rough ride yesterday. But she'd known he wouldn't protest, since he was as self-conscious about falling off a horse as she was about having diabetes.

Paisley shifted on the crinkly paper of the table in the doctor's office and tried not to kick Dr. Ratzloff in the face when he accidentally tickled her. Though ticklish feet were not the worst part of an exam.

"Circulation seems pretty good. Have you had your eyes checked lately?"

"I will," she responded automatically. She would if she ever had trouble seeing.

"And you're staying current on teeth cleanings with your dentist?"

She sighed. Dad used to stress the importance of her oral hygiene almost as much as he worried about his horse's teeth. "Yes."

"Good, good." Ratzloff rolled away on his stool and made a couple of notes in her file.

Yes, those things were good. They were also things she took for granted. Other Type 1 diabetics probably dreamed of good vision and dental health the way she'd longed to be non-diabetic. But nobody could have it all. She needed to focus more on gratitude.

"I know it's hard to regulate your blood sugar when you're active on the ranch, so make sure to take breaks and check it regularly." The doctor snapped his folder closed. "And if there's nothing else I can do for you today, I'll plan to see you in the summer."

She wouldn't ask Ratzloff any more questions. She wouldn't think about the things that troubled her. There was nothing he could do about it. "Sounds good. Thank you."

The doctor headed out, and Paisley glanced at her watch. If she dressed quickly, she'd have time to make it back to the ranch before the sun set and take Butch and Cassidy out wearing their jingle bells once more before Friday's sleigh ride. Grandpa had conditioned them gradually, first with a single bell then by wearing the bells himself when grooming and feeding them. But she still wanted another trial run before attaching them to a sleigh full of people for the first holiday ride of the year. Especially after Josh's last ride on Butch.

Paisley grabbed her socks. If she took the sleigh out tonight, would it be safe for her to go alone? Normally she'd want to take a ranch hand, but Josh was her only ranch hand at the moment. Gliding through a winter wonderland with him would probably be riskier than riding by herself. Especially after the way they'd talked about kissing—or more accurately, the way they'd talked about *not* kissing—the night before.

She stopped to fan her face before tugging on her boots. What was she going to do? Josh wanted to kiss her to get over his ex. And she wanted not to kiss him so she wouldn't have to get over him again.

It was tough when they were working so closely together. Even taking the sketches of her cabins into the office would have her working side by side with him. They'd both be leaning over the same table. Sharing the same vision for the ranch. Laughing at jokes. Making eye contact. Smelling his musk.

Then there was breakfast, lunch, and dinner. Three meals a day. When had she ever shared three meals a day with a man? Not even Nick had eaten three meals a day with her. He'd come out for breakfast on weekends, but Dad had always been there, sipping coffee and clearing his throat if Nick so much as played footsies with her.

If Josh tried to play footsies . . .

Oh boy. She'd have to kick him.

Her heartbeat sped up like she was ready to go into fight or flight mode even though nothing had even happened. What was she going to do?

She was going to have to send him to Sun Valley. That would leave her alone on the ranch until she could hire someone new, which could be a problem since she hadn't even gotten any calls on her flyers yet. Hopefully after the loan went through, she could afford to pay employees a little more, and she'd have a better selection of cowboys to choose from.

The room grew darker as the sun ducked behind a cloud. Or maybe that was her mood growing dim at the thought of saying goodbye to Josh, but it was for the best. Even if his presence made her insides shiver like an unexpected cold front sweeping in—snowmageddon in her soul.

Sliding her arms through the sleeves of her parka, Paisley headed out to Big Red. She wouldn't think about Josh. She'd think about the blueprints being designed for the four cabins to be built on her property that spring. That was her future. That's what she had to look forward to.

But she still wanted to show them to Josh. She wanted him to be excited for her. The best part of joy was sharing it.

She slid behind the wheel of her truck and turned the key to let the old boy warm up a second before asking him to do any heavy lifting. She checked her phone to see if the bank had called. Nothing. Except another message from Dad.

Did she listen to it now and let him ruin her enthusiasm by telling her she'd never be able to handle the ranch without Nick? Or should she wait until a time when she was already feeling down? She'd wait. Maybe after Josh left.

She wouldn't be *all* alone when Josh left. She had Dot and Annabel as cheerleaders. She had her horses. She'd have lots of kids come summer—thanks to Josh and his marketing skills. Could she really kick him out after all he'd done for her?

She considered banging her head onto the steering wheel, but she'd save her agonizing indecision for later. At the moment she needed to get home to take Butch and Cassidy for a sleigh ride.

She shifted into reverse and backed out of her parking spot to head home. Big Red whined and jolted a few times, but like a tamed mustang, he finally obeyed. She waved to the concerned faces peeking through the window of the doctor's office, before pulling onto the highway.

The roads were clear, though with the ocean of grey clouds on the horizon, it looked like they might have another snowstorm headed their way. Customers would enjoy the snow as part of the sleigh ride experience, but Josh wouldn't be happy about having to shovel off the pond again. She laughed at the look he might give her. It would be a mixture of frustration and disbelief. Exactly the way she probably looked at him when he appeared in the door of The Coffee Cottage that first time.

Was she glad he appeared now? Yeah. He'd designed a great logo for her ranch. His eyebrow wiggle the night before made her feel desirable again, which was always a nice feeling. Even if it couldn't last, she'd have the satisfaction of knowing she wasn't completely invisible to men like him. Though this was probably where she should remind herself he was a player. It wasn't about her at all. It was about him wanting to be liked.

If they kissed, he'd forget about her the very next day the way he had in high school. She'd feel like he'd taken a little piece of her heart with him, and she couldn't be whole without it. Yeah, she needed to send him packing.

She slowed at the sign for the turnoff to her ranch. It was a little sign. Something Grandpa used to tie balloons to so it would be visible for birthday parties. But once she got her loan, she'd put up a large sign that couldn't be missed. Everyone would know how to get to Bright Star Ranch. And they'd all talk about the ice skating and the sleigh rides. Maybe next year she'd run extension cords out and decorate a few pine trees with twinkle lights.

She pressed the brakes and turned onto her private gravel road. She might consider getting it paved eventually, too. Then city slickers in Mercedes sports coups could experience ranch life for themselves without needing her to shuttle them back and forth from the coffee shop.

Yes, she was thinking about Josh again. She let herself smile since he wasn't around to witness it.

She stepped on the gas. Big Red jerked but didn't speed up. She pressed down harder. The engine sputtered. She checked the gas gauge. Half tank. She frowned as the speed slowed to a stop. Did she have another faulty fuel line or seal problem in her engine block? She'd been laughing about Josh's car, but at least his wouldn't die in the middle of nowhere.

She rolled to the side of the road and shifted into park to try the engine again. Nothing. Now was a good time to bang her head on the steering wheel. Because she'd either have to call Josh to pick her up on a horse or hike the two-plus miles home. If she chose Plan A, she'd have to make sure to specify he bring Cassidy for her. It would be like him to expect her to ride behind his saddle with her arms wrapped around his waist.

She willed her heartbeat to slow down as she picked up her phone. No signal. Looks like she was stuck with Plan B. Which was just as well. *You know exactly what I need, right Lord?*

She pulled her fur-trimmed hood over her head and zipped up her jacket before opening the door and dropping down into a snowdrift. She reached inside the cab to retrieve her purse with her blood testing supplies. She felt fine at the moment, but she hadn't had anything to eat or drink for a while. Hopefully her sugar levels wouldn't drop too low during her trek.

A low, electric hum sounded in the distance. She slammed Big Red's door and looked for the sound. There. A snowmobile. Maybe she could hitch a ride.

She stepped around the truck and waved both hands overhead. Did the rider see her? It bounced over the snow in her direction, but that didn't mean the driver had noticed her yet.

The snowmobile grew larger. The buzzing louder. It roared toward the truck then turned to come to a smooth stop parallel to her park job, shooting snow across the road. The driver took off his helmet, though shaggy dark hair covered his eyes.

"Paisley. I can't believe you're still driving this old thing."

Paisley took a step backward. Of course she was still driving Big Red. The whole town knew she drove Big Red. So who was she dealing with here?

He flipped the hair out of his face and his smile flashed. Registered.

Her jaw dropped. "Sam?" He'd grown out his buzz cut required in the military.

"Sam I am." The joke had started the week of Dr. Seuss's birthday when Mrs. Hodges read Green Eggs and Ham to the first grade class. That's how far back they went.

What was he doing there? Did it matter? Because not only could he give her a ride to the ranch, he'd be there with her and Josh. A chaperone. If Sam stayed, she wouldn't have to send Josh away, and she wouldn't have to worry about him getting too close.

She bounced a couple times before leaping to wrap her arms around her old friend. She'd seen him when he returned from serving in the Army, but she still wasn't used to his bulk. She squeezed as tightly as she could though he probably barely even felt the pressure. "It's so good to see you."

Sam slapped her on the back hard enough to knock the wind out of her, if she hadn't been wearing the protection of a thick coat. "I'll bet. Big Red having trouble?"

"Always." She surveyed his mode of transportation. "Are you on vacation? Are you staying for the holidays?"

"I didn't think Josh should be without family on Christmas. Especially with the mess he's in. Do you mind if I stay?"

Was he kidding? "You're like my family, too. The brother I never had. I'd love it if you stayed."

Sam's cheeks flushed. Or had they already been that way from his ride? "Josh also mentioned you need ranch hands, and I'm between jobs right now, so I figured I could help out. I'll start by giving you a ride." He patted the seat.

It had been a long time since Paisley had ridden a snowmobile. She grinned and swung a leg behind him, clutching his sides for balance. "You couldn't have ridden this thing all the way from Idaho."

"Oh, I could have." That mischievous grin erased any embarrassment she thought she'd spotted a moment ago. "But I flew in and took a shuttle to the resort then decided to rent this baby instead of a car. Thought I'd surprise you."

What a great surprise. "Does Josh know?"

Sam cranked the ignition. "He will when he sees us."

JOSH SCRAPED THE SHOVEL across the ice covering the pond one last time, his shoulder stinging where it had been pierced with a twig the night before. He leaned his weight on his good leg to give his injured knee a break while finishing up. Had Paisley really needed the ice shoveled today, or had she simply been trying to keep distance between them since he'd talked about kissing her? Frustration brewed within like the grey clouds bunching up over the mountains.

Why had he even mentioned kissing? He should have just done it. Then she wouldn't have had time to reason herself out of it.

Of course, Mom had taught him and his brothers that a gentleman asked for permission first. Josh had always abided by such an ideal, but with Paisley, he knew she'd say no. And he also knew with as much certainty that she'd like it if she tried it. Last night, when she'd been adjusting his overalls, it was like they were two puzzle pieces that would fit perfectly together.

What would it have hurt to step closer and wrap his arms around her and dip his lips to hers? All right, she'd mentioned the whole rebound thing, and she had a point, but if he could go back in time and not propose to Bree, so he could romance Paisley, he would.

The thought stopped him. He propped his shovel in the snowbank and leaned on it as he looked across the field toward the lodge. Did he simply want to kiss her, or did he want something more? He'd been planning to marry Bree. And now his feelings for her didn't even compare to his adoration of Paisley. That was weird.

The hum of a snowmobile in the distance broke through the silence. He used to snowmobile with his brothers a lot as a kid. Now he rode the L to work in Chicago. Not quite the same.

Maybe Paisley would join him if he rented one before he left. Except that took money. And well, he was out of the green stuff. So it was a nice idea, but they'd have to stick to sleigh rides.

The buzzing grew louder. Why would somebody be riding on Paisley's land? If he saw the snowmobilers, he'd ask them to leave. If they didn't, he'd suggest she hang up NO TRESPASSING signs. There were enough snow parks and trails in the area that people with time for recreation could respect her boundaries.

There. Riding along the snow packed road. Two riders. Maybe they weren't trespassing. Maybe they were coming to the ranch for a visit. Josh stepped forward, using the shovel like a walking stick.

The snowmobile turned to pass him then slowed. Josh stopped. Because the second rider looked familiar. Wasn't that Paisley's plum-colored coat?

The machine stopped. Paisley dismounted and removed a helmet. A full smile lit up her face.

His gut itched. Why was she riding on the back of a snowmobile? Who was the guy with her? Nick, the former fiancé she refused to talk about? Or someone new?

Josh eyed the intruder. He looked familiar for some reason. Had Josh met Nick back in Sun Valley and not known it?

The man removed his helmet. The man wasn't a man at all. He was Josh's little brother. Okay, he was in his twenties now, too, and he'd filled out when serving the military, but still, Josh thought of him as a kid. And he loved that kid.

"Sammy." He held out his good arm to welcome his brother into a hug as soon as they got close enough. "What are you doing here?"

Sam made it down the hill faster than he could make it up. But he didn't stop there. He leaped from a distance, and it was seeing the kid mid-flight that told Josh he was being tackled. Though he should have expected such a greeting.

Down they both went. The snow cushioned their fall, but it also stuffed ice down the back of Josh's collar and up his sleeves. "You came all this way to tackle me? I'm honored." He ignored the throb in his ribs, as he twisted to grab a handful of the fluff and rub it into Sam's face.

Sam rolled over, packing the snow with his body as he went. He shook his head to send small chunks of ice flying. "Sorry. I couldn't resist."

"It's okay," Paisley called down. "Josh is used to getting knocked down around here."

Josh glared playfully up at her and reached for a mound of snow to form into a ball.

She giggled and backed away.

Sam sat up, watching the exchange. "Don't tell me you let Paisley take you down, too. I know you're used to working at a desk, but come on, bro."

"Paisley didn't take me down." Though that would have been fun. Maybe he should tackle her. He'd start with the snowball and see how she handled that. Josh rolled over to his knees then pushed to his feet for better aim.

"So who took you down?" Sam wanted to know.

Paisley had ducked behind the snowmobile, but she popped back up to answer for him. "Butch," she called.

Sam blinked. "Wow. Who's Butch? Do I need to get him back for you?"

Josh chuckled. Sam's arrival made his whole situation seem lighter somehow. Even the kid's take on his injury the day before made it feel a little less serious. "Butch is a horse. And I'm sure he could take you down, too."

Sam dropped back into the snow with a chuckle. Josh knew from the sound of the snow crunching flat, not because he was watching. He still had eyes on Paisley.

She peeked up. "Why are you looking at me? Sam's the one who tackled you. Throw the snowball at him."

Josh pretended to consider her point. He frowned at the snowball in contemplation. "True. But you laughed. And while he's already covered in snow, you're not."

She pointed. "He's the one laughing now."

Sam laughed again on cue.

Josh glanced over his shoulder. Was the kid really that tickled, or was he trying to protect Paisley?

Sam's eyes sparkled. From adrenaline? The freedom of ranch life? Seeing family again? Or did he have the same reaction to Paisley's natural beauty that Josh had?

Josh would stake his claim. "Good try." He turned back to face Paisley. "But you're mine."

He climbed to his feet and stepped forward like a pitcher, cocked his good arm back, and hurled the snowball. It exploded on the top of the snowmobile the way he'd planned. The remnants rained down.

Paisley squealed. She wasn't the type to normally squeal over a little snow, but she was playing along. Sam's fun-loving nature had brought that out of her, and Josh would take advantage of it.

He reached down to scoop another handful. One more snowball, then he'd charge.

A snowplow rammed into his back. Or was it Sam again? Josh should have known not to turn his back on his brother. They tumbled through the snow like they were caught up in an avalanche.

"Run, Paisley," Sam shouted as if they were a team against him. "I'll protect you."

Not the snowball fight Josh had in mind. Sure he was happy to see his brother, but having the kid on the ranch was going to change everything. The last thing he wanted was a chaperone.

CHAPTER NINE

"Warm enough?" asked Josh.

Paisley rubbed her mittens together and watched the snowflakes drift to the ground around them. Such peace was in direct opposition to how she felt inside. If only the sun were shining, it wouldn't be so cold sitting in the cab of the truck, waiting for Sam to get there with the Mercedes to jump Big Red's battery. And if only Josh had been the one to ride the snowmobile to The Coffee Cottage to drive his Mercedes back, then she wouldn't be alone with him. She wouldn't have to act like she didn't want him to put his arms around her to help keep her warm.

But Sam's rental insurance only covered him driving the snowmobile, and thus, she was cold and uncomfortable. "I'm a little chilly."

At least when the brothers rode Butch and Sundance out to check the truck's engine the night before, they'd determined it had a bad alternator. An easy fix. After jumping the battery, Sam would follow Big Red into town where they'd wait while Charlie restored him to health at Canyon Auto Repair.

Josh rested his arm along the back of the bench seat. If he was offering to put his arm around her shoulders, she'd ignore it. "While we wait for repairs in town, we could head over to The Coffee Cottage, and I'll buy you a cup of . . ." He turned to face forward again, his hands dropping onto his lap, a grim look on his face. "Never mind. I keep forgetting I don't have any money."

All he'd been offering was coffee? What a relief. "Coffee sounds good. And don't worry about it. I'll buy both you guys a cup for rescuing me and Big Red."

"Thanks," he said, though he didn't sound thankful. And he didn't look thankful, either. He kept staring straight ahead.

Was money that important to him? She'd read once that people had a spending style. They used money in one of four different ways: stability, enjoyment, control, and status. Josh would have to be a status spender. So without his ability to spend a lot of money, he wouldn't feel important. He wouldn't have the confidence to keep hitting on her. Which was good.

"Any word from your boss?" she asked.

He looked down at his hands. "Nope. I should call him again."

Now she felt a little bad. She didn't want him hitting on her, but she also didn't want him to be so depressed. "If he doesn't have good news for you yet," —she stressed the *yet* because she needed him to go back to Chicago as much as he needed to— "then you get to spend more time hanging out with Dot and Annabel. And that's priceless."

His gaze flicked her way, a wry smile on his lips. "You still think I should let Dot give me a tattoo?"

She smiled back and shrugged. "I'm sure she would if you really want her to, but when we see her today, I promise she'll have a whole new hobby to pursue."

His eyes bugged. "You could have told me this before."

Too cute. She laughed. "Where's the fun in that?"

He shook his head and turned toward her as if to enact retribution. "You want fun?"

Uh-oh. Maybe he wasn't a status guy so much as an enjoyment guy. And maybe he was going to remember they didn't need money to enjoy each other's company.

She leaned into the door and held up a hand to block his progress. But as much as she tried not to smile, her nervous laughter probably made her look happy. "What are you doing?"

"I think it's time we finish that snowball fight from yesterday. Now that you don't have my brother here to play bodyguard."

He reached past her for her door handle. Maybe she *should* get out. Then they wouldn't be in such a confined space. And she wouldn't have to feel the warmth of his breath or smell the mossy scent of him. It was probably his expensive hair gel. But still.

Hurry, Sam, hurry. "You don't think I can hold my own?"

He looked up then, the twinkle in his eyes challenging her in more ways than one. "I know you can."

Her pulse shimmied in her neck. She wasn't cold anymore. What were all those reasons she shouldn't kiss him again?

A horn blared.

She jerked in her seat. Her emotions scattered like birds at the sound of a hunting rifle. "My bodyguard is back."

Josh dropped into his seat, looking past her to where the Mercedes rocked violently over the mounds of snow covering the uneven dirt road toward a spot where Sam would be able to pop the hood next to Big Red. "He's really got the worst timing."

She wanted to disagree. But while most of her emotions had flown away, they'd left a little disappointment behind. So she wouldn't feel. She'd act. "Jumper cables are under your seat. I'll pop the hood if you go connect the batteries."

Josh went to work without a word, disappearing behind her hood. Sam lifted the hood of Josh's Mercedes and gave her the thumbs up. She turned the key. Big Red's engine sputtered to life. She patted his dashboard.

Josh slammed her hood shut and then marched back around to the passenger side. The door squeaked open.

Her heart thumped in protest at his return. "You're not driving your car?"

Josh stepped up into the cab. "Sam was having too much fun."

She looked him in the eye. Had Sam really wanted to drive the Mercedes, or had Josh picked spending time with her over his luxury vehicle?

His steady gaze told her nothing. She didn't want to think there was a chance he'd pick her over the life he'd created for himself because that would just lead to trouble. Though the way her toes curled told her she was already asking for it. She reached for the knob to turn down the heat, since it was shooting cold air at them, but then realized a blast of cold air might do her good, so she left the heater alone and shifted into reverse instead.

Sam followed her down the highway, and she focused on getting Big Red to the mechanic's safely. Thankfully, Josh didn't try to make conversation. He was either lost in thought or enjoying the scenery. The gray cloud cover hadn't diminished the splendor of their surroundings. It only gave the frosted trees a soft, timeless look as if they'd stepped into an Ansel Adams black and white photograph.

Paisley sighed as she turned into the repair shop. She may live in a beautiful place, but that didn't make life any easier. She still had a truck that liked to break down. And she didn't want to get rid of it any more than she'd wanted to put down Ranger when he broke his leg. But maybe it was time. Or it would be when her loan came through.

Charlie greeted Paisley with a smile underneath her grease-smeared cheeks. "So the old boy needs a new alternator?"

Paisley grabbed her purse and slid to the ground. "Hopefully that's all he needs."

The passenger door creaked shut, and Josh joined them. He looked a little skeptical about handing over Paisley's vehicle to the tiny, Asian woman.

"Who's this?" Charlie asked, dark eyes radiating curiosity.

Had the mechanic really not heard the gossip from Dot and Annabel? Surely Charlie would have gone for coffee and noticed Josh's car. "Mercedes owner." Paisley pointed toward Sam pulling into the parking lot.

"Oh yes." Charlie nodded. "Your old friend from high school. Joshua, right?" She wiped her hand on a rag to extend it in greeting.

Paisley didn't correct Charlie's assumption. She didn't want to make a big deal about how she and Josh hadn't been friends. People might think she was protesting too much.

Josh shook hands, concern etched even deeper into his brow than before. He probably wasn't put off by the label of "friend" like she was, though. He'd probably forgotten what it was like to live in a small town. He didn't realize he'd be news simply for parking at The Coffee Cottage. "And you are?"

"I'm Charlie Kwan. Paisley and Big Red pretty much keep my business afloat all by themselves."

Paisley shrugged. That was a relationship status she couldn't argue with.

Josh nodded, confusion melting away.

Sam slowed next to them. The passenger side window buzzed down. "Do we know how long this is going to take?"

Charlie stooped to peer in. "Who are you?"

"I'm Sam."

Charlie looked back to Paisley for explanation.

"Josh's brother."

"Nice." Charlie stood. "I might have to come out to your ranch after all. Still wanna trade car repair for a sleigh ride?"

Paisley blinked. She wasn't sure how to take that. A trade would be wonderful, but Charlie's offer obviously wasn't so much about the sleigh ride as it was about the Lake brothers.

Sam's chuckle drifted out the window. Josh pretended to cough.

"Yeah. Great. What time can I pick up my truck?"

Charlie glanced at her watch. "It shouldn't take me long. A couple hours. So be back around eleven."

Josh climbed into the Mercedes.

Charlie leaned forward and lowered her voice for a little girl-talk. "Which one is with you?"

Which brother? With her? Paisley checked her peripheral vision to make sure the men hadn't heard the mechanic's question. Neither was looking her way. "Uh—"

"Paisley, you don't mind sitting on Josh's lap, do you?" Sam called out.

What the what? Sit on Josh's lap? Josh's car was a two-seater. Josh's car. So he should be the one driving.

Charlie squeezed her arm. "I gotcha."

No. She didn't get anything. But what could Paisley do? Wait in the cold, cement, grease-filled mechanic shop and read old copies of *People Magazine* for two hours? She'd promised to buy the guys coffee. They'd helped her get her truck to the garage. And because of them, she wouldn't even have to pay to have it fixed.

She stiffened but squished into the front seat anyway.

"I'll be your seatbelt." Josh pulled the door closed and wrapped his arms around her waist.

She wasn't going to lean back into him. She couldn't let him feel the speed of her heartbeat or hear the depth of her breath. And she couldn't allow herself to feel the solidity of his chest or her hair getting caught in his stubble, because then her heart might beat even faster and her breathing grow even shallower.

She balanced gingerly on Josh's knees and held a hand to the roof of the car to keep herself upright as Sam swerved around to exit the repair shop.

Charlie was wrong. Josh wasn't with her. He was getting over being dumped by his fiancée. And he wasn't even her friend. Sam was her friend. She'd hang with Sam once they got out of the car.

But then Sam would drive his snowmobile back to the ranch, and Josh would be left to return her to the garage. At least she wouldn't have to sit on his lap then.

MAYBE JOSH COULD GET Sam to drive them back to the auto repair shop before he took off on his snowmobile, because Paisley certainly wasn't going to relax on his lap this trip. He'd thought there had been some attraction back in her truck, so why was she so distant now?

Could she still be hung up on her ex? Just because *he* wasn't hung up on his ex, didn't mean that she hadn't felt more for the Nick guy than he'd felt for Bree. Or was she scared of getting hurt again? He sighed, remembering that he was planning to return to Chicago as soon as possible, so she was probably right to stay away from him. But that fact didn't at all diminish his desire to kiss her. To rub a hand up her rigid spine. To swipe her hair over one shoulder so he could see her profile.

Sam flipped through radio stations as he drove, singing to a couple random Christmas carols then barking along with Jingle Dogs. He grinned over at them at a stop sign. "Comfy?"

Josh shot him a look that said, *Really?* Because the kid didn't have to act like Paisley's guardian.

"I'll be glad when we get there," Paisley said stiffly.

All right. Josh wouldn't blame his brother. Just because Josh was drawn to Paisley's baby powder scent and passion for nature and hard work and concern for others and goals for the future and independent air didn't mean…

Hey, could it be her independent air that he found the most appealing? Could it be that he knew he wasn't ready for a relationship, either, so he picked a woman to woo, knowing subconsciously she would never fall for him? That had to be it.

Sam flipped on his blinker then rolled over the compact snow in front of The Coffee Cottage. He returned the Mercedes to its spot. The passenger side door flew open before Sam cut the engine.

Paisley practically leaped off Josh's lap. "Sam, did you meet Dot and Annabel when you were here earlier?"

Sam tossed Josh the keys before climbing out his door. "The lovely ladies who run this establishment?"

Josh rolled his eyes. It had to be nice to be the baby in the family. Not being tied down by life. Sam could show up to visit any one of his brothers and be treated like a celebrity, not a care in the world.

Josh wasn't jealous was he? Maybe over the lifestyle. Not over losing Dot and Annabel's attention. He pocketed his keys and followed his brother and Paisley toward the entrance.

Paisley clung to Sam's arm. She smiled openly up at him. "Did they love you?"

Josh tilted his head as he studied the pair. Paisley had all of a sudden begun to gush as if she were turning into one of the coffee shop owners. She was gushing over Sam. What had Josh been thinking about her being an independent woman? She didn't look like one anymore.

Was that friendship? Familiarity? The two had grown up together. They knew each other. But she'd mentioned love. Was she in love with Sam?

Josh slowed and crossed his arms to smother the feeling ballooning inside as he watched the two enter the coffee shop. It was a feeling he didn't want to name. And it was a feeling that might not even be warranted. He'd stand back and find out for sure.

He climbed the steps and reached for the door handle. It swung open again before he touched it.

Paisley stopped inches from running into him. "Oh." She looked up, and her smile startled away. "Annabel is making our drinks while Sam gives Dot a ride on the snowmobile."

Dot appeared behind Paisley and clapped her hands. "Step aside, Joshua. I have to try out this doohickey now before I get scared."

Josh turned sideways to allow everyone else to descend the stairs. But if Sam was giving Dot a ride, Paisley would be left standing there with him. He'd ask a couple of probing questions to find out if her walls with him were really about wanting to be with someone else. And if the attraction he thought he read in her eyes earlier was simply because he looked a little like Sam. He ground his teeth together at the idea. Because that would really stink.

He followed Paisley down the stairs to stand next to her. "Is this going to be her new obsession?" he asked.

Paisley didn't look over. "Yes. Though I'm not sure if it's better or worse than the tattoo idea."

"Paisley," Dot called from where Sam parked the machine. "Come ride with Sam first so I can see how you do it. If it's like riding a motorcycle, I'm in trouble. My ex-husband left me here on his last motorcycle ride because he got tired of me leaning away from the curves instead of into them."

The information jumbled in Josh's brain. Dot's ex rode motorcycles? And he rode away without her? That was harsh. But it shouldn't require Paisley to ride with Sam.

"It's easy, Dot," he called. "You'll be fine."

His words didn't beat Paisley across the snow. She pulled on a helmet and swung a leg behind Sam. She flipped her visor open. "It's fun, Dot. You'll love it. Hang onto Sam like this." She wrapped her arms around his waist tighter than Josh had been holding her in the car. What was up with that?

Sam turned the key and the two took off, swerving slowly through the trees. Sam circled back. Paisley waved a hand overhead and whooped as they passed the shop a second time. Was she really having that much fun?

Dot held her little fists up in the air as if victory was about to be hers. "I can do it."

Annabel stepped out onto the porch with a steaming cup of coffee. "Here you go, Joshua."

Josh forced his shoulders down and back so he could relax and smile at the redhead. "Thank you, Annabel. Are you going to go for a ride?" If so, he could yell at Sam that Annabel was also waiting for a turn. It would then be rude for him to keep Paisley on longer.

"Me? No. Absolutely not."

Of course not.

"Your brother is quite a daredevil, isn't he?"

"He's something all right." Josh sipped his coffee. The warmth barely registered.

"He's been friends with Paisley for a long time?"

"Yes." Josh had been stupid to think he could simply show up and a few days later have some kind of amazing connection with Paisley. If the woman who'd pledged to marry him couldn't even trust him, and his boss questioned his success, and he was dumb enough to blow his money in celebration before his contract got signed, why would anybody want to be with him?

Rejection shouldn't be any surprise. And this small one shouldn't even matter at all in the grand scheme of things. It was stupid to feel competitive with Sam. The kid was an American hero. What woman wouldn't love him?

Sam slid to a dramatic stop. Paisley climbed off and helped Dot on. She adjusted the helmet over Dot's spikey hairdo.

Watching her tore at something inside. His confidence? That should have already been ripped to shreds. But somehow she'd found one more little piece to destroy.

Paisley was only one woman. Josh had dated lots of women. So why should this one matter? Why did he want to stalk over and ask her on a date? Which was even stupider, since he didn't have any money to take her out. He couldn't even buy her a Christmas gift if he wanted to.

Hmm...a Christmas gift. What would he buy her if he *did* have money? An ornament? A scarf? Or something more personal? Something with meaning?

Gah. It didn't matter. Well, it didn't matter to *her* anyway.

CHAPTER TEN

PAISLEY WIPED THE SNOW OFF THE four rows of seats in the red sleigh and laid out the Sherpa lined blankets. Josh held the reins as a couple of kids petted Butch and Cassidy. He smiled for the picture their mom was taking. Sam passed out Styrofoam cups of hot chocolate and apple cider to their riders. How had Paisley ever thought she could do this without help?

Sam glanced her way. "What are the days and times of sleigh rides again?"

She climbed down into the snow, trying to remember the new schedule. Josh had posted it on the website. What was it?

Josh looked over as if to check on her. "Fridays at six and seven, and Saturdays every hour from noon to five."

She nodded in agreement. If she filled all the slots, her ranch would break even, and all the money from parties and boarding horses and ice skating would be able to fund her camp.

The mom with the camera leaned around the horses to get a better glimpse of her. "You're the owner?"

She patted Butch as she passed and held out her right hand to introduce herself. "Yes. I'm Paisley Sheridan. Nice to meet you."

The mom switched her phone to her other hand to shake. "I'm Elizabeth Rodimel. It's nice to meet you. Though you must not be related to the old owner, Johan Borstad."

The woman knew Grandpa? "I am actually. He was my mom's dad. He passed away earlier this year, and I inherited the ranch."

Elizabeth Rodimel held her hand to her heart. "Oh, I'm so sorry. He was such a wonderful man." She wiped her eyes. "Only last year he was telling me about a special lady friend. I wondered if maybe you were related to her."

Paisley tried to keep her eyebrows from shooting to her scalp. Grandpa had a lady friend? And he'd told a stranger, but he didn't tell Paisley? "How . . . how did you know my grandpa again?"

"Oh." The woman shook her head. "We always come up here to ski for Christmas. One year we won a free sleigh ride through the resort, and we loved it so much I've brought my kids every year since. Your grandpa seemed so happy and healthy last time I saw him. I was surprised to find the ranch under new ownership."

Paisley's lips parted, but no words came out. She shook her head in shock.

The woman's eyes widened, and she looked back and forth between Paisley and Josh. "I'm sorry. I hope I didn't say anything wrong. You look like a lovely couple, and I'm sure you'll do a fantastic job taking over."

She and Josh a couple? And the Rodimel woman thought the two of them were taking over the ranch together? If she'd been speechless before . . .

"Paisley." Josh motioned her over. Was he trying to rescue her? Then he should correct the misconception since he still had the ability to talk.

She stepped toward him to whisper as much.

He put his hand on her shoulder to turn her toward the clueless lady. "Mrs. Rodimel, would you take a picture of us to post on the website?"

The website? He wanted to be on her website?

"Sam." He waved at his brother. "Come join us."

A picture with her and the two brothers. That wasn't a bad idea. But her head was still swimming with the shock of Grandpa having a special lady. She'd have to ask Dot about that. Surely the busybody would know who might have been spending extra time with him.

Sam stepped to her other side. Each man wrapped an arm around her shoulders. She adjusted herself in the center and lifted arms behind both their backs, careful to keep her touch light on Josh. She didn't want him to get the wrong idea. Or perhaps the right idea.

"Say 'sleigh ride'."

Paisley pasted on a smile. "Sleigh ride."

A light flashed. They were done. She untangled herself and twisted away from Josh before she got too comfortable.

Charlie stomped through the snow toward her. A couple of guys from her repair shop followed with their wives. Paisley had agreed to let the mechanic bring the Canyon Auto Repair crew as a Christmas gift in exchange for the new alternator.

"Hey, girl." Charlie winked. "Do you need me to take one of these gentlemen off your hands?"

She did. She really did. She started to point toward Josh, but he reached out and grabbed her hand before Charlie noticed her gesture.

He tugged her toward where he stood with Mrs. Rodimel. "Isn't that a great photo?" he asked.

She focused on the screen. The beautiful snow-covered trees in the background. The red sleigh. Butch and Cassidy. Her with Josh's arm around her. She didn't look as overwhelmed as she felt.

How did he look? She studied the tiny image of Josh's face. He looked like a cowboy, rugged and strong in Grandpa's coat and hat. The photo could fool anybody. And she was certainly a fool.

"Don't you think it would look good on the website?" he asked.

She nodded. "Thank you, Elizabeth."

"Certainly. I'm honored to help keep the tradition alive."

Paisley's heart sank. She was keeping Grandpa's tradition alive, but it wasn't going to be a family endeavor the way Elizabeth Rodimel thought. Paisley had no one to share it with and no one to pass it down to. A tickle inside her nose warned of impending tears. She sniffed and turned away to face the rest of the crowd and give her spiel.

"Welcome, folks. If you've got your warm beverage, go ahead and climb in the sleigh. It's a beautiful evening to go dashing through the snow. And while I'm on the subject, I hope you enjoy singing Christmas carols." Her tour guide persona took over, empowering her to interact as entertainment rather than on a personal level. "But Sam, no matter how much you like Jingle Dogs, there is no barking allowed."

Sam howled in response.

Laughter floated around much like the large, wet flakes dotting her cheeks and getting stuck in her eyelashes.

She met Sam's gaze and tilted her head toward the driver's seat. She needed him to sit by her so Josh didn't.

He registered her request and smiled a knowing smile. Had he noticed the tension between her and Josh?

"Oh, Sam." Charlie stepped between them. "You're so funny. Come sit in the back with me so I don't miss any of your jokes." She grabbed his hand and tugged.

Sam sent a shrug Paisley's direction before following Charlie like the puppy he'd pretended to be.

Paisley grimaced. She should have paid cash for the repairs to Big Red.

She felt Josh's presence beside her before she saw him. Her lungs sucked in enough icy air to cause her chest to sting.

Then his warm gaze melted her insides into a puddle. "Climb up, and I'll hand you the reins."

"Okay." A part of her was jittery with excitement about sitting next to him, having his shoulder bump hers or his thigh press against her leg. The other part would rather leave the sleigh behind and get dragged around by wild horses.

She shot daggers at Sam as she stepped up into the front row. He'd known she'd wanted to sit by him. At least there were only a total of eleven riders, which meant she and Josh would have the whole row to themselves. They'd have room to move without being squished together.

Josh stepped in and handed her the reins. He lowered onto the seat next to her, his knee bumping hers despite the space. "What's up?" he asked.

"Hm?" She gave her best innocent look.

He didn't buy it. "You don't look very happy about your mechanic friend sitting with Sam."

Rather than respond, she twisted her face into puzzlement. Because it wasn't like she was going to say, *It hurts to be near you. And I'm afraid that like frostbite, if I'm with you too much, I'll grow numb to the pain and get comfortable, and I won't even realize it's killing me until you're gone.*

She'd ignore Josh as long as she could. She was good with sleigh rides. Not so good with emotional roller coasters. "Everybody in?"

Positive responses. She twisted to double check. They were ready.

She faced forward, the reins light in her gloved hands. "Butch, Cassidy, walk."

The horses took their first steps. The bells jingled. The sleigh slipped through the snow. The kids in the back whooped.

She used to ride with Grandpa when she was a kid. He smelled like pipe smoke. And he told stories of her mom when she'd been a barrel racing champion. And he protected her from Dad's disdain. He'd been her hero. Yet how well had she known him if she hadn't known he'd been dating?

"I can't believe Grandpa had a girlfriend. I used to always be his girl." She'd said the words aloud without meaning to. She smooshed her lips shut. She didn't want to talk to Josh at all. And especially not about relationships.

WHY HAD HE WANTED to sit by Paisley again? First she was fuming over his brother leaving her in favor of Charlie. Now she was pining over memories of riding in the sleigh with her grandfather. She would obviously rather be anywhere else but next to him.

"Well, honey." He leaned back and extended his arms along the top of their seat. If it made her uncomfortable, then good. "Your grandpa was a big boy. He had every right to date. As do you."

Her chin snapped higher. Cassidy whinnied like she sensed the change in Paisley's mood.

"What's that mean?" she demanded.

He shrugged, his arm brushing against her coat. "I mean if you want something, say you want it."

She sat up straighter. Her fingers tightened around the reins. "And what do you think I want?"

Josh tried to catch her gaze, but she wouldn't look his way. "I really have no clue."

They rode in silence even though Paisley opened her mouth a couple of times like she was going to say something. Once she did instruct the horses to trot. And she also answered a couple of questions about the ranch. Her patrons didn't catch onto her uptight attitude and continued to laugh and talk amongst themselves. She was really pretty skilled at hiding her emotions. Which could be why he had so much trouble reading her.

Snowflakes continued to melt against his skin, not so much cold as it was festive. Like nature's confetti. Montana didn't have the wind Chicago had, so even when the temperatures dropped, they were more like a walk into the freezer section of the store rather than joining a polar bear plunge into the lake on New Year's.

"I . . . I . . ."

She couldn't get out whatever she wanted to say to him. Maybe he'd pushed her too hard. Maybe he'd come across too forceful. He just wanted to shock her façade off. Did she truly dislike him? Was her on-again-off-again connection to him more like a fishing lure designed to trap him into promoting her business? Or had she kept him on the ranch in hopes of getting Sam to come for a visit?

One look at her biting her lip and he softened. Okay, he knew she wasn't like that. She was honorable. If she was hiding something, it had to be out of fear. And he didn't want her to be afraid of him. So he'd ease up. He'd change the subject.

"That photo Elizabeth took will look good on your website, and you should consider getting more done. Maybe you could do a trade with a professional photographer like the trade you did with Charlie."

She glanced at him for the first time since they'd left the barn. "I will check that out."

He surveyed the area. She had a great view of Lone Peak. Today it disappeared into a ceiling of clouds, but on a sunny day—

"You can't always get what you want."

Was Paisley talking to him? He looked back down.

Her gaze was hard. Unflinching. Maybe even a little judgmental like she thought he was selfish for pursuing dreams.

He leaned away. "I know. But that's different than being honest about it."

She faced forward again. "*How* do you know? You've always gotten what you wanted."

He scratched his head. "Did you forget why I'm here?"

She gave a bitter laugh. It wasn't a flattering sound. "You've had a minor setback. Your boss will figure out what happened. Your fiancée will apologize for not trusting you, if you decide to marry her after all. And you'll get your big deal."

He studied her profile. He'd never seen this side of her. Was this who she really was? Was that what she really thought of him? "I hope you're right, but you sound upset about it."

"No." She shook her head to get rid of any cynicism. "It's great for you. But life doesn't work out that way for everybody."

Why did she think his life had worked out so well? If he knew what he wanted, he went after it. Sometimes it worked, sometimes it didn't. Like right now when his most prized possession—his car—was a joke. When he didn't have a cent to his name. When his career was on hold indefinitely, possibly forever. When he'd never been able to find the woman of his dreams. And when the one woman who intrigued him the most seemed to be lecturing him on having it all.

"How does it work then, Paisley? Tell me."

"Sometimes . . ." Her tone lowered. The lines on her face softened. She wet her lips with the tip of her tongue. "Sometimes you want the impossible."

He didn't get her. What was so impossible? She had a pretty great life, and she hadn't even had to work for it. She'd been groomed for it from birth. It had been handed down to her from a relative.

Unless she'd never wanted to leave Sun Valley. Unless this was all about her broken engagement. Unless she still wanted to marry the Nick guy. She hadn't seemed heartbroken, but he knew she was hiding something. "Is this about your ex?"

She laughed again. This time it tinkled lightly as though she was surprised. "What does it matter? My ex. My grandpa. My mom. All gone."

Whoa. He hadn't thought of it that way. She might not be hiding emotions. She might simply be numb with grief. Her mom had died a while ago, but that still had to be rough. Paisley hadn't mentioned her dad. He was a pretty cool guy. But he lived in a different state.

"I'm sorry," he said. Even though that wasn't enough.

She nodded acceptance. "If there are things I want that I can't have, I'm not going to focus on them. I'm going to focus on what I can make happen. Like turning my ranch into a camp."

She was smarter than him. She was kinder than him. She was less selfish than him.

"That's awesome." He should focus on her camp, too. Because making it all about himself had him looking like a jerk.

"What do *you* want, Josh?" She'd turned the question around. That wasn't how this thing was supposed to work.

After his whole lecture on honesty, how honest did he get? When he knew what he wanted, he always spoke up. Like the night he said he wanted to kiss her. But so often when he got what he wanted, it wasn't enough. There was this restlessness inside. Like the multi-million-dollar deal wouldn't even satisfy. "I want to figure out what I want."

Her posture relaxed. She studied the horizon as if in contemplation. As if she couldn't imagine not knowing what she wanted. "You don't know?"

"I think I'm just a little lost right now." His answer continued to spill out. "I thought I had it all, and it turned out to be an illusion. And now I have nothing, but it's real. And as painful as it is to be broke, I'm doing okay. It's confusing."

She gave him a small smile, and in that moment it didn't matter that he had nothing. "That makes a little bit of sense," she said.

He let the calmness of their surroundings envelope him. The split rail fence leading them along the property. The crystals of ice covering tree branches. The fresh powder puffing up behind them. The snort of horses and tinkle of bells and swooshing of runners. The conversations about snowshoeing and how to stuff a turkey and that time Uncle Fred built a snowman in the street so he could drive through it.

Paisley tapped his leg. "We're headed back. This is the part where I usually have the horses trot while we sing 'Jingle Bells.' Do you want to start us out?"

Josh studied Paisley. She'd dropped her defenses. She'd overcome whatever was bothering her when they first climbed into the sleigh. Maybe it had helped her to vent a little. Maybe she only needed to get back into her element.

"Sure," he said. He still had his arm behind her. Earlier it had been to irk her, but now with the coziness of the moment, he wanted to tuck her underneath his shoulder.

"Hya."

He rocked back in his seat as the horses picked up speed. The breeze invigorated while the dimming light blanketed him with peace.

He cleared his throat. "Dashing through the snow . . ."

Paisley joined him. "On a one horse open sleigh . . ."

More voices. Some rough. Some off key. Some clear and powerful. Was that Charlie? She was good.

The chorus came to an end. Sam finished with a, "Hey!"

Which led straight to Charlie's solo. "Sleigh bells ring, are you listening . . ."

Peace settled over Josh. This was what he'd needed. Had God allowed him to be accused of stealing advertising ideas to get him away from the commercialism of life so he could remember what it was like to enjoy the moment? So he could reconnect with family? So he could focus on the true meaning of the season?

That's what would draw other people to Paisley's ranch. That's the route he should take for her advertising campaign.

He studied her profile again. Leather cowboy hat, freckles, long wavy hair. She was different from the kind of people he worked with in the city. She was refreshing. And if he was honest with himself, what he wanted more than anything in that instant was to get to know her better.

Should he tell her? How could he not after the conversation they'd just had?

Charlie's voice lowered. Her tone dropped. She sang the first line to "Silent Night." The rest of the sleigh joined in, including Paisley. The melody wrapped around him, warm like a fire.

"Paisley?"

She gave him a soft smile, though she probably wasn't thinking of him. She was being carried away by the sweetness of the lyrics. But if he was going to ask her out, she was in the right frame of mind to accept.

"There *is* something I want."

Her face tilted his way. Curiosity? Interest?

"I want to take you on a date."

Her head dropped back slightly. She focused her eyes straight ahead. Losing the heat of her gaze left him chilly.

She scrunched her nose before answering. "Remember when I said some things are impossible?"

He snorted. Of course he remembered. But he hadn't understood then, and he didn't understand now. "Did I come with the same warning label for dating as I did for kissing?"

She shifted away, but she might as well have stayed pressed up against him with the way that little space between them vibrated with an electric current.

"That's one way to put it," she allowed. "But taking me on a date is literally impossible."

Oh, this ought to be good. He waited.

"You can't pick me up because your car won't make it down the road. You don't have money to take me anywhere. And then, you couldn't even invite me back to your place—not that I'd go—because your former fiancée is living there."

He stared at her. Everything she'd said was true. And cruel. And an excuse. Because she was the kind of girl where money didn't matter. If she'd wanted to go out with him, she'd be happy stargazing or taking a quick road trip to see Old Faithful in Yellowstone. Which was probably why she wouldn't look at him. Her eyes would reveal the rejection to be based on more than monetary requirements.

"And you live in Chi-ca-go," she added, drawing the word out for emphasis.

"Are you going to keep going?" he deadpanned. She'd made her point. And maybe that was the only point she needed to make. He lived far away. Getting involved was senseless. Only that fact didn't make him any less drawn to her.

"Do I need to keep going?" she asked.

The lights inside the barn loomed. In a minute they'd be unloading passengers, unhooking the sleigh, feeding horses. As they sailed across the pasture, Charlie led the rest of the riders in a rendition of "We Wish You a Merry Christmas."

Josh didn't feel merry anymore. How presumptuous of him to think God had brought him to the ranch to restore his joy. God must have brought him there to continue the humbling process. Not a fun lesson. He'd thought he'd lost everything before running into Paisley again. He'd been wrong.

He shook his head at the situation. Why did he have to run into her? Was she a carrot to keep him going? To show him that there was more to life than promotions and sports cars? He knew something had been missing. And now he knew it existed. But it was still out of his reach.

"No, Paisley. You're right. Dating you sounds impossible."

CHAPTER ELEVEN

THERE HE WAS, SHOVELING SNOW AGAIN at the beginning of another week. Only this time Paisley also wanted him to sweep it. Repetition was not his strength. He liked to do creative things, social things, and exciting things. Yet Paisley had him doing the exact same thing he'd done the day before the snowstorm. Only today they were going to start flooding the ice to create a smooth surface. They'd have to repeat this process five times before she opened it for ice skating.

If Sam and Paisley helped him out, it would go faster. But they were too busy carrying benches and burn barrels to strategic locations while he did all the grunt work.

"She's the boss," he muttered to himself. She'd allowed him to stay on her ranch when he had nothing to pay her. And their trade was beneficial to both of them. But he kept hearing her statement from the day before ringing through his head. *You live in Chi-ca-go.* There really was nothing for him here.

Paisley grabbed a couple of buckets and headed his direction. Sam held her hand as she stepped out onto the ice as if she needed help balancing. Josh rolled his eyes. The girl had the balance to jump a horse while standing on its back if she wanted. They weren't fooling anyone.

She let go of Sam and slid her boots purposefully along the opaque surface of the pond. Sam cheered as if she'd completed a triple jump.

She glanced Josh's direction, a huge smile on her face. He'd take what he could get. Plus, seeing her smile made him smile whether he wanted to or not.

"Great work, Josh. You checked to make sure the ice is thick enough?"

"Five inches." He leaned on his shovel. "I also chiseled off the bumps as you requested."

She nodded. "Flooding the ice should fill in any holes and level the surface, but it wouldn't have covered those kinds of imperfections." She held out her arms for balance and made her way toward the other side of the figure-eight shaped pond where a small fountain kept the water from freezing. "So you think we can safely walk to the edge to fill our buckets and pour them across the ice?"

Josh strode after her. He'd mounded a blockade of snow to keep skaters from crossing onto thin ice, but he didn't want her leaning over it by herself. "It should be safe, but just in case, we'll have Sam stay on the side with a rope."

"I'm here for you, bro." Sam plunked onto a bench and extended his long legs to cross at the ankles.

"My hero."

Paisley handed Josh a bucket before leaning over the ledge of snow to demonstrate the flooding process her grandpa had told her about. Cold water splashed up, wetting the tips of her gloves. "We'll have to do this every night after skaters leave."

"Every night, huh?" Life on a ranch was all about manual labor. But she was nothing if not a hard worker. Hopefully she'd make time to enjoy the rink, as well.

Their last splash hadn't yet reached the other end of the pond. If they were going to enjoy the rink at all, they should do it before they finished the flooding process. He took her bucket and set them both down in the snow. "Come here."

She stood slowly, a palm to her lower back for support. "Why?"

He held out his hand for hers. "Because owning a skating rink should be a fun job."

She looked at his offered hand out of the corner of her eye. "I haven't ordered skates yet."

"That's okay. We'll slide around in our boots."

She didn't move.

He dropped his arm and slid his feet back and forth like working out on a Nordic Track. "Not impressed?"

She shook her head, but one side of her lips curved up.

"I'm not impressed either, bro," Sam called.

Nobody was trying to impress his brother. But maybe they should. "You think you can impress Sam more than I can?"

She lifted her arms overhead like a ballerina and spun on one foot. "Yes." She stepped down, and her foot slipped out from under her. She teetered his way.

Josh caught her around the waist, her chest leaning into his. This was working out better than expected. He tilted his chin down to inhale her sweet scent and tease her before letting her go. "Smooth move."

She smiled but pushed against his chest, sliding backward and creating more distance between them.

He slid his feet forward and shoe skated around her. "You get five moves. Sam can be judge." Which meant Josh was going to lose, but winning wasn't his goal here. He spoke louder to alert his brother of the role. "Sam, you get to judge us on a scale of one to ten. Paisley goes first."

"She gets a perfect ten," Sam called back.

Josh held out his hands in exasperation. "You can't judge her until *after* she skates."

"Oh, right."

Paisley stood in place, tapping her fingers against her legs. "I haven't agreed to the competition yet. What does the winner get?"

Josh rubbed his hands together. This was working out a *lot* better than expected.

She pointed a finger to stop his train of thought. Though since they'd agreed dating was impossible, her eyes shouldn't have been dancing with the pleasure of being pursued. "Let's just say the winner gets to choose, since I'm going to be the winner," she said.

He really wanted to win now. Though… "The judge does seem to be a little bit biased."

"Yep." She smiled in agreement. "Ready, Sam?" she asked, but her eyes never left Josh.

"I'm practically breathless in anticipation."

Josh shook his head. He didn't have a chance.

She scrunched up her freckled nose. "Here I go."

She scooted backwards, waving her arms in front of her. Move one. She stepped wide to turn herself around twice. Move two. She lifted a foot and balanced like a flamingo. This caused her to tip precariously, but she set her foot down before falling. Move three. Not bad. She did a little jump. Move four—and that one would be hard to top. She finished by striking a pose with legs wide and an arm pointing to the sky.

Sam clapped. "Bravo. Bravo. Though because of the wobble when you were standing on one foot, I'm going to have to give you a 9.5"

"I meant to wobble."

Josh guffawed. "Puh-lease. You're just scared I can beat you now."

Her eyes narrowed in mock challenge. "You are not going to beat me."

He crossed his arms. "We'll see."

"Hurry it up, Josh." Sam called from his spot. "I'm getting hungry. All this sitting here and doing nothing is wearing me out."

Josh had absolutely no idea what his five moves would be. In fact, he had no idea what his first move would be. The only time he'd watched ice skating was when he took clients to Blackhawk games. That would have to be a start.

He ran across the ice and slid. Move one. Now what? He ran across the ice and slid faster. Move two. And actually kind of fun. Maybe once more.

Paisley watched him pass her a third time. She laughed. "Is that all you've got?"

His feet slowed, and he looked over his shoulder. If she was laughing, he'd keep going. "No, I can do it faster."

He ran. Wind stung his cheeks. He planted his feet and sailed past, holding his arms out for balance.

"This is great stuff." Sam whooped. "I think you could sell tickets for such a show, Paisley."

She covered her mouth, but the corners of her eyes crinkled, giving away her smile. She pulled her hands down to her chest. Definitely smiling. "Yeah, I don't need a loan anymore. I've got the Josh Lake Capades to bring in big money."

Josh faced her across the pond. His heart swelled. Because it wasn't about money. It wasn't even about getting her to go out with him. It was about bringing her joy. "If you liked that, wait until you see this."

Not that he knew what *this* was going to be. He had a good thing going with the running and the sliding. Maybe he could run and slide and turn at the same time. Why not? She'd done a turn as one of her moves.

"How long do we have to wait?" Sam shouted.

If the guy was so hungry, he should go raid the fridge. But Josh had made him judge. He took a deep breath, charged, gave one last mighty push, and careened forward. Now for the turn. He looked over his shoulder, twisted his hips, turned his toes...spun out of control. Right towards Paisley.

"Whaaa . . ." He yelled a warning, arms flailing.

Her eyes grew wide. Her mouth opened. She leaned backward as if trying to get out of the way.

Then his body connected. He gripped her shoulders to keep her from going down. His momentum carried him forward and her backwards. He slid his feet wider to try to keep balanced, but they tangled with hers.

They tipped right. He flexed. Overcorrected. They tipped left.

She gripped his jacket. They balanced themselves out but ended up in a spin. Gravity pulled. Josh continued the spin to throw himself down underneath her, gritting his teeth in preparation of impact.

The snowdrift caught them. Cushioned him. Paisley's body rammed into his, an elbow to his ribs.

He grunted. All went still. He waited for a throbbing to alert him to an area of pain. Nothing. Nothing except for Paisley smashed on top of him.

Josh lifted his chin to check her for injury. Her freckles stood out even more than usual against her pale face. But it was her eyes that had all his attention. Awareness. Then fear. But shouldn't the fear have come before the awareness that they were okay?

He'd check. "You okay?"

She nodded. Still no words.

Sam's voice rang out. "If I deducted half a point for Paisley's wobble, I'm going to have to deduct at least a whole point for a fall. And as you took someone else down with you, Josh" —Sam clicked his tongue— "I'm going to have to take at least nine points off for that. That gives you . . . uh . . . zero points."

Josh lost. Like he knew he would. But somehow he'd ended up with his arms around Paisley. She hadn't moved yet. "What do you want?" he asked.

Her body tensed against his. "I told you yesterday some things are impossible."

He still didn't know what she meant by that. She'd made it clear that she wasn't going to date him. Though with his arms around her and her lips so close, it seemed like the most possible thing in the world. His gaze studied hers to read between the lines. What wasn't she saying? "You're the winner, Paisley. You get anything you want from me. You just have to ask."

Her huff warmed his cheek. "In that case . . ."

He inhaled. His fingers dug deeper into her jacket. Was he feeling light-headed from hitting his head too hard or was it from being so near to her?

His pocket vibrated. His phone rang out the insurance commercial jingle he'd written. It sounded so out of place in their peaceful environment. He'd have to change it.

Paisley pulled back into a kneeling position, brushing snow off her pants and refusing to look at him. "You'd better get that. You don't know when you'll have coverage again."

What a horrible time for phone coverage. He stared up into the blue sky. Not quite the same as looking into her eyes. He remained on the ground as he stuck a hand into his pocket to retrieve his phone. If it was Bree, he was so blocking her number.

But it wasn't. It was the office. His pulse pounded harder in his wrists and behind his knees. He hadn't heard from his boss since he'd arrived. Was it going to be good news or bad news? Maybe he wouldn't have to go back to Chicago after all. Then dating Paisley wouldn't be as impossible. But that's not really what he wanted, was it?

"This is Josh."

"Josh. I left a message at the number you gave me but decided to try your cell, as well. Are you still in Montana?" Marcus's voice sounded jovial. Was that a good thing?

"I am. What's up?" He looked over to check on Paisley who had Sam joining her to finish flooding the ice. What had she been about to tell him she wanted?

"We found evidence of your designs being leaked to a competing company. It looks like you didn't steal their ideas. They stole yours."

Josh sat straight up. "I knew it. Who was it? Craig? He always seemed a little too interested in what I was doing."

"Uh . . ." Marcus paused. "I wouldn't go pointing fingers yet. You don't want to make any enemies. We don't know who it was, so we're going to keep you on suspension for a little longer to make the culprit think he got away with it. We'll catch him when he lets down his defenses."

Josh climbed to his feet and ran a hand through his hair. There had to be something he could do to help out the investigation. "Do you want me to come back right now?"

"Isn't Bree at your place?"

"Yes, but if I tell her that you're clearing my name, then she'll realize she can trust me, and she'll work with me to get a new place rather than blame me for ruining her life."

Marcus huffed. Or someone huffed. Maybe it was Marcus. "No, don't do that yet. I don't want your patched relationship to tip off the suspect."

Josh nodded. He hadn't thought of that. Not that he was going to start back up where they left off, but he could see how others might expect that. "Well, how long do you think it will be?"

Marcus cleared his throat. "Hopefully before Christmas, Josh. I want this mess cleaned up as badly as you do."

Of course he did. It looked bad for the company. Josh would have to keep trusting in Marcus's investigation. Keep trusting in God's justice. Isn't this what Paisley had prayed for over dinner the other night. She'd be thrilled.

He glanced her way. She must not have overheard because she didn't look very thrilled.

PAISLEY WISHED SHE HADN'T overheard Josh's exuberance about leaving—and right after he'd been teasing her about asking what she wanted. Some chaperone Sam turned out to be. He'd been sitting on the bench watching the whole thing.

She poured a bucket of pond water across the ice. What she needed was another layer of ice to freeze around her heart. That way it wouldn't be so easy for Josh to melt it.

Water splatted next to her as Sam dumped out his bucket. "So, Ice Skating Champion of Bright Star Ranch, what are you going to ask Josh for?"

Paisley pursed her lips. She hadn't had anything in mind earlier. But she'd thought Josh had something in mind. Which had her trying to come up with arguments against it. It was hard to come up with arguments when he was holding her close. Maybe that had been his plan all along.

Well, good thing she'd won. Because she had other plans. "I want him to cook dinner. And clean up after it." She nodded in agreement with herself. That sounded like a great idea. A great way to avoid him anyway. Then she could do something relaxing for a change. Maybe watch a Christmas movie. She hadn't done that in a long time. "Wanna watch *It's a Wonderful Life* with me?"

Sam grimaced. "The old black and white movie? Maybe I should trade places with Josh to get out of it."

Paisley tilted her head. Were they talking about the same movie? "Have you ever seen it?"

"No."

"Then hush. You'll love it."

"I call the couch. Then if I fall asleep, I'll be comfortable."

She punched him in the arm.

Josh strode over. "What'd he do?"

"What did *I* do?" Sam played innocent. "She's the one who punched me."

Paisley returned to her bucket. She couldn't play along. Because then she'd be smiling and laughing and somehow end up in Josh's arms again. "He doesn't want to watch *It's a Wonderful Life* with me."

Josh gasped as if his brother had done something truly horrific. "Sam."

Paisley tucked her chin to hide her smile. Why couldn't she feel sisterly toward both of them? Then she'd be able to join in the fun without risking her heart.

Sam bent toward the pond to retrieve more water but looked over his shoulder. "Don't act all offended, bro. I know if it were up to you, we'd be watching *Ernest Saves Christmas*."

Josh nodded thoughtfully. "True. Don't you want to watch Ernest with us, Paisley?"

Ha. Even if she wanted to watch Ernest, it would not be with him. She stood and poked him in the chest. "You're not watching a movie."

His gaze flew to hers.

Oops. Too close. She backed up, ready to head to the lodge. The pond was wet enough. "You're making dinner and cleaning up the kitchen."

His jaw dropped. "Hey."

She shrugged, though it felt more like raising her arms in victory. "You said you'd do anything I wanted."

He trotted to catch up then took her bucket and tossed it back to his brother.

Paisley looked at Sam for help. She needed him to come to the lodge with them, not stop to put the buckets in the barn.

"You did win. But you know what? I won, too. My boss called to say they've found evidence someone stole my ad ideas." He sounded like he'd unwrapped the largest gift under the tree. "So if I'm cooking dinner, it's going to be a huge dinner to celebrate."

She turned her focus to the lodge and marched forward. If they made it to the lodge without Sam, she'd excuse herself to shower. It would warm her up. Plus, it would be a good place to hide her tears. Then she could pretend to be happy for Josh. This is what she'd prayed for, after all. And it was proof that had she let him kiss her, she'd be forgotten the moment he was free to head back to his life.

"Congrats. What are you going to cook?"

He chuckled, lost in his own world. Probably imagining how he would have celebrated if was he back in Chicago. She didn't have any thousand dollar bottles of wine at her place. "I can make spaghetti."

Shemarveled at Josh's sweetness. The guy didn't know how to cook. Probably ate out every night. If he'd stayed longer, she could have given him lessons. They could have worked together in the kitchen, sampling flavors, wearing aprons, and sidestepping one other until they couldn't avoid each other any longer.

She groaned. Why was she doing this to herself?

"You don't like spaghetti?"

She climbed the steps to the front door and put on her brightest smile. "Spaghetti is great. Let us know when it's ready."

His smile slipped. He studied her. "You're going to start the movie with Sam?"

What else would she do? "Yep. I'm sure you wouldn't even be able to concentrate on a movie with all the excitement. You've got your own wonderful life to think about."

CHAPTER TWELVE

Paisley tightened her arms around Sam's waist as the wind stung her neck above her scarf and underneath the helmet. The ride back to the ranch on the snowmobile wasn't nearly as crazy as the ride out into the forest, since they were now dragging the giant Christmas tree behind them and had to go slower. "Thanks so much for doing this, Sam. Grandpa Johan loved putting up a tree in the windows of the lodge for people to see from the barn, but I didn't have the energy to do it on my own."

"You have to have a tree." Sam gunned the engine to make it up the hill to the lodge. "This is my first Christmas home after being deployed to Afghanistan."

Paisley kept forgetting Sam had lived a whole different life since they hung out in high school. Afghanistan at Christmas was about as far away as one could get from the beautiful snow-covered mountains of Montana. "Did it even feel like Christmas over there?"

Sam's back stiffened with his shrug. "It was a normal day with better food. And I dressed up like Santa—Santa with a sidearm."

Paisley pulled off her helmet and smiled at the image. "You *do* take Christmas pretty seriously."

"I do." Sam chuckled as he cut the engine. "Now that we have a tree, we need to build a fire and play Christmas carols and make a popcorn string and eat ice cream."

Eat ice cream? Maybe if he was still in Afghanistan. "It's a little cold for ice cream." Paisley swung a leg off the snowmobile and pulled out the knife on her Leatherman to cut the rope that held the tree.

Sam followed. "It's never too cold for ice cream." He reached between the branches at the top to grab the trunk.

Paisley kept her mittens on to protect her skin from the rough bark as she grabbed the base. "I think I might have a pint of vanilla I never finished."

Sam started forward. "You better. Because I would seriously have to leave your ranch if you didn't serve ice cream."

Paisley tromped after him up the stairs onto the deck. She knew Sam was joking, but the thought of him leaving made her stomach twist into a knot. Right beyond the doors of the lodge, Josh would be working in her office on an advertising campaign, and he'd join them as soon as they got the tree through the door. Setting up a tree alone with Josh was too cozy an image for her to allow herself to picture. "You can't leave, Sam. I need you to be my chaperone."

Sam dropped his end of the evergreen. The weight of the tree tugged Paisley lower. He turned to face her and crossed his arms. "It's about time you admit you have feelings for my brother."

Paisley stubbornly held onto her end of the tree. She'd made a statement rather than opening up a new topic of conversation. Especially with Josh awaiting their return. "It doesn't matter. He's leaving soon. Now grab the tree and take it inside before my toes turn blue."

Sam held up a glove. "One sec. Why do you think Josh is leaving soon? He looks pretty comfortable here from what I've seen."

Paisley sighed. She might have agreed with Sam if she hadn't seen Josh's excitement the day before when he got the message from his boss. "He's going back to Chicago as soon as his name is cleared."

"Hmm." Sam tilted his head and narrowed his eyes. "Josh is good at what he does, but he's also a romantic at heart. He left Sun Valley because of a woman. I wouldn't be too surprised if he came back west for one, as well."

Paisley twitched. She couldn't even allow such a notion to implant in her mind. "Me? You think Josh would leave everything and move out here for me?"

"He'd be a fool not to."

Ahh . . . kind words. And they meant even more coming from the ultimate commitment-phobe. "That's very sweet of you, Sam, but Josh can find a woman wherever he goes. Sure, he's here right now and wants to kiss me again . . ." Her numb cheeks blazed back to life. ". . . But that doesn't make me anything special."

"Oh?" Both of Sam's eyebrows arched like question marks. He unfolded his arms to lean against the deck railing. He crossed one leg over the other like he wasn't moving until he got answers to his unasked questions.

Paisley dropped her end of the tree. She didn't want to stand around discussing her love life, but she couldn't very well carry the whole tree into the lodge by herself.

"Josh certainly got over Bree quickly if he's kissing you."

What? No. "He hasn't kissed me since he's been here." Because she pushed him away, but that was beside the point. "He kissed me back in high school."

Sam's expressive eyebrows dipped down. "In high school? He was a senior when we were sophomores. How did I not know you were kissing upperclassmen? That would have been big news."

She hadn't told Sam because she hadn't told anyone. She glanced toward the windows to make sure Josh didn't overhear her talking about it now. "I don't think Josh wanted people to know."

Sam studied her eyes. His voice softened. "Why do you think that?"

She didn't mean to make Josh sound like a jerk. They probably both just got caught up in the moment, and Josh didn't want to embarrass her by rejecting her publicly. How did she explain? "Remember how I passed out in the cafeteria in fourth grade?"

Sam's eyes rolled toward one side to look back through his memories. "I think I was sick that day, but I heard about it."

"Well, that's when I was diagnosed with juvenile diabetes."

Sam stood up straighter. His arm dropped down to the side. "I didn't know."

It had been degrading enough when Dad found out about her disease. She wasn't going to give her classmates the same reason to look down on her. "Yeah, I was embarrassed and tried to hide it, which made it even harder for me to monitor my sugar levels."

"Oh, man."

He didn't know the half of it. But she'd tell him this part to gain his support in keeping her from falling for Josh again. "A friend from 4-H invited me to go with her to prom during Josh's senior year. I fainted and Josh caught me."

Sam's lips parted. "You?"

"I know." Paisley shook her head at the irony. "I'm supposed to be this strong cowgirl who can shoot a rifle and take care of myself, then I passed out in a man's arms like the cliché damsel in distress."

Sam ran a hand through his hair. "This is crazy."

"It gets worse." She grimaced. And not simply because of the situation but at how she'd reacted to the situation. "He carried me out into the lobby of the Sun Valley lodge so he could lay me down on a couch. I was out of it and scared. And I was afraid that if he called an ambulance, I'd get in trouble with my dad. So I clung to him." Paisley couldn't look Sam in the eye. "And he asked to kiss me."

"Holy buckets."

Paisley peeked up. "Finally he convinced me to let him go get a cup of water. After he left I remembered where I'd put my purse with my insulin. I retrieved it and injected myself in the bathroom where nobody would ask questions. When I went back, he was gone. I felt really dizzy and had Evangeline take me home right away."

Sam blinked repeatedly as if in shock. But the fact that Josh never told him about kissing her was proof his older brother wanted to keep it a secret.

She shrugged off the lingering disappointment. "I thought Josh would want to talk about it when he came over to work at our ranch the next weekend, but he acted like it never happened."

"That's incredible. I don't . . . I don't know what to say," Sam stammered. Sam didn't stammer.

"You don't have to say anything. I'm not trying to badmouth your brother. He dated a lot of girls so, who knows, maybe . . . maybe he doesn't even remember."

Sam motioned toward the lodge, a look of concern washing over his face. "Have you loved him all this time?"

Love? Paisley pulled her head back at Sam's overreaction. "No. It was a school girl crush. I'm over it. I was engaged to marry Nicholas Riley, remember?"

"Yeah, but you didn't."

Oh no. Sam was supposed to be on her side here. What if he really *did* think she loved Josh? What if he said something? Then Josh felt forced to talk to her about it? She'd feel even more pitiful than she already did.

She pointed a finger and stepped closer until she could dig it into Sam's chest. "Don't you dare say a word to him."

Sam grabbed her hand and laughed one of his I'm-innocent laughs. "What would I say?"

She knocked his arm away and poked him with her other hand. He had to know how serious she was. "Sam, if you want ice cream tonight, then you will promise."

The laughter died. He lifted three fingers in the sign for Scout's Honor. "I promise."

The door creaked behind her. "It's warmer in here, guys."

Paisley's heart lurched into her throat. She had enough to worry about without the threat of Josh bringing up their past. She sharpened her glare to stab Sam with it one more time.

He pressed his lips together to symbolize them as sealed.

The pressure in her chest eased away on an exhale. She could trust an American soldier, couldn't she?

She pulled her hand from his chest and scratched at the hair tucked underneath her beanie to appear nonchalant. "We're coming." She spun and gave Josh a candy-coated smile. Why did he have to look so perfect in overpriced sweaters? "If you'll help Sam set the tree in the stand, I'll go dig some vanilla ice cream out of the freezer."

So what if Paisley had stood outside talking to Sam in the cold? Josh was planning to leave soon. But he hadn't left yet. He was just being treated like he wasn't there.

He twisted the bolt on the Christmas tree stand, while lying on his belly underneath the prickly branches. Sam simply stood next to it and held it in place. Josh grunted. "How's that?"

The tree swayed toward the wall as Sam let go. He righted it again so Josh could screw the far side in tighter.

Josh's fingers pinched against the hard metal until the bolt refused to move farther. "Try again."

The tree stayed in place. Success. And it smelled so much fresher than the fake tree Josh pulled out from storage now and then.

He dug his elbows into the nubby carpet to belly crawl backward from underneath the branches. He stopped in front of the stone fireplace and surveyed his handiwork from the floor. Beautiful. Maybe he should spend every Christmas in Montana.

Paisley padded into the room wearing fuzzy, striped socks. He should definitely spend every Christmas in Montana.

She nodded at a white, ceramic bowl in her hands. "Do you want ice cream, too, Josh?"

He shot a knowing look Sam's way. "It's too cold out to eat ice cream."

"That's what *I* said."

"You guys are pansies." Sam took the bowl and sprawled out on the rustic leather couch. "Thanks, Paze."

Paisley moved past the couch to pop open the plastic crates of decorations they'd brought up from the storage room. "Paze? I haven't been called Paze in a long time."

Sam's familiarity gnawed at Josh's gut. He'd known Paisley in high school, too. Well, he knew the dirty looks and snide remarks she shot his way when he tried to talk to her at her dad's ranch. And he hadn't made much progress since. He climbed off the floor to help her string the lights she'd found.

Sam scooped a spoonful of his favorite dessert into his mouth. "What do people call you now? Any new nicknames?"

Paisley plugged the white lights in to make sure they still twinkled before uncoiling the strand to pass it around the tree to Josh. He looped it over a low row of branches and handed it back. His fingers brushed hers—still cold from the snowmobile ride or maybe from scooping ice cream. If Sam weren't sitting there watching them like a Christmas movie, Josh would have cupped her hands in his until they warmed.

She retracted from the touch, her gaze flitting up to his before she continued looping the lights. "Uh . . . no new nicknames. Although . . ."

Sam's spoon scraped the bottom of the bowl. Already. "Although what?"

She handed the strand to Josh once again and left him to open another box. Had she been aware of his hand-warming plan?

"My grandpa had a name for me." Paisley dug through an assortment of ornaments until she found a paper heart woven together out of green and red cardstock. "He taught me how to make Norwegian heart basket ornaments when I was in kindergarten. He called it a *julekurver*." She pulled an old photo from inside and held it up for Josh to see.

He squinted at the faded image of a little girl sitting on her grandpa's lap. Same long, wavy hair, but in pigtails. Same freckled nose, only smaller. Same smile except for an empty space between her teeth.

"Ahh . . ." Josh finished winding the strand so he could take the snapshot and get a closer look. He turned it over. Was that English? "What's *'min skatt'*?"

"It means 'my treasure' in Norwegian." Paisley wrinkled her freckled nose at him. "That was Grandpa's nickname for me, which I guess is a big thing. Mom said in Norway it's very rare to use a term of endearment."

"How cool." Sam set his bowl on a side table to reach for the photo. "I love it."

Josh's gaze slid sideways to study his brother as he handed over the picture. Sam sure used the term "love" an awful lot in conjunction with Paisley. Was it simply a figure of speech or was his relationship-shy brother starting to fall for someone? The thought made the bottoms of Josh's feet itch.

He rubbed the soles of his stockings against the rough, stone hearth. "That seems to be a common sentiment," he said. "Annabel described you as a treasure, too."

Paisley looked up at him, eyes searching to see if he was speaking the truth. Though she wasn't looking at him as if he were a liar. She was looking at him as if she had trouble believing anyone else would consider her a treasure. "She did?"

Such sincerity made his own heart feel as fragile as if it were also made out of paper. "Yes."

"Of course she did." Sam handed the photo back for Paisley to stuff inside the ornament and hang on the tree. "I knew you were a treasure, Paze, but I didn't know about the nickname. I'm learning all kinds of things about you today."

Josh tilted his head. "What else have you learned?"

Paisley's wide eyes turned Sam's way. Sam cleared his throat before diving into a second crate and coming out with a Santa hat. He stuffed it on his head then grabbed a couple of stockings to hang on the mantle. Josh looked back and forth between the two of them. Did he even want to guess what they weren't saying? If he saw anybody else acting that way, he'd assume they were romantically involved. But the cramping in his gut wouldn't let him make such an assumption here.

Sam was his brother. Sam would tell him privately if anything had happened.

Christmas music floated in from the kitchen. Paisley hummed along as if Josh was going to forget he'd asked a question.

"Grandpa Johan used to play Christmas songs on his guitar when I was little," she said.

Josh spied a twelve-string resting in the corner. His own grandpa used to play, too. Taught him a few chords. But that wasn't the reason she'd suddenly gone all hush-hush.

"Oh yeah?" he asked. He'd play along verbally with her change of subject but challenge her with a knowing look.

"Yeah." Paisley refused to meet his gaze and left the ornaments to him as she retrieved pine garland for wrapping around the log support beams separating the living space from the dining space.

If he was going to get any information, it would have to be from his brother. Finally, Sam got tired of fiddling with the stockings and took his bowl to the kitchen. Josh hooked an ornament on the tree, so he was free to follow and demand if Sam had kissed her, but Paisley beat him to the kitchen alcove. Josh could see the two of them from his position at the fireplace, but the kitchen area was far enough away that the sound from their conversation didn't carry.

Seriously? Did they think they were being covert?

If they wanted to leave him out, fine. He should be getting used to the feeling by now. First his job. Then his engagement. Now his family. Josh plopped down on the couch with his back to the kitchen and stared into the plastic crate where Sam had removed the stockings. A manger scene awaited display.

Josh wasn't the only one who'd gotten left out this time of year. At least he'd been allowed in the house and wasn't forced to sleep in the barn like Jesus. He leaned forward and pried the lid open to remove a crèche. One by one he unwound bubble wrap from each wooden carving and set them inside the stable.

What do I do, Lord?

How often did the answers to his life's questions stare him straight in the face the way they were right now? Josh was supposed to worship. The way the magi did. No matter what his problems were, Jesus was the answer. And focusing on the answer always made the problems seem smaller.

He crossed the room, picked up the guitar, and sat in front of the hot, crackling fire. It took a few minutes to strum, tune, and feel at home with the instrument. He'd start with the beginner version of "Silent Night" until the rust wore off his skills.

Having grown up on a Christmas tree farm, he'd heard a lot of Christmas music and knew all the verses to the song by heart. But it wasn't until he got to the fifth verse that the words came alive.

"Silent night, holy night, wondrous star, lend thy light . . ."

Wondrous star. The logo he'd designed for Paisley's ranch. It meant much more than a horseshoe or the bull horns so many other ranches used. It was a sign from God that He had a plan for redemption.

Josh needed redemption. He didn't know what that would look like. With the phone call he'd gotten earlier, it could very well involve his old job. He knew now that it would never involve Bree. He wanted someone more like Paisley. Someone with depth and heart and the ability to keep up with him and his four brothers.

But no matter what it looked like or what happened between the youngest Lake brother and Paisley (eye roll), Josh had to find some way to thank her. She'd taken him in even when she hadn't wanted to, and through the beauty and simplicity of Bright Star, he could celebrate the holiday season with hope.

CHAPTER THIRTEEN

PAISLEY PICKED UP A TURQUOISE COWGIRL boot with white floral embroidery to read the price tag on the bottom. Annabel could use a new pair for Christmas. Two-hundred-and-fifty-nine dollars? She put the boot down. Annabel's pink boots matched everything in her wardrobe. Paisley shouldn't mess with that.

She frowned across the store to where Josh was in a deep conversation with a Native American who made jewelry. He'd talked her into going shopping, but unless she wanted to buy art, ski equipment, or fur coats, there really wasn't much of a selection in Big Sky. As for Josh, how did he even have money to shop in the first place?

Hangers screeched against metal, and Sam appeared between two overpriced ski jackets hanging on the coatrack in the middle of the store. "I lent him money so he could buy you a gift."

Paisley's gaze slid up to meet his. Was he serious? Josh had nothing. He shouldn't be spending money on her. And she definitely didn't need anything—especially any reminders of him after he left. "You didn't have to do that."

Sam's huge smile overtook his face. "I know."

"You *shouldn't* have done that."

Sam's dark eyes flashed like a train signal, warning her laughter was headed her way. "I wanted to see how romantic he could get. I'm not the most romantic guy, you know. I could use a few pointers from my big bro."

"You're horrible." She couldn't keep from laughing along with Sam despite the heat flooding her cheeks. "Did I not lecture you enough in the kitchen last night? You're supposed to be understanding and supportive, but you're making everything worse. I'm getting you a bus ticket home for Christmas."

"Or maybe you're sending me back to Sun Valley so you can be all alone with Josh." Sam pretended to check out a display of sunglasses next to him, but the wicked grin told her he was impatiently awaiting her response.

So this was what it was like to have a little brother. Well, then she'd act like a big sister. "If you don't knock it off, I'm going to plant some mistletoe over you and Charlie."

Sam's expression turned serious. He waved a white t-shirt. "Truce."

Paisley smiled triumphantly. "Truce." She made her way down another rack away from Josh. She didn't want him to know she knew he was buying her a gift. But she did know it. Which meant she should probably buy him something.

She sighed. What did one get a guy who used to have it all? A mug with a moose on it? A cheeseboard in the shape of Montana? A bear sculpture designed to hold toilet paper?

Sam looked over the other side at her. "I know what I'm getting you."

She narrowed her eyes. "I already have the bathroom bear. Grandpa Johan put it in the master bath a few years ago."

Sam's eyebrow arched then his gaze dropped to the bear in question. "As *awesome* as that is, I found something even better."

"The matching toilet brush holder?"

"It's not for the bathroom. It's for Big Red." Sam wiggled his eyebrows. "What is something your truck needs?"

"New paint?"

"Well yeah, but that's not available here."

"A new transmission?"

"Again, I'm pretty sure a gift store doesn't carry such items."

"New brake pads?"

"Well, *that's* scary. But still way off." Sam held up a plastic package with a picture of Rudolph on it. "Big Red needs a big red nose."

Paisley's brain registered the large antlers and squishy red ball. It was actually pretty cute, but would seem tiny on her giant truck. "I usually put a wreath on the front of Big Red."

Sam dropped the package to his side. "I didn't notice it."

She hadn't made the effort so far this year. And she'd be lucky if she got around to it at all. With throwing Frozen parties, driving sleigh rides, and preparing an ice skating rink, Sam should be thankful she went with him to get a tree. "It's still in a box somewhere."

"It's December twelfth, Miss Scrooge. You need to get that wreath out."

Paisley bit her lip to keep from replying "bah humbug." She might as well find the wreath for Sam. It really wouldn't take that long. And it was the least she could do for everything he was doing for her—everything except loaning money to Josh for a gift. Speaking of gifts, did Sam really want to get her the Rudolph thing? "Do you want me to put the wreath on Big Red, or do you want to dress him up like a reindeer?"

Sam's gaze dropped to the package in his hands before bouncing over to his brother. "I could always give this to Josh for his car."

Paisley smirked at the visual of antlers on the luxury sports coupe. "He would never use them."

Sam leaned forward over the shelf and lowered his voice. "We could decorate the Mercedes for him."

Paisley guffawed then slapped a hand over her mouth when Josh twisted his head their direction. His eyes met hers. Paisley's heartrate picked up speed. But that could be because they were talking about pranking him. Did he know?

Josh's brows lowered before he turned back to the salesman.

Paisley's pulse returned to normal. She pulled her hand away from her mouth but cupped it by her cheek to keep their discussion more private. "How are you going to do that?"

"Not me. *We.*" Sam looked out the window into the parking lot. "You distract Josh while I buy this. And figure out a way to get his keys so I can roll down his windows far enough to insert the antlers. I'll borrow Big Red and be back before he knows I'm gone."

Paisley's heart lurched forward once again. "You're joking."

"I'm serious. You both need to lighten up and get into the Christmas spirit. Plus, I think I owe Josh for pranks he's pulled on me in the past."

Paisley understood the Christmas spirit part, as she and Josh were probably both downers for the youngest Lake, but she didn't want to get into the middle of a prank war. She lifted her hands in a shrug. "How am I supposed to get his keys?"

"Be resourceful." Sam took off toward the cash register.

He was buying it? Then she'd have to get Josh's keys right away. But . . .

"Find anything?" Josh spoke from behind her.

She jumped and spun, almost knocking down the cheeseboard. She grabbed the smooth piece of wood to right it. "Do you like cheese?" she blurted.

A corner of his lips turned up. "That is the cheesiest pickup line I've ever heard."

Ohh . . . not at all the tone she was going for. But it was almost impossible not to flirt with Josh. He made her insides melt like a snowman. She had to regain her original prickliness. "Did you already forget the pickup line you used on me at The Coffee Cottage?"

Josh titled his head as if it would jog his memory. "I was pretty out of it from lack of sleep, but I think I called you an angel. Most women like that kind of thing."

"I'm sure." A great reminder why she had to pretend she wasn't falling for him.

"So." Josh glanced over her shoulder toward his brother at the cash register. "You think I should take lessons from Sam on how to hit on women? He seemed to have you laughing pretty hard over here."

"Sam?" Paisley had to get Josh away from Sam before he saw what Sam was buying. She grabbed his arm and pulled him toward the door. "Let's go next door. Sam can catch up."

Goodness, Josh's bicep was solid for a white collar worker. Was it possible for him to be even stronger than he was when he worked for her dad? What would it feel like to have those arms wrapped around her again? She had to get him outside and let him go before she caved into the temptation to try to hang on. Forever.

The bell jingled as she pushed outside into the snow. Josh looked down at her, his face only inches away since she hadn't released him yet. The stubble on his chin suited him. She retrieved her lip gloss from her pocket and twisted it open.

His breath puffed warm against her cheek. "What's going on?"

She froze with the applicator halfway to her lips. Had he overheard the Rudolph plot?

Josh pulled away. "If you have a thing for Sam, don't use me to make him jealous."

Paisley's arms dropped to her sides, half of the lip gloss container still in each hand. She searched his eyes. Rejection glimmered underneath the hazel surface. She knew that look because she'd looked at him that way for years.

She'd been rejected by him, not the other way around. Now she was protecting herself. And he considered it rejection because he'd already been hurt by the woman he'd planned to marry. He was hurting, sure, but not because of her. As for her having feelings for Sam . . . "That's ridiculous."

The accusation in his glare wavered. "You obviously have a thing for him."

Her face scrunched up in disbelief. "Because we're friends?"

"You guys talked until midnight last night."

She'd needed a distraction from Josh. And from the way her heart ached with loneliness when he played Grandpa's guitar. But she couldn't tell him that. "He's easy to talk to."

Josh lifted his chin, unwilling to accept her explanation. He turned his back toward her, but she could make out the reflection of his face in the window of the camera shop. His eyes roamed the display aimlessly.

Why was he making such a big deal out of her relationship with Sam? Was it because he was used to getting all the female attention before Sam joined the Army? Or was it because he wanted her attention alone? Had he really bought her a gift to woo her the way Sam suggested?

Her belly clenched tight over her insides at the idea, but even if he wasn't playing her, she'd end up losing in the end. Big Sky wasn't his home.

Paisley stepped next to Josh and looked at her own reflection in the window as she applied the lip gloss. How did she assure him Sam was only a friend without giving the impression she was still available?

She pocketed the tube. "I threatened to hang mistletoe above him and Charlie if he didn't stop acting like an annoying little brother," she said.

Josh didn't smile, but a muscle in his jaw twitched. "It's his specialty."

Paisley's shoulders relaxed. There may never be solid ground in dealing with Josh, but at least she'd regained her footing. Time to move forward, away from that dangerous cliff of a conversation. "I should see if there's a photographer here who can come take pictures of the skating rink. That would look good on the website, huh?"

Josh nodded. "Now you're starting to think like a business owner."

A bell jingled, the gift shop door flew open, and Sam charged out as if headed to fight a three-alarm fire. A clump of snow from the eaves overhead slipped from its perch and smacked the back of Paisley's head before splashing down her collar and riding her spine like a waterslide.

Paisley shivered and shook the ice away. Too bad she hadn't worn her parka with the hood. "Remind me not to leave my coat at home the next time I come shopping with you, Sam."

"Here." Josh shrugged out of the barn coat he wore.

He was offering her his coat? Probably to mark his territory rather than to be a gentleman. Hadn't he gotten anything from Paisley's comparison of Sam to a little brother?

Paisley held up a hand to decline.

Sam cleared his throat. Bugged out his eyes. Jingled the keys in his pocket.

Oh. She had to wear Josh's coat to get his keys. Of course. So much for keeping her distance.

The warmth from Josh's body heat trapped in Grandpa's old jacket enveloped her as he slid one sleeve up her extended arm. She reached her other arm inside the oversized coat and stepped away to keep Josh's hands from brushing her skin, but his mossy scent clung to the material and followed her into the camera shop.

Photographer. She needed to focus on asking the proprietor about a photographer. She stepped to the glass counter to wait her turn.

The warmth of the jacket mixed with the heat of the shop ignited her from the inside out. Or was it the intimacy of knowing Josh had worn the coat that caused her to flush? It just smelled so . . .

Sam stepped behind her. "Are you sniffing his coat?"

Paisley slammed an elbow into his ribs. He needed to keep his distance so Josh didn't get any more ideas about the two of them together.

Sam clutched his gut. "I wasn't going to tell him."

"Cut it out, Sam. I'm trying to warm up from that snow you knocked down my shirt, that's all."

Sam stepped closer behind her. "And I'm trying to covertly get Josh's keys from you. Remember Operation Rudolph-the-Red-Nosed-Mercedes?"

Oh yeah. The whole reason she was wearing the big coat in the first place. She pushed her hand out the end of the long sleeve and rubbed the side of the rough material until she found an opening. Her fingers closed around hard, ragged metal. Bingo.

She retrieved the keyring and passed it behind her without turning around.

Sam's rough hand clamped down and pulled the keys away silently. Wow. If Sam ever needed a new job besides the military, forest fire fighter, and freelance ranch hand, he could always become a spy. "Give me fifteen minutes," he whispered.

Fifteen minutes until what?

He jogged away. "This shopping thing is wearing me out," he announced loud enough for Josh to hear from where he was browsing on the other side of the room. "I'll wait for you guys in the truck."

Paisley turned to gauge Sam's performance then glanced at Josh to see if he might suspect anything. Josh's gaze was already on her. Watching her watch Sam.

Her heart slammed into her chest as if she'd been caught doing something wrong. Which was worse? Josh suspecting they were playing a prank, or Josh getting jealous because he thought she was attracted to his brother?

She rolled her eyes back to the counter. It was going to be a long fifteen minutes.

JOSH SHIFTED HIS WEIGHT side to side to jostle loose the growing pressure inside his chest as he watched Sam take off out of the store. Maybe Paisley had been honest when she'd described Sam as a younger brother, but that kind of closeness could easily turn into something more. Josh might have felt chemistry with her, but his presence seemed to repel her like a magnet, whereas she told Sam secrets and laughed at his jokes.

Would this be bothering him so much if he hadn't recently been dumped by his fiancée? If he hadn't been planning on getting married and settling down? Paisley accused him of being on the rebound, but could it be more than that?

Paisley was the one girl in high school who'd been immune to his charm. She challenged him to analyze his life. She made him want to be a better person.

But she was right about their relationship not being able to go anywhere. It had been silly of him to special order her a necklace pendant designed after her new ranch logo. He should be happy for Sam. Especially since Sam normally avoided commitment. If the kid did commit to Paisley, he'd be free to move to Montana. And he'd fit in great on the ranch.

The pressure expanded against Josh's sternum like a balloon as he imagined himself serving as best man in Paisley's wedding. How could watching Paisley marry someone else make Josh the best man? Wasn't the best man supposed to win?

Josh spun away from the tripods section and marched over to the glass counter where the shop owner wrote down information about a local photographer for Paisley. She looked tiny and outdoorsy in the huge jacket he'd given her to wear. Yeah, he'd wanted her to wear it like a shield to protect her from Sam's advances, but maybe he should talk to her and tell her how he felt rather than get all chicken-breasted and try to compete for her affection.

Paisley glanced up hesitantly as he approached. The uncertainty in her eyes sucked the wind out of his sails.

"It's over a grand for professional photos of the ranch," she said. "I'm going to have to wait for my loan to go through before I can afford this."

He slowed. Because he had nothing to offer her. He was as broke as a joke. Not that she needed money from him. She was capable of starting the ranch on her own, but by the time she was able to get the pictures taken, he'd likely be back in Chicago.

He studied the sweet determination on her face. Was there anything more beautiful than a woman who wanted to change the world? Maybe he'd stick around until after Christmas. "That should be soon, right? You'll be able to get the pictures taken before the snow and ice melt?"

"I think so, but it would be even better with the Christmas lights up." Her eyes came alive, and her gaze danced with his. "You know what would be really fabulous? A star at the top of the barn. It would go perfectly with the theme of the ranch, and also, it's Christmassy."

With the way Josh's heart responded, she might as well have been an angel singing about joy to the world.

"Sam would have to stop giving me a bad time about not wanting to decorate," she added.

The Christmas carol playing in his mind came to a halt as with the scratch of a record. "You put up the tree for him. What more does he want?"

Her eyes blinked wider. She waved a hand between them and looked away. "I told him I usually put a wreath on the front of Big Red, but I haven't yet this year. I probably should. I will. Yeah, I will." She wandered toward the exit. Did she have another destination in mind, or was she trying to get away from another conversation about his brother?

This wasn't about Sam. This was about them. He followed her. "Sam's still a little kid when it comes to Christmas. He doesn't feel the weight of the kind of responsibilities on our shoulders. He hasn't lost a job or a fiancée or a grandpa. He hasn't ever had to come up with a business plan."

She pushed open the door, allowing the cold air to remind him he wasn't wearing his coat. But that was one more way he had a connection with Paisley that Sam didn't have. "There's no rule you have to put a wreath on your truck. I say if it causes you more stress, then don't worry about it. I like the star on your barn idea, but decorating cars is a bit over the top."

Paisley stopped. Tilted her chin toward him. Her eyes studied his, searching for something. "Yeah, you don't need that." She gave a little head shake. "Your car is already over the top."

He looked up toward heaven beyond the bright blue sky then smirked down at her. There she was—repelling him like a magnet again. But the thing about magnets was that if you turned one around, they'd connect. "Will you ever let me live that down?"

"Mm . . ." She twisted her mouth to one side as she thought. "Not today."

What did she say? He was too busy watching her lips in fascination for the words to register. Maybe he didn't have to turn her around. Maybe *he* could turn around. Maybe he already had. Because there was some kind of magnetic pull going on. Scientists called it attraction.

A giant red truck crunched through the snow next to the curb. A loud honk jerked Josh back to reality. The reality of Sam behind the wheel of Big Red.

He looked up to find Paisley's wary eyes watching him. Her last words penetrated and rang through his skull. *Not today . . . not today . . . not today . . .*

That didn't mean never. Did it?

CHAPTER FOURTEEN

THE ONLY WAY THEY ALL FIT in the truck was for Paisley to be squished in the middle. Josh hadn't minded letting Sam drive earlier, but now he was wishing his younger brother had taken the snowmobile. Because every time Paisley's thigh brushed against his, he knew Sam was feeling the exact same thing. And Sam seemed to want to prolong the experience.

"Anybody else need coffee?"

"Oh, I do," Paisley responded before Josh could even shake his head. Did she really need coffee, or did she simply want to ride the extra mile out of the way to The Coffee Cottage while sitting next to Sam? Because usually she was an all-work-and-no-play kind of person.

His breath puffed out and fogged the window beside him. He'd need to have that talk with her soon. But for his own peace of mind, he'd give her the benefit of the doubt. She needed coffee as fuel and to warm her for when she got home and had to work in the barn.

The sun was already starting to set, so she'd have to make dinner, too. Maybe he could help her in the kitchen. Maybe he could accidentally slice his finger when dicing potatoes, and she'd have to bandage him up again.

The crunch of tires on snow grew louder as Sam turned into the makeshift parking lot, and Josh realized how quiet the cab had become. He looked over at Paisley who seemed to be watching him out of the corner of her eye. Had he made her uncomfortable with his brooding? He'd prefer to talk to her alone, but it wouldn't hurt to join her conversation with Sam. "I'll take some coffee, too."

She didn't respond. Sam didn't respond. What happened to their earlier giggling and elbowing? Were they waiting for him to get out of the truck first?

Sam shifted to park, but they both sat there. Could the moment be any more awkward? Maybe Josh didn't have to talk to Paisley at all. Maybe he was already history. Fine. He yanked the old metal door handle and dropped to the ground. Too bad he couldn't drive his car back to the . . .

His car? Sam had parked nose to nose with it. Only the nose of his Mercedes looked a little brighter than usual in the glow of Big Red's headlights. He did a double take.

"What in the North Pole . . . ?"

Paisley collapsed forward in giggles. She filled the seat he'd vacated.

Sam hooted in laughter.

"You guys did this?" His luxury car had become even more of a joke. But Josh couldn't help chuckling, himself. Because if this was what Sam and Paisley had been talking about back at the gift shop . . .

Paisley wiped her eyes. "In case your car wasn't over the top enough."

Josh shook his head. The whole time he'd been acting like a jealous idiot, she'd been pulling a prank on him.

Sam smiled at him over Paisley's head. "This is for the time you replaced all the filling in my Oreos with toothpaste."

Paisley's jaw dropped. "You did not."

"He did. Another time he filled all my donuts with mayonnaise."

Paisley gasped. "Did you eat one?"

"A couple."

Josh shook his head in mock regret. "You really shouldn't have dragged her into this, Sam."

Paisley held up her hands in surrender. "It was Sam's idea."

Josh nodded to the coat she was still wearing. "Sure. And you went along because you were cold and wanted to wear your grandpa's jacket?"

She twisted her shiny lips to one side in guilt. She'd pretended to be cold to get the keys out of his pocket. As for Sam knocking snow down her shirt, that was probably no accident.

"Maybe," she said.

Sam patted Paisley on the back. "Don't worry. We taught him a lesson. Now he knows not to mess with my food."

Josh eyed Sam's hand on Paisley's back. "Speaking of food." He motioned his head toward the coffee shop. "I could use a croissant. How about you, Paisley?" He held the door open for her. No way would he leave her behind with his brother.

She unbuckled and slid his direction. "From what Sam said, I don't think I should trust you with food."

"That was a long, long time ago."

She landed with a plop in front of him and erupted with laughter. "In that case, will you order me a sugar-free cream cheese croissant? I have to run to the bathroom." She reached into her wallet to dig out some cash.

So embarrassing that she had to pay. Before Josh left Big Sky, he'd make sure to take her out for a huge meal. On his own dime.

Sam slammed the driver's side door and sauntered around the truck. "I've got it, Paisley. Since the whole Rudolph thing was my idea, I'll pay."

Josh ground his teeth together and looked away. Paying had always been his thing.

"Thanks, Sam." Paisley snapped her purse shut and ran toward the front door. Her continued giggles floated back to them.

Josh wanted to enjoy the relief that came from knowing Paisley hadn't been trying to make Sam jealous earlier by hanging onto his arm. He'd talk to Sam about it, if there really was something to talk about, but he needed to hear it from her first.

He pulled the coffee shop door open. Jingle bells announced their entry.

"Samuel Lake." Dot welcomed his little brother like Santa reading the kid's name off the nice list. "The ride on your snowmobile inspired me. I called on an ad in Craigslist, and I'm going to sell my car to buy a snowmobile."

Sam's mouth hung open, but Josh smiled. He knew Dot's hobbies never lasted long enough for them to worry about.

"I'm not going to ride it, though," Annabel chimed in. "I was not inspired by your snowmobile but by your practical joke. I'm making candy cane reindeer to stick in hot chocolate for the kids."

Dot faced her friend with an exuberant frown. "You promised me you'd try out the snowmobile if I helped you make candy cane reindeer."

Annabel pointed to the two miniature candy canes Dot had formed into the shape of a heart. "But you're not making reindeer."

"Kids can have Rudolph," Dot argued. "This is for adults." She set the heart down on the side of a red saucer holding a red mug. "What do you think?"

"Nice," Josh offered.

"Looks like something ladies would like," Sam added.

Dot beamed. "What can I get for you boys?"

Sam rattled off his order along with Paisley's. "And what do you want, Josh?"

Josh wasn't going to take charity from Sam no matter how much the kid had in savings after serving oversees and spending a summer helping out the United States Forest Service. "I'm fine."

"Bro. I thought you wanted a croissant."

Dot rose to her feet. "I'll be offended if you aren't at least tempted by our brew. At least let me give you that free cup of coffee I owe you for being Paisley's friend."

It did smell good. And it would warm him up.

"Paisley's friends get free coffee?" Sam asked.

Josh grunted. "Long story. I'll take that cup, Dot. After all, you're the whole reason I'm still here." Sam may have gone to high school with Paisley, but Josh had a bit of a history with her, too.

"Goodie." The older woman scrambled behind the counter to pour drinks while Annabel retrieved pastries.

Paisley joined them from the back hallway. She held a hand to her belly. "Is my food ready? I think I need something to eat."

Josh frowned at the lack of color in her face. She'd been so happy a moment ago. Was the stress getting to her? Getting sick was the last thing she needed before the holidays.

"Here." Annabel rushed over with a candy cane. "Peppermint helps with a queasy stomach."

"Thanks." Paisley sucked on the end of the stick and sank into a chair.

The older women kept up a dialog with Sam over the prank he'd pulled, something about "reindeer games." Josh grabbed the cream cheese croissant as soon as Annabel placed it on a plate and hurried it over to Paisley.

What was he doing? Was he really the best thing for her? If she was stressed over the ranch and creating stability for her future, she didn't need him fighting for her attention. The whole reason she pushed him away was because she knew he was leaving. And he was.

So what if his blood heated up every time her golden brown eyes glanced his way? He'd made a lot of mistakes in his life, and he needed to turn that around. He had to stop thinking about himself all the time. It had gotten him nowhere.

He gulped his coffee and resolved to let her go.

"THANKS." PAISLEY PROPPED UP her heavy head with one arm and took a deep breath before pinching off a piece of her pastry.

"Anything else you need?" he asked.

She gave him a small smile and shook her head. If her blood sugar was low, eating would raise it. Too bad she'd left her testing supplies in her parka back at the ranch. "This should help."

Josh glanced over his shoulder to where Sam was still caught up in retelling all the pranks from their past. Dot and Annabel were just as enthralled as she had been at the kind of childhood the brothers shared.

"I, uh . . ." Josh took another sip of his coffee. Had it made him hot enough for his forehead to shine with sweat already? The coffee shop was warm and cozy. Maybe that's why she felt so tired all of a sudden.

"I want to apologize for getting jealous back at the gift store."

She peeked up, taking a moment to assemble his words into a sentence that made sense. What was wrong with her?

Oh no. She'd been here before. Ten years ago when her blood sugar went out of control at the masquerade ball. She couldn't end up in Josh's arms again. No matter how sweet and protective he was acting.

"I admire you, Paisley."

The words hushed her doubts to sleep like a lullaby. He wasn't only trying to stroke his ego with her admiration. He. Admired. Her.

"Even though I know you're right to push me away."

She rocked back in her seat. This wasn't what he'd said when he carried her into the hotel lobby at the ball.

"As much as I'd like to get to know you better, I'm going to be leaving soon."

She knew that. Why did he have to say it? Why couldn't he kiss her despite the fight she liked to put up? Why did she have to put up a fight in the first place? She may not get forever, but that would have made their short amount of time together even sweeter.

She rubbed her temple and squinted at him through the fog. Normally she chose to corral her feelings with logic, but now she couldn't think past her emotions. Why wasn't the food helping?

"So I have no right to get jealous."

He didn't. But at the moment, his confession made her feel valuable—like that pair of turquoise cowboy boots she couldn't afford.

She could give him the right to be jealous if she wanted to. She reached across the table planning to lace her fingers with his.

He held up his hands to release any claim he might have had. She couldn't reach him if she tried.

"Sam's a great guy. And even if you aren't attracted to him now, then—"

"No." He was trying to set her up with Sam? He had no idea she ached to slide her hands up the sides of his face into his messy hair and pull him close enough to crush his mouth with hers and recreate that magic moment that had haunted her for so long.

A tendon in his throat twitched as he lowered his hands to his lap. "Well if not Sam, then somebody. You have to date somebody, Paisley. Because . . ." His eyes dropped to her mouth.

She curled her fingers into her palms to keep from clutching her throbbing heart and giving away her every emotion. This was why she'd kept up her guard. Where was it now? Why was she suddenly okay with images of melting against Josh despite the consequences? Blood pounded in her ears at the idea of being together.

Blood. Her blood sugar. It wasn't low. It was high. That's why she was tired. Why she'd had to go to the bathroom so bad. And why her resolve had weakened to that of a needy barn cat.

Oh no. The carbs she'd eaten would make her blood sugar rise even higher.

Worse than ending up in Josh's arms would be ending up in a hospital. She had to get back to the ranch to inject insulin.

She pushed palms against the scarred wooden table and rose to her feet. "We need to go."

Later she could finish her talk with Josh. Later when she wasn't tempted to have the conversation by whispering her responses into his ear and nuzzling his neck.

"All right." He stood, shoved his hands in his pockets, and looked away.

No. It wasn't all right. Without realizing it, she'd rejected him again. Later on she'd probably rationalize this to be a good thing. He was not supposed to have slipped so easily past her defenses. She was not supposed to be wishing to faint so she could wake up in his arms. It was not supposed to hurt so bad to know she'd quite thoroughly quenched the fire that burned between them.

Her legs carried her across the room. Away from the pain. Toward medication. That's what you did for pain, right? You medicated it. She reached through the fog for the man with the keys. "Sam." Every second counted when dealing with diabetes as well as matters of the heart. "I need to get home. Please."

CHAPTER FIFTEEN

SAM KNELT ON THE ROOF OF the barn and held the top edge of the ladder steady, high above Josh's head. "Come on." He shouted down. "What are you waiting for? Christmas?"

Josh gritted his teeth. "Don't give up firefighting, Sam. You'd make a lousy comedian."

"And you'd make a lousy firefighter."

Josh had never been a big fan of heights, but what was the worst that could happen? If he slipped, he'd only fall into mounds of soft snow. After falling from a horse, getting tackled by Sam, and then crashing on the pond with Paisley, this was nothing.

He gripped the icy rungs and climbed up after his brother to help hang Paisley's star. After that he'd have to help Sam muck stalls and unload the hay being delivered. Paisley hadn't been feeling well the night before, and when she still looked dazed at breakfast, he'd insisted she head back to bed. After he and Sam left, she'd hire ranch hands to help her out with the horses, but who was going to be there to take care of *her*?

The ladder jostled. Josh leaned into it to wait for it to steady before climbing higher. His stomach somersaulted as he looked down at the ground far below. Hopefully Paisley would applaud the end results of his effort. Because then this would all be worth it.

He reached the edge of the roof.

Sam sprawled flat on his stomach, huge grin on his face. Of course, the kid had always loved the thrill of danger. One of the Olympic trainers in Sun Valley had seen him on the halfpipe in high school and tried to talk Sam into training with him, but the youngest Lake decided to join the military instead. The choice had shocked his whole family almost as much as Josh was shocked that Sam hadn't mentioned boarding in Big Sky.

Lone Peak was known as one of the best places in the world for extreme snowboarding. Was this evidence Sam preferred to be around Paisley? Josh would have to find a way to ask casually.

Sam swung the frame of the star over the tip of the roof. He'd hold it in place while Josh hammered the nails that would keep it there.

Josh retrieved the hammer from where he'd hooked it to his pocket. "You planning on snowboarding at all while you're here?"

Sam grunted and shifted to align the star. "Of course. You?"

Josh grunted in return. "I'm broke, remember?" He pulled a nail from his jacket and leaned to the side of the ladder to place the end under the point of the star.

"Oh yeah." Sam's teeth flashed in his trademark grin. "I never imagined I'd have more money than you."

Josh swung the hammer. The clink of metal on metal rang out through their silent surroundings. "Enjoy it while it lasts."

"I will." Sam chuckled. "Hey, how about we go skiing tomorrow. Dot mentioned something about a free ski day on Friday."

That didn't sound like the resort Josh knew. "Dot also thought she was going to become a tattoo artist when I met her."

"She still could." Sam's voice rose as he defended his biggest fan.

Josh smiled at the relationship his brother had with the older woman. But it was Sam's relationship with Paisley he wanted to talk about. "Why don't you take Paisley skiing? I'll stay here and feed the horses and flood the ice."

Sam snorted. "Right."

Josh lined up a second nail. "What do you mean 'right'? I know more about horses than you do."

Sam moved his hand out of the way so as not to get smacked by the next blow of the hammer. "I mean you don't want me to go skiing with Paisley. You didn't even like me taking her out on the snowmobile alone to get a tree."

Josh frowned at the nail. Had he been that transparent? Here he thought he was going to be able to casually question Sam about Paisley, and he had Sam questioning him. He might as well be honest.

"I like her." Yeah he did. Especially the way she'd been looking at him the night before. There'd been something different in her eyes. Something vulnerable. "But I'm going back to Chicago soon. And she's not the kind of girl who starts a relationship she knows will end." He slammed the hammer against the head of the nail once more, forcing it to sink into the wood.

"Huh."

Josh grabbed another nail. But how was he going to reach the other end of the star? "Here, you take this, Sam. I'll hold the star in place while you anchor it in on the other side of the roof."

"'Kay." Sam grabbed the hammer and nail before belly crawling over the peak of the barn. He brushed snow out of his way and looked back at Josh. "You know you don't have to leave, right?"

Josh stiffened. He wasn't the same free spirit as Sam. He had a career. He had a mortgage. And besides, even if he would rather live in the middle of nowhere and give people horsey rides for a living, Paisley hadn't even wanted him there. "You're one to talk. Out of the two of us, you have more freedom to pick up and move. Yet moving here would be too much of a commitment for you, wouldn't it?"

Sam squinted in confusion. "You want me to move here? And what? Marry Paisley?"

The knot in Josh's stomach hardened. He hadn't meant to go that far. Though who wouldn't want to marry her? "Why not? You said you love her."

Sam held out a free hand. "Not like that."

"Maybe not yet." Josh's back muscles throbbed from the way he'd twisted around the ladder to push the star firmly into the red planks. And his heart throbbed at the resistance Sam was putting up at the idea of romancing Paisley. He nodded toward the nail Sam was supposed to be hammering so they could hurry up and finish the job and move on. Was Sam really going to make him spell it out? "You guys have been awful close lately. Whispering. Laughing. Pranking me."

Sam set up the nail before pounding. "Dude," he admonished.

Oh, like Josh was imagining things. They'd been standing within inches of each other on the deck when he'd interrupted them the other day. He had to know . . . "Have you kissed her?"

"No. Have you?" Sam shot back.

"No." Josh grabbed hold of the ladder with both hands to climb down. He wasn't going to admit she'd rejected him.

Sam rolled his way and handed him the hammer. "What about in high school?"

High school? Sam had known Paisley better in high school than Josh had. Josh hooked the hammer and checked to make sure Sam had the ladder anchored securely before he rattled it in descent. "No."

"You dated a lot of girls."

Josh gripped the lower rung and bent a knee to lower down to the next step. "You know why."

Snow rained down as Sam swung his legs over the edge of the roof. Wait. Sam was supposed to be holding the ladder in place, not joining him on it.

Josh scaled down quicker. "Stay up there for a sec, Sam."

Sam responded by climbing onto the top rung. He'd never been a good listener. "You're not getting out of the conversation that easily, Josh," he yelled over his shoulder.

Josh would have held out a hand in a confused shrug if he hadn't been hanging onto a wobbly ladder for dear life. "I thought our talk was over." A few more feet and he'd be able to jump to safety.

The ladder shook. Sam's body dropped past him to the ground. Oh no. He'd slipped. Josh would borrow Paisley's truck to rush him to the—

Sam landed in a squat then stood to grin up at him.

"Show off." Josh criticized but smiled to himself as he turned to face the ladder again and descend the normal way.

"So." Sam waited at the bottom. "What if Paisley is the girl from prom?"

Josh stepped into the snow as the idea swirled through his brain like a blizzard. Paisley would have been the right height. And had the right hair color. He'd never seen her in a dress, so it was hard to imagine. If she was the girl in the mask that he'd kissed, then it would make sense that none of the upperclassmen he'd taken out knew anything about the mystery girl. But if he'd kissed Paisley, why hadn't she said something when he saw her again at her dad's ranch?

He looked toward the lodge curiously. His pulse throbbed in his neck at the thought. His face warmed. Had he already kissed Paisley without even realizing it?

The image of her as a teen flashed through his memory. Long, messy, golden brown hair. A challenge in her amber eyes. Turned up freckled nose...

"She didn't have freckles." Josh's hope deflated. He clicked his tongue and looked back at Sam. "The girl in the mask didn't have freckles. I would have totally recognized those."

Sam frowned and scratched his head. "Are you sure because I think girls can cover those up with makeup?"

Was he sure? If there was any chance Paisley had been the girl from prom, he'd march right into the cabin and . . . and what? If she'd once shared a kiss with him but then was able to completely avoid him at the ranch, it must not have meant the same thing to her as it had to him. And that would have been a crushing blow. He'd be too embarrassed to even face her again. Besides . . . "It couldn't have been her. The dance was only for upperclassmen."

Sam's eyes narrowed in thought. "She could have gone with an upperclassman."

Josh sighed and watched as the little white puff of breath floated away. "If any of the guys I knew brought her as a date, then she wouldn't have been kissing me."

No, her date would have been there to catch her when she'd fainted. And goodness, the girl had fainted because she had high blood sugar from being diabetic. Paisley wasn't diabetic. And even if she was, she wouldn't have been scared of having Josh call her dad. Mr. Sheridan was one of the coolest men he knew.

Sam motioned with his arm as if trying to come up with another argument from thin air. "Maybe . . ."

"Maybe not." The mystery girl had to have been with the Boise Ski Club that had stayed at Sun Valley Lodge and crashed the event. Otherwise Josh would have found her by now. As for all Sam's arguing, it was a little suspicious that his brother was trying so hard to force the issue. Could it be that Josh's little brother really did have feelings for Paisley but was afraid to settle down? That sounded like Sam. "Ask her out, Sam."

Sam held up his palms. "Whoa."

Josh shook his head. "Stop trying to come up with excuses for why you can't be more than friends with Paisley."

Sam's mouth fell open. "I don't—she's not . . ."

Right. "She practically ran to you in the coffee shop last night, Sam. She obviously has feelings for you. And you couldn't do any better than Paisley."

PAISLEY WAS DOING BETTER. She wasn't as tired anymore, and the fog had lifted from her mind. Which was good if she was going to try to stay away from Josh.

She peeked out the window to where the brothers and Pastor Taylor unloaded the hay from the pastor's trailer underneath the large star they'd hung for her on the barn. It was perfect. It fit with her logo and her goal for camp. Josh was great at branding. And that's all it was. Even if her heart skipped a beat at the sweetness of his offer to hang the star.

The problem with keeping distance between her and Josh was that it gave her the opportunity to watch him covertly. His body may not be used to the manual labor anymore, but his knowledge and experience enabled him to make unloading the stack wagon look easy.

She had to stop looking. She closed her eyes, and the memory of Josh gazing at her lips the night before warmed her to the core.

Okay. Back to work. Physical work would be a good distraction. And if nothing else, the chill in the air would at least cool her down. She grabbed her coat, gloves, and the cowboy hat Grandpa Johan bought her last Christmas.

"Hey, Paze," Sam greeted as she crunched through the snow.

"Hey." She jumped up on the trailer to help Pastor Taylor hand down the sweet, earthy-scented bales.

Josh paused and studied her up and down. He was distracting her from her distraction. "Are you sure you're up for this?"

"Are you?" she shot back. She'd be better off if he headed inside to work on her website some more.

"Oh yeah. I got this." Josh retrieved her bale to stack inside the barn. He brushed his hands together when coming back for more. "In fact, I can cover the ranch tomorrow if you want to go skiing with Sam."

Skiing with Sam? She handed Josh another bale then looked over his head to see if his brother had heard.

Sam shrugged as if to say skiing hadn't been his idea.

Paisley pressed her lips together. Josh must have been serious the night before when suggesting she date someone so he wouldn't be tempted to kiss her. Maybe that wasn't such a bad idea. Then Sam would be more than a chaperone. He'd be "the other man." Josh would never make a move on her if that were the case. And Sam wouldn't, either. He was safe.

She grabbed another bale and pivoted to pass it to Sam. His eyes told her he didn't like being put in the middle. She'd explain later. "It's been a long time since I've gone skiing."

Pastor Taylor paused to wipe the sweat from his brow and look between the two of them. "You were in the military, right Sam?"

"Yep." Sam carried his bale toward the barn.

"Then you should definitely go skiing tomorrow. It's free for vets."

Sam paused. "That must be what Dot was talking about."

Josh took the bale from him.

"Yeah, I'm going." Pastor Taylor shoved the few remaining bales to the edge of the trailer. "I served in the Army for a few years right out of high school."

Sam strolled back to the trailer as if they'd already finished the job. "What position?"

Pastor Taylor's wide smile split his face. "Barber."

"No kidding." Sam pulled off the Seahawks beanie and ran a hand through his thick dark hair. "I might need a trim here soon. This is the longest my hair has been in years."

Josh rejoined the group, hands on hips, eyes on Paisley.

She longed to toss him another bale to get him to turn around and take away the prickly awareness that warned her whenever he was near, but Pastor Taylor and Sam blocked the hay with their manly talk of hairdos.

"So, you gonna go?" Josh asked her.

The weather report had predicted clear blue skies for Friday, which would make for glorious skiing, but even if she didn't want to ski, she'd still go to avoid being alone on the ranch with Josh. "If you think you can handle . . ." Darn. The ranch. She had another meeting at the bank. Hopefully to sign loan papers. She rubbed a hand over her face.

"What?" Josh's gaze burned into hers.

"I can't go."

Wariness shaded his expression. Did he not trust himself to be alone with her? Well then she definitely shouldn't trust him. "Why not?" he asked.

The other men looked her way at the question. Apparently they'd run out of topics of conversation after the "buzz cut."

She motioned for Pastor Taylor to move so the two of them could hand the brothers the last bales of hay. "I have an appointment at the bank."

Paisley handed over the last bale with the reluctance of putting down a shield. How was she going to protect herself from Josh, now?

CHAPTER SIXTEEN

Two weeks after her first trip to the bank, Paisley was headed back in to discuss her paperwork and hopefully finalize the loan. She pulled down the passenger side visor to fix her lip gloss to prepare for her second trip. And she'd gone all out this time, replacing her jeans and sweater with a business suit. She rubbed her lips together and studied herself with makeup on. It felt weird but hopefully looked professional.

Something made her fingers and toes tingle. Was it nerves about borrowing thousands of dollars to pursue a dream that may or may not work out?

Josh's gaze caught her attention. The tingles grew. That was it. "Don't stare at me. You're making me nervous."

Josh shrugged. "You look good. You have nothing to worry about."

If he thought she looked good, then she had a lot to worry about. But not right now. Right now she was headed into the bank. While he was going to pick up groceries. "Thanks. You've got the shopping list?"

He held up the folded piece of paper. "Check."

So weird having someone else go to the supermarket for her. And Josh wouldn't have been her first choice since he could barely boil noodles, but Sam was skiing. And her mind really wasn't concerned about food at the moment. Once she got her loan she'd be so happy, she'd probably forget to eat for a week.

"Okay." She nodded. "I don't think I'll be here that long, so if I get done before you, I'll wait in the lobby."

Josh nodded. The hinges squeaked as she pushed the truck door wide. Cold air swirled into the vehicle before she closed it again. And despite the chill, she stood and waved through the window as he rolled away out of the shopping complex.

A smile started deep within Paisley, and she couldn't keep it from reaching her lips. But that was because she was about to have her dreams become a reality, not because she was picturing Josh in the fabric softener aisle or trying to pick out the right size ham for Christmas. No, he was simply the exclamation point on her excitement.

Allen, the banker, was about to hand her a check that would open up the door for her to build and hire to her heart's content. And soon Bright Star Ranch would open, and she'd have hundreds of kids running around and laughing on her property.

Josh had nailed the logo design. There was no way the lender wouldn't approve her now with such a solid business plan. Which made letting him sleep in her bunk room until Christmas worth the risk of being close to him. Worth the risk of a broken heart.

She faced Big Sky Western Bank. Clasping the smooth manila folder with her new marketing materials, Paisley shook off the snow clinging to the wretched black pumps. She hated them, but Josh had made a quip about feeling like he was back in Chicago when he'd joined her in the kitchen for breakfast that morning. His former fiancée probably dressed like this all the time. Not that Paisley wanted to compare herself to the other woman.

No, she was absorbed with running a ranch and retreat center. Or she should be. She held her arms out for balance to keep from slipping on any ice as she made her way to the front door.

God, I know Christmas is about following Your direction so we can share our treasure, and I'm so excited for the opportunity. Please, please, please help me make this happen.

Her stomach clenched in determination. Dad had offered the money, but to him, money was all about control. And she'd never let him control the ranch where Mom grew up.

She swung the glass door open and wiped her heels on the thick, black mat before stepping into the warmth of the bank. This was it. She approached the counter.

"Good morning, ma'am, I will be right with . . ." Heather's long blonde hair flew over her shoulder as she did a double take. "Paisley? I didn't recognize you. Are you going to a funeral?"

Well, that wasn't the impression she'd been trying to create. "I hope not."

"Oh." Heather smacked her head with a palm. "You're dressed up to meet with Allen, huh? You look so chic."

"Nice save."

Heather giggled. "No, you really do. You should let me set you up with my cousin in Bozeman. He likes business women."

Paisley drew her eyebrows together. Not only was she avoiding dates, but with the way her toes were being pinched, she'd pretty much decided never to wear heels again. "I think you've forgotten who you're talking to."

Heather leaned forward as if telling secrets. "Oh, that's right. You have a couple of brothers staying at your ranch, don't you? Well, if nothing works out with one of them, know you clean up nice enough to pass as a business professional."

Paisley couldn't even go there. She'd pretend it was a compliment. "Let's hope Allen Marshall is as easy to fool."

A deep throat cleared behind her. "Miss Sheridan?"

Paisley closed her eyes. Of course Allen would have heard her comment about fooling him. How would she make up for that mistake? She'd have to be herself. Because though she may not be good with selling ideas and crunching numbers, she knew how to run a ranch.

She pivoted and held out a calloused hand. "Yes. Nice to meet you, Mr. Marshall."

"Likewise. If you'll follow me, please."

Paisley wobbled after the man. If anybody felt like a fool, it was her. She'd been ridiculous to exchange her jeans and boots for a stiff suit, but at least the new logo design was authentic to her identity.

"Please have a seat, Miss Sheridan."

"Thank you." Paisley folded herself onto the hard plastic chair, though it wasn't like she could be any more uncomfortable.

Mr. Marshall sat behind the desk and grimaced at his computer as if he were uncomfortable, as well. But perhaps that was because he wore a suit to work every day. With a tie pinned down the center of his shirt. "I've looked over your file, but I see you brought something to add to it."

"Oh yes." Hopefully her application had all the information he needed to approve her loan, but if not, he was sure to love the business plan changes Josh had inspired. She slid the folder across the table. "I've recently acquired the assistance of a marketing professional from Synergy Ad Agency in Chicago. He's redesigned my logo and come up with new ways to promote the ranch. Plus, my ice skating rink opens tomorrow." Okay, now that sounded professional at least.

Allen Marshall slid glasses up his nose before opening the folder. "Nice. Very nice." He pulled the readers off and poked the tip of one glasses arm into the cleft of his chin. If he thought the business plan was nice, why did he frown rather than smile? "And by what means did you acquire such assistance?"

Means? Like money? He wanted to know where she got the money. "I offered the man a trade—room and board at the ranch."

Allen Marshall nodded. "I admire your resourcefulness."

He did? Because she couldn't find any admiration in his eyes. "Thank you, sir."

He slapped the folder closed. "And I'm glad you are resourceful, because you don't have the credit needed for Big Sky Western to grant you a loan today."

What? She wasn't going to get the money? But . . . but . . ."I should have great credit. I don't have any credit cards or late fees or anything."

"Miss Sheridan, the problem isn't late payments and huge amounts of debt. It's that you've never made any payments at all. No car loan. No student loan. No mortgage."

Her heart sank. They were rejecting her because she was smart enough to drive Big Red rather than to get into debt with a new car loan every five years? And because she worked her way through college? And because she'd inherited a ranch? She scooted to the edge of her seat. "Doesn't that fact show how responsible I am? And isn't my property collateral in case I default?"

"I'm sure you're very responsible." Mr. Marshall attempted to placate her. "Which is why I believe you can find other ways to start your business without a business loan."

If he believed in her, he'd give her the loan. He had to work with her here.

"I can go buy a new truck today if you want. How long then? How long until I'll have enough credit to be approved?"

Allen Marshall glanced over her head. Probably at his clock. Because he had other things to do, other people's dreams to destroy. "Miss Sheridan, your best bet is to find a co-signer."

A co-signer? Who? Not her dad. He'd rather she borrow the money from him.

Who else was there? Dot? Annabel? Sam? Josh?

Goodness, she wasn't that desperate.

God? She glanced toward heaven. How could this be His will? Did God really not want her to get the loan? She was going to use the money for His glory. Was that not enough?

He had to have some other plan for her life. What were her options? Run the ranch herself? She was barely making it as it was. Go back home? Never. Sell it? No way, except . . .

"Can I mortgage my land?" That's what she did in Monopoly when she needed money.

Allen Marshall rose from his chair. "That's still not a possibility without credit."

She'd been giving Josh a bad time for driving a car he couldn't afford. But at least he had credit.

Her temples throbbed at the unfairness of it all.

"It was nice meeting you, Miss Sheridan." Allen Marshall held out his hand. "I wish you the best with your ranch. It would be a wonderful addition to our community."

Paisley stared. Numbness spread through her body. If he really thought the ranch was such a good idea, he'd offer her more than well-wishes.

When she didn't respond, the man used his extended hand to motion toward the door.

Paisley stood in her wobbly shoes. It was all she could do. Because ripping them off and throwing them through the window like she wanted to wasn't considered acceptable behavior. And she wanted to be accepted by the bank so she could start the kids' camp more than anything.

"Thank you, Mr. Marshall. Merry Christmas," she murmured.

Though Christmas was ruined for her.

JOSH LOADED THE GROCERIES into the coolers in the back of the truck to keep them dry from the snow. Walking across the store parking lot hadn't left him as cold as climbing stairs to the L station in Chicago wind. The blanket of snow seemed to insulate the way a blanket should. He would miss this when he returned home. And the beautiful mountains that surrounded him. And, of course, the big sky with its fresh air.

He climbed behind the wheel of Big Red and turned the key. It started on the first try. "Good boy." He patted the dated dashboard. He might even miss this old truck.

If only Marcus had reinstated his pay. Then he could take Paisley out to celebrate her loan. And he could celebrate the good news he got from work on Monday. His spaghetti hadn't been much of a celebration. The pasta was sticky and the sauce runny. And Paisley had expected dinner to be some kind of prize for winning the skating competition.

When she'd fallen on him at the pond and he'd asked what she'd wanted, she hadn't looked like she wanted spaghetti. Unless, of course, she was thinking about Lady and the Tramp and the way they'd shared noodles. Which had been on Josh's mind the whole time he'd made dinner. And it was still on his mind now even though he'd given up the idea of pursuing her.

He was headed home. Well, at the moment he was heading through the parking lot to pick up Paisley. But soon he'd be headed home to Chicago. Which meant he shouldn't be thinking about kissing her at all. And even if he did have the money to take her out for a celebration, she'd probably consider it a date and turn him down. They both knew she was better off with Sam.

He sighed and listened to the tires crunch over hard-packed snow.

A figure in black waited in front of the bank. Paisley? Why hadn't she waited inside the bank like she'd said? Miserable golden eyes locked onto his through the windshield. Oh no. She hadn't gotten the loan.

Josh rolled to a stop. His heart ached for her. She'd been counting on this. Planning on it for weeks. And now all that work and excitement he'd put into her logo design and business plan would amount to nothing. Unless there was another way. There had to be another way.

Could he loan her money? Would she let him consider it an investment? It couldn't happen for a little while. He'd have to get his job back and renegotiate the huge contract he lost, but it could be done. Maybe this was why God allowed him to lose his job in the first place. Maybe he was supposed to run into her in Montana. Maybe it wasn't about finding himself at all. Maybe it was about being there for someone else.

She yanked the door open but wouldn't look his direction.

He might as well test her out to see if she'd even be willing to take a private loan. "What happened?"

She didn't make eye contact but the sniffing gave her away. She was crying. Now what should he do?

"Hey," he consoled.

"Drive. Please drive."

He shifted gears and stepped on the gas. A high heel flew past his face. Was she aiming at him? He hadn't done anything. He was trying to help. He did a double take to check on her while driving.

"Sorry." The other shoe plunked to the floor without presenting any threat of harm. Paisley turned backwards to sit on her knees, her feet bare and her arms straining to reach behind the seat.

Josh scratched his head. "Did you lose something?"

"My mind apparently." She tugged at something just out of view, but she met his gaze long enough for him to see that her tears had dried into a shimmer of anger. "I can't believe I dressed up for that guy. I'm never wearing high heels again."

Rubber squeaked and a pair of red galoshes appeared from behind the bench seat. The sight of them made Josh want to laugh and pull her into his arms for a comforting hug at the same time. But he refrained. Because she was as tough as she was cute.

She righted herself on the bench seat and pulled the boots over her slacks. She glanced up as if to challenge his opinion of her attire.

"Much more practical," he offered, swallowing a smile. Her situation really wasn't anything to smile about. "What happened in there?" It appeared that the Scrooge she met with didn't think she was capable of running a ranch on her own, but he needed to hear it from her if she was going to accept any consoling and/or money from him.

She strapped on her seatbelt as he pulled out onto the highway. He didn't blame her for wanting to get as far away from the bank as possible before talking.

"I didn't get the loan. I don't have enough credit. I don't know what I'm going to do." She stared at her hands. "Though I guess I should start with taking down all my flyers about hiring. Stop at The Coffee Cottage."

"Hon." He'd meant the endearment to be comforting, but she shot him a look that told him she experienced it as condescending. He'd try again. "I'll take the flyers down for you. You shouldn't have to worry about it right now."

"I've got nothing better to do." She pointed at the shop on their left. "Stop."

Against his better judgement, he pulled off the road and shifted into park. His Mercedes mocked him. How much money he'd wasted in the past when he could have been using it to make a difference the way Paisley wanted to. Lending her money would be the least he could do. "I don't think you should give up on the ranch. I want to help. Keep the flyers up, and by the time you have ranch hands applying, I'll be able to loan you money and—"

She growled. Actually growled. "Absolutely not. I'm not taking money from my dad, and I'm not taking money from you. This is my ranch. My dream. I'm not giving over control."

Control? Josh held out his open hands to show he wasn't trying to rein her in. "I don't want control."

Her eyes narrowed. "Oh, that's right. You're not about control. You're about status. Will it impress your friends back in Chicago if you own part of a ranch in Montana?"

His face froze in confusion. "Status?" So maybe he had expensive taste, but he was willing to give up some of his luxuries for the greater good. He thought she'd be thankful. He'd thought it was God's will.

"Yeah. Status." She yanked her door handle to shove the door open. She paused and looked back toward him, toward the high heel sitting between them. "I'm going inside to take down my flyer. You can wait out here, so I don't embarrass you with my unprofessional appearance." She dropped to the ground and slammed the door.

Her behavior would be much more embarrassing than her appearance, but he'd keep his mouth shut and grant her grace over the loss she was experiencing. Her ranch was her everything. Maybe Dot and Annabel could calm her down. Or convince her to consider his offer. He shoved his door open and dropped lightly to the ground to follow her bright rubber boots down the shoveled walk.

She stalked ahead and pulled the front entrance open before he even reached the steps. Country music blared from inside. Not the usual coffee shop atmosphere, but then again, Dot and Annabel weren't the usual coffee shop owners. Josh grabbed the doorknob to follow Paisley in.

Annabel shoved chairs and tables toward the wall, their legs screeching against scarred, wooden planks. Dot stood in the center of the room with her thumbs in her belt buckles and her sparkly, gold boots tapping. A few customers stood around with their mugs and bemused expressions.

Josh slowed to stare. Paisley strode past toward the bulletin board, unfazed.

"Joshua." Dot clapped when she saw him. "I'm so glad you're here. Annabel was going to try to be my partner for swing dancing, but she's not strong enough to throw me in the air."

How did he get out of that one? He held up a hand as he followed Paisley. "Another time."

Paisley stared at the bulletin board. Brightly colored flyers and business cards advertised everything from craft bazaars to holiday parades. But he didn't see any hiring signs.

Paisley's shoulders slumped. "It's not here."

Josh ran a hand over his face. Was it safe to talk to her yet?

Paisley's rubber boots squeaked against the floor as she spun to face the shop owners who were now holding hands with each other and galloping around the room. "Where's my flyer?"

They galloped by. Dot waved and yelled back over her shoulder. "What flyer?"

Paisley's eyes flooded.

Josh pressed a hand to her spine to let her know she wasn't alone.

She shook it off. "My flyer for hiring ranch hands," she yelled across the room.

The women circled back their way. "I took it down," Dot squealed, her voice as gleeful as before. "You don't need ranch hands when you have Joshua and Samuel."

Except that he was leaving. Sam should have been standing there with her. If she wasn't going to accept Josh's money, then Sam was the only one who had anything to offer her.

Paisley turned to him then, her expression hopeless. Did she want help? Did she want him to yell at Dot for her? Or did she only want someone who understood?

He'd start by offering empathy in the form of a wrinkled brow and sad smile. She didn't snap at him or throw things this time. He lifted a hand slowly to run it down the sleeve of her blazer. She let him.

The front door swung open, bringing the familiar chill along with a couple of stout older men with mischief in their eyes. "How dare you start dancing without us," said the one wearing a red buffalo checkered hat with ear flaps.

"How dare you be late." Dot spun Annabel into the man's arms.

The man in the trucker hat pulled off his jacket to reveal a snake tattoo wrapped around one arm. He stuffed his hands into his pockets and chomped his gum.

"You're not getting off that easy." Dot yanked his hand out of his pocket and pulled him onto the dance floor.

Both couples spun their direction.

"What are you two waiting for?" Annabel glided by as if on skates. "If you're here, you might as well dance."

Her dance partner clumsily cha-chaed beside her. "Oops. Sorry. I think I got your toes."

Josh held up a hand again to wave them away. Of all the times for The Coffee Cottage to be turned into a dance hall . . .

Paisley turned, her hand covering her mouth, but her eyes didn't seem as shiny. "I don't know whether to laugh or cry."

Relief surged through Josh's veins. If she hadn't lost her sense of humor, there was still hope. "At least you're not throwing shoes at me anymore."

She bent her head and leaned into him, her crown pressed against his chest. He lifted his hands to hug her in tighter. But he couldn't. Not after how hard she'd fought to keep him away. Not after he told her he'd be heading home soon. Not after he realized she was a better fit for Sam. That would be taking advantage of the situation. He dropped his hands to his sides.

She didn't move. He rolled his head back to send an "ah, come on" look heavenward. Because if she stayed there, he'd be a heartless jerk not to hug her. He lifted his hands, flinched from the coming impact, and gingerly placed them on her shoulders.

Not bad. It was a kind gesture. He could do this. It wasn't like he was going to . . .

His fingers massaged the muscles at the top of her back. Gah. He needed to stop. But she was so tight. So tense. Only one moment longer. He wouldn't think about the way her hair tickled his chin. Or how he wasn't sure if the sugary smell was coming from her or fresh-baked cookies. Or how if the music slowed he could slide his arms down around her back and rock with her to the melody.

It was a good thing Dot and Annabel's dance floor was soon going to be returned to a coffee shop. And there weren't any holiday dances coming up that he knew of . . .

He froze as memories invaded. Bree had taken him to a Holly Ball last year. The ticket prices were ridiculous, but he justified it since all the money went to a charity.

What if Paisley put on a ball as a fundraiser for her ranch? His mind listed off resources and timeframes and the publicity involved. Together, they had what it took to make it happen. And people traveled to Big Sky for Christmas—people with money to spend. They'd see the value in helping fund a youth ranch. If not, he'd make the event something that they'd want to be seen at. He could invite Emily up from Sun Valley because her celebrity status always drew a crowd.

Paisley pulled away and lifted her chin to look at him. Her eyes were wary like they thought he might be about ready to nuzzle his nose against her temple. Not that he didn't want to, but his mind had been elsewhere. His gaze bounced with the energy of his thoughts.

She tilted her head. "What?"

"We're going to host a Cowboy Christmas Ball."

CHAPTER SEVENTEEN

"You want us to what?" Tracen's voice blared over the phone the next morning.

Josh glanced out the office window. A reporter from Big Sky News would be there any second, and he had to ensure his brother and famous sister-in-law were going to make the trip up for the Cowboy Christmas Ball and a silent auction fund-raiser the following Saturday, before he did the interview. "It's only a five-hour drive," he reasoned.

"Do you know how much time we spend traveling?" asked Tracen. "Mercy. We only got home yesterday from filming another Wonder Woman movie, and we have to go to Sundance Film Festival in Utah in a month. I finally built my cabin, but I'm never here to enjoy it."

Yeah. His life was rough. "Put Emily on the phone."

"That's not cool."

Josh smiled.

"If you talk to Emily, she will . . ." Tracen's voice faded away as if he'd covered the mouth piece. "It's Josh. He's trying to take advantage of your celebrity status."

Nice. Josh shook his head.

Muffled bumps and scratches echoed over phone wires.

"Josh? How are you?" Emily's sweet voice rang out. At least she cared.

"Hey, sis."

Paisley carried in a couple mugs of coffee. Her eyes widened at his use of the word sis. She set one mug down and pointed at the landline telephone before mouthing, "Emily Van Arsdale?"

Emily Van Arsdale *Lake* was more accurate, but Josh nodded. The thrill he got at seeing Paisley's awed expression beat out the excitement of his first meeting with the actress.

"I'm doing pretty well," he said. Did Emily still think he was suffering from being suspended from his job and dumped by his fiancée? He'd fill her in later. "I was actually wondering if you would want to come to Big Sky next weekend for a Cowboy Ball and silent auction. It's to raise money for my friend's ranch that she is turning into a camp and retreat center for families and kids."

"That sounds really cool." Emily paused. "Tell me more about the friend."

How did he explain? Maybe he best leave that to Paisley. "Here. I'll let you talk to her."

He held out the phone.

Paisley stepped back and waved her free hand in protest. Funny, he never would have expected the cowgirl to get tongue tied over a movie star.

The doorbell rang. He stood and set the phone down so Paisley would have to pick it up to talk to Emily or be considered rude for leaving the phone on the desk.

When Paisley realized what he was doing, she set her mug down and raced him to the office door. He reached it first and shot an arm across to block her path. She ducked to squeeze under. He shifted over so they were face to face. That should scare her away.

She didn't move immediately as he'd expected, but she wrinkled her freckled nose in defeat.

"Don't be rude," he admonished before leaving her to talk to Emily. He'd get the door and let Paisley work out the details of Emily's visit the next weekend. Which they would. And Tracen would come along and hang out with his brothers and eventually admit he was glad to be with family for the holidays.

Josh jogged to the front door and swung it wide to find not only a newspaper reporter but a film crew. He squinted at the van parked below the balcony. Channel Seven? They had to be from Bozeman. He'd emailed a press release but hadn't expected such a quick response.

The man who looked more like a college kid than a reporter held out his hand. "I'm Kyle Gray with KBZK. I was in the area for a piece on ski patrol and rescue dogs and figured I'd stop by to find out about your Cowboy Ball. Is it true actress Emily Van Arsdale will be attending?"

Josh grinned as a second car pulled up. Might as well make it a press conference. He'd been in over his head with life as a ranch hand, but he was in his element now. "Oh, it's true. And I'd love to tell you more about it. Come on in."

By the time Paisley joined him in the great room, he had two journalists along with the television reporter seated on the leather couch. He held out his arm to usher her to the leather armchair next to the Christmas tree. "Here she is now. This is Paisley Sheridan, the new owner of Bright Star Ranch. She's turning the place into a retreat center and kids' camp. Tickets for the Cowboy Christmas Ball will be raising money to help her get it started. I'll let her tell you all about the event."

Paisley eyed the row of interviewers then gazed at him, her mouth slightly open. It had to be a shock to go from talking to a celebrity to practically becoming one. He nodded toward the chair to get her to move. She closed her mouth and stepped forward slowly as if taking time to mentally prepare for what she was going to say.

"Ms. Sheridan, have you always wanted to run a camp?"

"And how did you come up with the idea for the ball?"

"Where are you from again?"

Josh stepped behind the couch to watch as Paisley got comfortable then began to share her passion. He crossed his arms, feeling proud of both her and his ability to help her. Though the real test would come that night after the news was announced, when they saw how many tickets had been sold from her website.

Sam joined him, on a break from his job of recruiting donations for the silent auction. "Pastor Taylor called. He's gotten the whole worship band on board to play at the ball. They are having an extra practice tonight to work on country songs and Christmas carols."

Josh nodded. That was a relief. A ball needed more than him on Grandpa Johan's guitar.

Paisley tucked a strand of hair behind her ear to keep it out of her face as she leaned forward, earnestly sharing her vision for the ranch. "As a little girl, I had two favorite places in the world. One was summer camp with my friends. The other was here with Grandpa Johan. I'd never imagined I would get the opportunity to combine both of those, and now that I do, I'm so excited to make a difference in the lives of other children."

His heart swelled for her. She may still be mourning her grandfather's death, but she'd used a tough situation to make the world a brighter place. She had a purpose.

His heart deflated a little. Because though he loved what he did, he'd never had the same kind of purpose. He helped giant corporations make money by selling products. Was anybody going to have their life changed by a product?

The ring of the phone interrupted his thoughts. Which was fine. They weren't comfortable thoughts anyway. He shook away the feeling of discontentment and trotted down the hallway to take the call in the office.

"Bright Star Ranch," he answered.

"Josh? This is Charlie. My guys have all agreed to act as parking attendants and a shuttle crew for your ball."

"Perfect." One more answer to prayer. Because they could decorate the barn with twinkle lights and bring in a dance floor and heaters, but if they couldn't get the guests down the two-mile dirt road, then any tickets sold would be worthless.

"We'll come out Saturday morning to plow the snow out of the field by the highway. Then we can park cars there."

Brilliant. Josh had never had a promotional event come together so easily. "I don't know how to thank you, Charlie."

She laughed. "Have Sam save me a dance."

That meant at least one dance where Paisley would be free to dance with him. "I'm sure Sam would love to dance with you."

Sam leaned in the doorway from the hallway. He shot Josh a dirty look and shook his head. Was it because he didn't like Charlie or because he preferred Paisley?

"Gotta go, Charlie. See you Saturday." He set the phone in the cradle and turned to face his little brother. "Did you need something?"

"I need you to let me choose who I want to dance with."

Josh wasn't going to ask who Sam would choose. He was having too good a day to ruin it with thoughts of Paisley in Sam's arms. "Anything else?"

"Paisley is taking the reporters out to the barn for pictures. I thought you might want to go."

Josh jumped up. "Thank you."

He'd join her so she knew she wasn't alone in this. If he'd gotten bruised and scraped up when getting on a horse for the first time in years, she could certainly get hurt when dealing with reporters for the first time. He grabbed the old coat he now thought of as his and jogged through the snow.

Paisley stood in front of the barn pointing up at the star he'd helped Sam hang. "The star isn't only a symbol of Christmas, it represents the name of my ranch, which I named because I want people to be drawn here and find hope the way the wise men found hope in Jesus."

Photographers focused their cameras on her, their whirs and clicks punctuating her speech. And there was nothing Josh could have added to make her words more beautiful. Had she just described him? Had he been drawn to the ranch for a divine reason?

Paisley spotted him. Her cheeks dimpled. "Josh hung the star. He helped me design the logo, too."

Heads turned his way.

"Can we get you in the photo, Mr . . . ?"

"Lake." Would Paisley want him in the photo? The reporters didn't know he'd be leaving soon. Paisley made it sound like he was as involved with the ranch as she was.

Kyle Gray faced him, his head cocked. "Lake? As in Emily Van Arsdale Lake?"

Josh flicked his gaze past the man toward Paisley. She still hadn't said anything about him being in the photo with her. She watched him with a dazed look in her eyes. She probably wasn't even thinking about him. She was focused on the fund-raiser and her dreams of opening a camp. Which was what he should be focused on, too. "Yes. Emily Lake. She married my brother, and they will both be here for the ball."

He had their full attention now. They'd want to note the connection in their reports. He didn't want the story to be about him, but he wanted to help Paisley's cause. He'd join Paisley if she didn't protest.

Josh walked across the snow to stand beside her, and it didn't feel weird at all. It felt like coming home.

She smiled up at him. "Thank you."

Cameras flashed. And he knew he should turn to pose for them. But he couldn't take his gaze off her sparkling eyes. Because though she was thanking him for what he'd done, he wanted to do more.

PAISLEY LOWERED GINGERLY TO the arm of the couch. Sam had sprawled across the whole thing, so there was no room for her, but it wasn't like she could sit still anyway. Her interview was supposed to come on the news any minute. And more importantly than what she looked like or how she sounded, was how viewers reacted. Would they buy tickets for two-hundred and fifty dollars apiece? So far, she'd only sold two. And that had been to Heather at the bank. Most of the people Paisley knew would be helping out at the ball, so it wasn't like she could sell tickets to friends. Not that many of them could afford it.

The fund-raiser had been a good idea. And Josh had been amazing at putting it together. But she still didn't want to get her hopes up. "You really think people will pay that much for tickets to a dance?" she asked.

Josh set his laptop on the kitchen counter so he could watch ticket sales. He stepped closer to the living area of the great room and leaned against a log beam. "People at Big Sky resort spend ridiculous amounts of money on fur coats, and they need a place to wear them."

That was a good point, but it didn't keep her from nibbling on a nail with nervous energy. The screen flashed to a rescue dog at Lone Peak. Somebody at the news station had thought rescue dogs were more important than her ranch. That couldn't be good. "The resort offers some events of its own," she countered, looking over her shoulder to gauge his reaction.

Josh nodded. "We're not limited to resort guests. People will drive down from Bozeman, as well."

Would they? "Maybe if they had more than a week to plan for it. You don't think they needed more warning?"

Josh lifted his shoulders. "Ideally, you could have been promoting the ball months in advance, but if people want to come they will come. Next year we can . . ."

His voice trailed off, but they left a burning sensation in her belly like a cattle brand. Next year? We? Why would he say that? She couldn't ask the questions aloud. But she couldn't take her eyes off his, either. His reflected the uncertainty she felt.

Was there a chance he wouldn't return to Chicago? She couldn't breathe.

"It's on." Sam rolled up, bumping her hip with his elbow.

She turned her back on Josh, but she could barely register the images on screen. Until the camera panned to a shot of them together in front of the barn. The way he strode over. The way she smiled up. The way they kept looking at each other rather than the camera. Oh no. She covered her mouth with her hand. The couple on screen made staring into each other's eyes look so natural. How could she face him again after that?

The screen flashed to a picture of her logo and the event information, but she couldn't even read it to make sure it was correct. She was still seeing the image of herself smiling up at Josh. Like she was in love with him.

"You guys, I left Sun Valley to get away from feeling like the third wheel," Sam joked.

But it was no joke. He'd seen their connection. That meant everybody watching the news would have seen it. Dot. Annabel. Charlie. Pastor Taylor. Josh.

What did Josh think? She couldn't see him. So she listened.

"If you don't want to be a third wheel, Sam, you should try dating someone." Josh didn't acknowledge Sam's insinuation. Which was good, right? Because it would hurt to have Josh dismiss the idea he had feelings for her. But she didn't want him to think they had a chance, either. Did she? No. That's why she'd avoided his earlier advances.

But this was so much different than an advance. Her throat constricted as if having trouble swallowing the idea.

"Pshaw." Sam kicked his feet back up on the couch to lie down again. "Right."

Footsteps. Josh was moving. Her mind blurred like the television screen during a snowstorm. Was he coming closer? Would she have to look at him in a moment? Feel his presence?

The footsteps carried him to the kitchen. Her body relaxed. She hadn't realized how tense she'd been. Maybe she needed to relax even more. She could say her body ached from the day and escape to a bubble bath. She really did ache but not the kind of ache that came from manual labor where it hurt to move a leg, or where her fingers stung from squeezing a shovel handle for too long. No, this was an ache that started inside her bones. Every bone.

"I'll check ticket sales." Josh's deep voice kept her in place.

She wanted to know if the news broadcast had affected ticket sales. And she wanted to hear his voice again. She sat as still as she could so she wouldn't miss anything he said.

"Oh, Paisley."

What? She twisted from her perch on the sofa arm, but she couldn't see him in the kitchen alcove. Why had he said her name like that? Was it only about tickets? Or could it be something else?

"You have to see this."

Ticket sales? He couldn't tell her? She had to go in there?

She pushed to her feet. Ticket sales. She was going to look at a computer screen and talk about ticket sales.

She walked gingerly as if testing out the ice on the pond. She could do this. She'd done it before.

He stood over the computer, eyes on the screen.

If he wasn't looking at her, she had nothing to worry about. She should be looking at the computer, too, but as she wasn't close enough to read the monitor, she let her gaze bounce back and forth between man and machine. "Is it good?"

It had to be good. Otherwise he wouldn't have called her in there. But good for the first day of sales on her first annual Cowboy Christmas Ball could be twenty-five people. They could have fun with twenty-five guests, couldn't they? It would make winning items at the silent auction even easier. She'd need to give Dot and Annabel an idea of how many to expect for the food they were catering.

Josh stepped to the side so she could get a better view of the computer screen. She couldn't resist peeking up at him first.

He beamed. The kind of beam she guessed he wore when getting the multi-million-dollar deal at Synergy Ad Agency. Was the news that good?

She held her breath and read the numbers on the screen. "Five hundred?" She couldn't have read that right. She bent forward to get a better look. She blinked. "That means . . ."

"We sold out," Josh said along with her.

She jerked upright, but the energy inside made her want to keep moving. "I can't believe it." She threw her arms in the air. This was happening. It was really happening. She hadn't gotten the loan, but God had provided another way. An unexpected way. A way she never would have gone without Josh.

She jumped a couple times then wrapped her arms around him for a hug. She was sharing the joy. She was congratulating him for a job well done. She was . . .

She was being hugged in return. His hands on her back pressed her closer.

The energy drained away. She couldn't think. She couldn't move. She couldn't let go.

His palms slid down to the small of her back. But she couldn't let herself touch him like that. She balled her hands into fists to keep from sliding her fingers up into his hair. She lowered her face into his chest so she wouldn't look up and accidentally nuzzle his neck. But still she couldn't let go.

His breath brushed her cheek. So warm, yet it gave her chills.

She shouldn't have hugged him. She shouldn't have let this happen. Because though she'd had memories of what it felt like to be in his arms, that wasn't the same. She knew Josh now. She cared about

Josh now. And having him hold her now wasn't about helping her get her blood sugar back to normal or calm her fears about calling her dad. It was about everything.

How could she experience this—to feel his heartbeat through his chest and the tickle of his fingers against her spine and have his muscles mold around her—and then live without it the rest of her life? What if she gave in?

Her toes curled in protest. Or maybe it was anticipation. But it didn't matter, she forced herself to pull her torso far enough away to meet his eyes. Only her gaze got snagged on his lips. They were so close. She tilted her head. But rather than close her eyes, she looked to him.

Big mistake. Because he was looking at her like he'd looked at her by the barn. The way she'd looked at him. The way that said she would never, ever get over him.

"Hey." Sam stepped past and opened the freezer. "I think you're out of ice cream. Can I borrow the truck to go get some more?"

Time froze, but it gave Paisley a chance to grasp her bearings. She was in Josh's arms—in the most passionate embrace she'd ever experienced, and Sam was talking about ice cream. Which was exactly what a chaperone should do. Maybe she'd thank him later when her mind cleared. Though her mind wasn't going to have a chance to clear if he was leaving to get ice cream, and she stayed in Josh's arms.

She stepped away. She couldn't look at Josh. She couldn't see his disappointment or let him see that she felt it every bit as deeply. And she couldn't remain in the room. "Yes. Go ahead, Sam."

Josh moved toward her as if refusing to let her get away.

"I'll grab you the keys." She spun. Keys. Where were they? Was her blood sugar dropping again, or was this how being in Josh's arms affected her? "I think they're in my purse."

The den. Her purse was in the den.

"I'll get them, then I'm going to head to bed. I'm not feeling well."

She strode forward, holding out her hands to help guide her along the hallway walls, because with as dizzy as she felt, she could easily stumble into furniture or down steps.

"Paisley," Josh called after her.

Josh. A second ago she'd been in his arms. She stopped and closed her eyes, reliving the moment. Then she said what she had to say. "Goodnight, boys."

CHAPTER EIGHTEEN

She didn't have to go to The Coffee Cottage in person after church to talk to Dot and Annabel about catering, but she needed to get away from Josh. Away from his smoldering looks and the questions in his eyes.

But there shouldn't be questions. She'd already explained everything. Unless he was considering staying in Montana for her. But with the kind of life he wanted, she knew that wouldn't be the best thing for him.

"Pais-ley," Dot greeted when she walked in the door.

"How are you, Paisley?" Annabel asked.

But the better question would be in asking how they were doing. Why were they sitting in rocking chairs? Why were they tangling yarn with long knitting needles? Had one of them pulled a hip muscle when dancing? Were they tired from staying out all night with their new male friends? Had they started drinking decaf?

"I'm okay. How are you?" she asked.

"We're ready to cater a ball for five hundred people," Dot said. She sounded like her usual energetic self.

"Are you sure?" Paisley looked around at the small groups of customers. She knew the older women preferred to be social over the actual business part of owning a shop, but if they were going to be feeding hundreds of people that weekend, shouldn't they be doing the work to get ready?

"Yes," Annabel answered. "We ordered all the food we need online. It will be delivered tomorrow."

"And we are learning how to knit so we have something to auction off at the ball," Dot added. "I'm making a Santa hat, though it's a little longer than I intended it to be. I just can't get the tip to come together."

Paisley eyed the knotted mess dubiously. She'd have to remember to place a bid so Dot wouldn't feel like a failure.

"It's very relaxing." Annabel held up her needles. "You should try it."

Paisley shifted. Could they tell how tense she was? If she didn't order coffee, they'd figure it out. They'd realize she didn't want the caffeine in her system because she already felt nervous enough. "I need something to help me relax," she said.

"What's going on with you, treasured one?"

The name melted her. Paisley sank into a stiff wooden chair as there were no more rockers available. "I'm in love with Josh."

Dot dropped her needles. "That's wonderful."

"No, it's horrible."

Annabel's eyes softened. Her gaze was a caress. "You don't think he loves you?"

Paisley stood back up. Her insides itched too much to let her stay still. She wandered away and gazed out the window at the Mercedes.

Josh was like his Mercedes. Gorgeous. Powerful. Exciting. But he wouldn't make it on her ranch.

"I don't know if he loves me," she said. But he didn't. He couldn't. She had to tell someone. Had to have them agree with her so she didn't feel like she was making a mistake. "He didn't love me in high school. He kissed me at prom then acted like it never happened."

"Oh . . ." Dot leaned forward. She was always one for juicy gossip.

Paisley blew out her cheeks. "Yeah. Broke my heart. But I was only sixteen. Now . . ." She shook her head.

"Fooey magooey." Dot pouted. "Has he kissed you since he's been here?"

Paisley laughed. Because it was absolutely ridiculous how scared she was of a kiss. "No. I won't let him."

Annabel set her yarn down. "It would be better this time."

"It would be worse."

"Why?" they chorused.

She'd never told anyone. Could she tell Annabel? Dot would probably blab. But what did it matter anymore? She was broken. No pretending otherwise. She moved back toward the pair to keep other patrons from overhearing. "I can't have kids."

Quiet. Because there was nothing they could say that would fix her.

"You can't have kids?" Annabel repeated softly.

Paisley looked at the landscape outside the window and bit her lip to keep it from quivering. She was like that landscape. The glistening snow made it look pretty and inviting, but underneath, everything was dead. "I'm diabetic. My blood sugar is really hard to control. Pregnancy could kill me like it did my mom when I was thirteen."

The rocking chair creaked. Boots tapped against hardwood. Annabel's frail arms wrapped around her. "I'm so sorry."

Dot joined them. More arms in awkward places.

But it was so beautifully awkward. Because she'd never told anyone. She thought if she did, it would be like confessing to a contagious disease. She'd be whispered about and avoided. Not loved. Not like this.

Paisley wiped at a stray tear.

Annabel looked up, her own eyes glistening. "I don't understand. Being barren is horrible, but that shouldn't make falling in love horrible."

Paisley sniffed then untangled herself to grab a napkin on the table next to her. "It's horrible because I can't marry him. Not that he's proposed or anything. I'm sure he's going back to Chicago soon, but if he knew I couldn't have kids, he definitely wouldn't stay with me."

"What?" Dot screeched. "Why would you think that?"

Annabel squeezed her hand. "Your ex. He found out and dumped you?"

"No." Paisley looked away. She hadn't expected their love the same way she hadn't expected her confusion. "I ended it with Nick before he found out."

Annabel's hand rose to her heart. "You never gave him a chance to choose you?"

Ha. Like her dad chose her mom? "Even if he chose me, I know what would happen. I wouldn't be enough."

"No, no, no." Annabel shook her head. "You *are* enough."

A ragged breath shook Paisley's body. "Before my mom died, she was never enough. Dad turned on her. Belittled her. Beat her. All because she hadn't given him what he really wanted—a son."

Dot gasped. "That's abuse."

Annabel tilted her head, a line deepening between her eyebrows as she leaned forward. "Paisley, an abusive man will abuse no matter how good or bad the woman is. This isn't about you not being enough. This is about choosing a man who will treasure you like you're more than he deserves."

Paisley shook her head. She hadn't expressed herself right. "I don't think Josh would beat me. It's that I know he came from a big family, and I'm sure he wants the same thing. He can't have that if he's with me."

"Oh, Paisley."

The compassion could undo her. She didn't need compassion. She needed support. Encouragement. "I'll be fine. I'll be like you two. I'll have a business, and I'll make friends." Never mind that Josh had somehow become her best friend.

Dot laughed. "There's a big difference between you and us. This is not what Annabel or I planned for our lives. This is Plan B."

Annabel pointed to herself. "My husband died before we had children." She pointed at Dot. "And Dot has grown kids, but her husband left her here on a motorcycle trip, and they've refused to come and visit because he told them all kinds of horrible things about her."

Dot gave a sad smile, which was the saddest Paisley had ever seen her. "I'm saving money to go visit them. If the coffee shop keeps doing as well as we are doing now, I should be able to go this summer."

Wow. Paisley couldn't imagine having a mom and not wanting to see her. But she was thankful to have the women there with her now. Both of them were an inspiration. Because Paisley would be like them. "My ranch is my Plan B," she explained. "I didn't only name it Bright Star because of Christmas. I named it Bright Star because of the promise God gave Abraham about having more descendants than stars in the sky. I won't have actual descendants, but I will have lots of kids at my camps. And I will pass God's promises on to them. They will be my heirs."

Annabel and Dot looked at each other. Were they planning some kind of secret initiation for her? Some grand welcome into their single-and-happy club?

Annabel looked down. "You know, Abraham didn't have faith in God's promise at first. He tried to take a shortcut by having a child with a concubine. He settled for Plan B when God wanted Plan A for his life."

They were so sweet. Even when they were living Plan B for themselves, they wanted Plan A for others. Paisley hadn't gotten the agreement she'd hoped from them, but she'd gotten the love. And that was better. Though she should probably avoid them until Josh left. Until it was too late for Plan A.

"Thank you ladies for listening. I needed to talk, but now I need to get back to working on the ball. So—"

"Wait." Annabel grabbed her hand. Her eyes intense and desperate. "Do you have a dress to wear?"

A dress? Paisley frowned. She didn't own a dress and hadn't even considered needing one. She scratched at her cheek. "Uh . . . I was going to wear jeans and help out behind the scenes. I'll help you guys with catering."

"Fiddle sticks," Dot declared. "You're the star."

"Ha." She was not the star. She was more like a charity case. "I'll wear a pretty sweater and curl my hair if it makes you feel better. But I don't have time to go shopping in Bozeman."

Annabel squeezed her fingers. "You don't have to." Her eyes sparkled. "I have an old dress I think will fit you."

Oh no. That meant Paisley would be wearing pink. She'd be so out of her comfort zone. "I don't think—"

"Wait here." Annabel clomped toward the back room then up the stairs.

She really didn't have time to wait. And she cringed at the idea of wearing a dress. When Josh had suggested a ball, she'd never considered the idea she'd have to dress up. How did she get out of this one?

Dot clapped her hands. "I know which dress she's talking about. You are going to be stunning. You're going to shine like an actual star."

Oh no. *Please God, don't let it have sequins.*

The thud of Annabel's boots grew louder. She appeared in the doorway, holding up a gown triumphantly.

Gold silk brocade. It was a halter dress with a sweetheart neckline and mermaid style skirt. Paisley only knew this from the rodeo queen pageants she'd attended with Evangeline in high school. But this was better than any pageant dress. It was classic. It was exquisite. It would make her feel like she was stepping back in time to star in a movie with Carey Grant.

"Where did you get it, Annabel?"

Annabel held the dress in front of herself and looked down. "My engagement party. Fifty years ago this month."

The red-head would have been a stunner. Like Maureen O'Hara. "I can't possibly . . ." Though maybe she could borrow it just to try it on and look in the mirror.

Annabel spun forward as if twirling with a dance partner. She swept the dress into her arms and held it out like a gift. "You must."

Paisley ran her hand along the sleek material. What would it feel like to have her whole body covered in such finery? "I don't have any shoes."

Dot pointed to her feet. "Cowboy boots, silly. It's a cowboy ball."

Well, that worked. It was better than heels. And she could always pull her denim jacket on if she got cold. That wouldn't be too fancy. Though who was she to go to a ball with a movie star and her high school crush? The image didn't even feel real. "You're like my fairy godmother, Annabel."

"Oh, Paisley. If I'm your fairy godmother, that makes Josh your prince."

JOSH LIFTED ONE LEG off the ladder to hook it over a barn rafter and reach far enough to grab the strand of twinkle lights. He hadn't considered this part of preparing for a ball when he'd suggested the idea, but helping Paisley get her camp started would be worth climbing the ladder again. Especially if he got the chance to dance with her.

Sam sauntered in, carrying a box of wreaths. He'd offered to take over the Christmas decorations, claiming he had the experience since he'd worked on the Lake's Christmas tree farm rather than a ranch when growing up. "Where do you want me to hang the mistletoe?" he asked.

Josh's gut warmed. He wanted it in the kitchen where Paisley would have to kiss him. He didn't want it in the barn where she could be kissing someone else. "Don't ask me."

"Thought you could use the help, bro."

Josh gritted his teeth in a fake smile. He'd never needed help in this department before. "Thanks, Sam."

Sam set the box down in front of a wood support beam and went to work, wrapping it like the red stripe on a candy cane. "I heard what you said last night about helping her plan the ball again next year."

What could Josh say to that? The words had slipped out before he'd realized how it sounded. And then when she looked at him . . . "Maybe I'll come back for Christmas."

"Maybe you shouldn't leave."

Was Sam right? He didn't want to leave, but if Marcus was able to prove him innocent of idea theft, and he still had the opportunity to sign the contract with the computer company, he'd have to be there to do the work. It would be the biggest sale Synergy ever made.

"Do you think Paisley would consider moving to Chicago?"

Sam shot him a dirty look.

Was it really that bad a thought? "We could keep the ranch and hire somebody to run it. We'd come back for the holidays."

Sam pulled a wreath out of the box. "Paisley would be miserable."

Would she? He liked to think she'd be miserable without him. Or would she have Sam there to dry her tears? "Well, since you know her so well, why don't you stay here with her?"

Sam dropped his head back to stare toward heaven in prayer. "God, why do my brothers have to be so stupid when it comes to love?"

Josh jolted at the word, knocking the ladder sideways. He wrapped his arms and legs around the rafter to hang like a wreath, as the ladder tipped in slow motion before slamming into stacks of hay.

"Love?" he asked. Because even with his thighs and pecs burning from the position and wooden splinters digging into his skin, he still had to correct his brother's misconception. "I'm not in love."

Sam sighed and kicked up dust on his way to right the ladder and rescue him. "Well, she is. So stop trying to get me to take your place."

Pin pricks traveled from his heart out his limbs. Paisley was in love with him? How would Sam know? Had she told him? "Why do you think she loves me? She wouldn't even kiss me last night."

Sam held the ladder steady. "I'm supposed to play chaperone so you don't break her heart."

Josh squeezed the rafter tighter, unable to move. Paisley wasn't attracted to Sam after all? She was using him as a buffer between the two of them? Josh *was* stupid when it came to love. "So that's why the whole thing with you marching into the kitchen and ranting about ice cream?"

Sam shot him a puzzled expression. "No. I really needed ice cream."

Josh closed his eyes in frustration. This was why Paisley never told him what she wanted on the sleigh ride. She believed a relationship with him to be impossible. And maybe it was. He still didn't know what he wanted. Except . . . "I don't want to break her heart."

"Then don't." Sam made it sound so simple. "Are you moving or not?"

Move to Montana? Live on a ranch for the rest of his life? That's what he'd wanted as a little kid. But now he was an adult. Which was something Sam wouldn't understand. "It's not that easy. I'd be letting down my whole company. I'd be giving up everything I'd worked for. I'd be—"

"Dude." Sam patted a rung, causing the metal to clang and echo through the open space. "I'm talking about climbing down from the rafters. I can't stand here all day. We've got a ball to prepare for."

Yeah, they did. But now Josh was even more unprepared.

CHAPTER NINETEEN

Paisley scrambled the egg mixture to pour into the pan still sizzling with hearty-smelling bacon fat. They'd worked hard all week since the tickets went on sale, and they still had a lot to do before the ball that evening, but making time for a big breakfast would give them the energy to do it. "Grandpa used to try to feed me fish for breakfast when I came to visit. That's one Norwegian custom I never got used to."

Josh set down a mug of coffee for her and sipped his own. "I have to say, your breakfasts sure beat my standard morning latte."

Paisley stopped and waited for the next line, holding the measuring cup over the frying pan.

"What?" he asked, mug halfway to his lips.

Dare she say what she'd been expecting him to say? It would be considered flirting, but flirting was only playing at love. It was a safe sidestep from the real thing. She couldn't keep from smiling. "I was waiting for you to say," she lowered her voice to use the coffee pun in a pickup line, "'I like you a latte.'"

Josh's eyes lit up at her impersonation. "Is that how I sound to you?"

She laughed and went back to cooking. She couldn't look into his eyes for too long, or she'd be in his arms again. Better to keep things light. "Yes."

His grin had to be the most charming thing she'd ever seen. If he'd been the one eating breakfast with her and Dad, instead of Nick, Dad would have never stopped clearing his throat. She was glad Dad wasn't there to control her anymore, but she'd keep her spatula between the two of them. Just in case.

Sam charged past in stocking feet. "They're here."

Her heart thumped. Emily Van Arsdale Lake was at her ranch. To help promote her camp. The two of them would be getting ready for the ball together. Like sisters.

Paisley glanced hesitantly toward the windows. Did the couple need help unloading? She couldn't go out and see or the eggs would burn. "She won't be offended if I don't greet her out there, will she?"

Josh snorted. "She puts up with my brother, which means she's hard to offend."

Paisley wasn't sure what he was saying about Tracen, but it sounded like Emily was a little less snooty than some of the other celebs who'd vacationed in Sun Valley.

Footsteps sounded on the stairs leading to the deck. Maybe the couple was going to bring in their stuff later.

"Here." Josh reached for the spatula. "I'll watch the eggs if you want to go introduce yourself."

Paisley didn't let go fast enough. His fingers brushed hers and jolted her awake more than a latte ever could. She sucked in a breath of his mossy scent and stared up into his dark, watching eyes. The mood wasn't light anymore. So much for keeping the utensil between them.

A throat cleared. Paisley jumped the way she used to at Dad's admonishment. Only it wasn't Dad this time. It was Sam. Along with a really tall guy and a tiny woman with dark, chin-length curls and eyes as blue as the Montana sky.

"Wanna introduce us to your friend, Josh?" Emily said, her voice low and teasing. She obviously wasn't offended, but she might have gotten the wrong idea about her friendship with Josh.

Josh let go of the spatula. Paisley used it to scramble the eggs so they wouldn't become an omelet . . . and so she had time for her blush to fade before facing Josh's family.

"This is Paisley Sheridan. I used to work on her family ranch in high school. Now she runs Bright Star."

"So nice to meet you," Emily maneuvered around the island for a hug. The woman might have been tiny, but her hug was strong. "This place is beautiful. Thank you for inviting us up for the ball, though we will have to return tomorrow for Christmas with my mom."

Paisley hugged back. She'd had nothing to be worried about. "Thank you for making time in your schedule. Did Josh tell you all the ball tickets sold out? And I'm sure it's because you're here."

Emily let her go to wave a hand. "Ack. Maybe they'll come for me, but they'll stay because you have so much to offer. Was that a skating rink I saw outside?"

"Yes. I let people use it on a donation basis, and I'm actually surprised with how much money people have left in the donation box since it opened a week ago." Paisley smiled past the little woman at Josh. He'd helped her get that going, as well. "You should see Josh's moves on ice. Pretty impressive."

Sam hooted. Josh smirked.

Tracen stepped into her line of sight and extended his hand. "I'm Tracen. I think we met once before when Josh was riding one of your dad's broncos at a rodeo."

"Yes." She took Tracen's hand. He was taller than his brothers and a little more rugged. "Nice to see you again. Do you guys want some breakfast?"

Emily waved her hand. "Oh, you don't have to serve us. We're here to help you."

Really? Paisley stared. Practically their whole family was here to help her. She'd never imagined such a Christmas. She thought she'd be watching The Grinch all by herself. Too bad this couldn't last forever.

Josh came around and put a hand on her shoulder. "Let's eat and show them around. Then the rental company will be arriving with the dance floor and stage and tables and heaters."

Paisley nodded, not trusting her voice to speak. It had all started with Josh. He'd showed up at The Coffee Cottage and turned her world upside down. Life would get really lonely after he left.

She fed the clan then ushered them down to the barn to explain how the place would be set up for dinner and dancing. They let the horses out into the field and cleaned out the stalls to use each one as a private booth with tables for dinner. They set bales of hay around for ambiance as well as additional seating. Linens and candles transformed the place. The band arrived to warm up. Dot and Annabel brought tangy-scented pulled pork and tri-tip. There wasn't much more Paisley could do other than head back to the lodge to get herself ready. And that would be the toughest part.

She debated on the way back up to the lodge—maybe she shouldn't wear the gown Annabel lent her. The last time she'd dressed up around Josh, he'd kissed her. The idea gave her a thrill, but at the same time it twisted her insides like that kitchen towel Sam was trying to snap at Tracen.

Paisley separated herself from the group in the kitchen. She wrapped her hands around a hot mug to thaw her fingers, while she watched the brothers wrestle and toss things around.

Emily slid down the bench at the table to sit closer. "It was a little overwhelming for me at first, too," she said. "But you'll get used to it."

No. Paisley wouldn't. The warmth of the moment shattered like an icicle in her soul. Why was she doing this to herself? Why was she letting herself get close to a bunch of people who'd soon be gone? Why was she letting herself fall in love with the idea of family when she could never have one? *What do I do, Lord?*

A window rattled by the balcony. The sun was already setting, but a couple of teen girls in pink jackets and beanies were highlighted by the light through the glass. They weren't dressed for a ball. Skaters.

The men all turned to stare in surprise. Paisley rose and breezed past them to answer the door.

The girls didn't even look at her. They peered inside the house, eyes squinting.

Paisley frowned. "Everything all right?"

The brunette with braces pointed. "Is that Emily Van Arsdale?"

The blonde shrieked. "It is. She's so little."

Paisley scratched her head. Was there anything wrong? Or were they only there to stalk a celebrity?

Emily glided over. "Hi, girls. Are you skating? Because if not, you're trespassing, and we'll have to ask you to leave."

Small, but forceful. A nice combination.

Shame washed over both faces in front of them. The blonde held up a palm to reveal her mitten torn with a pink scrape underneath. "We were skating. Honest. But there's a crack in the ice, and I tripped.

Do you have a Band-Aid?" Her grin returned. "And can Emily autograph it?"

A crack? Paisley looked out at the pond.

"I'll get a bandage," Sam volunteered.

"And I'll sign it," Emily agreed. "I'm glad you weren't hurt."

The teens giggled.

Josh appeared next to her. "I read about cracks. They can be fixed, but we'll have to shut down the rink."

Paisley ran a hand through her hair. This could be her answer to prayer. If she went out and fixed the crack, she wouldn't have to worry about putting on the dress. She wouldn't have to debate with herself about whether she was going to stand under the mistletoe or not. She'd seen it out there. Right at the entrance to the barn. It would be hard to avoid.

"I'll go ask the skaters to leave. Then I'll flood the ice again. I've got this," she said.

Josh pulled her to the side so they wouldn't be in the way, as Sam and Emily took care of the teenagers. "First of all, if you'd read all the info your grandpa compiled for starting an ice skating rink, you'd know water will go right through the crack. You'd have to make a paste to fill it in. Once it's dried, you scrape off the top to make it even again. Then you can flood it." Josh lowered his eyebrows. "Second of all, I'm going to do it. You're getting ready for your fund-raiser."

She shook her head. "No, you planned this fund-raiser."

Josh met her gaze. "For you."

Maybe this would work, too. Maybe now she'd be able to enjoy the ball without worrying about Josh. Of course she didn't want him to have to be out on the pond when she was having all the fun, but it was safer this way.

"Go get ready, hon." He looked at his watch. "It's after five already. People will start arriving by six. And as cute as you look in your jeans and plaid flannel . . ." He tilted his head and let his half smile say the rest.

Her heart hammered. God may have provided the escape she needed with the cracked pond, but He'd have to do better than that, because if Josh was able to finish in time to make it to the ball, there wouldn't be any need for mistletoe.

JOSH SCRAPED THE LAST of the dried paste from the ice with a shovel and grabbed a bucket to flood the top. Music and laughter drifted through the dark night from the barn. Light spilled out whenever a new vanload of guests arrived. None had left, so it had to be going well. He wanted to be in there with Paisley, but more importantly, he wanted her to shine.

He splashed another bucket of water. There. Done. Now to race to the bunk house and change for the ball. It was a good thing he'd packed a suit. At the time, he'd been hoping to receive a phone call from work and hop a first-class flight to Illinois, prepared to sign his hard-earned contract. But this was better.

He paired the suit jacket with Paisley's grandpa's buffalo checkered shirt and jeans then topped it off with a black cowboy hat. He barely recognized his reflection in the mirror. Actually . . . he peered closer . . . the guy reminded him of the kid he used to be in high school. Back before he left Idaho looking for bigger, better things.

Maybe the Montana sky was the bigger thing. Paisley was certainly better than any other woman he'd met. Was he really going to leave her? After the way she'd teased him that morning?

She was so hot and cold. Melting into him one minute, running away the next. But if Sam was right about her being in love with him and being afraid of getting hurt when he left, it made sense. What if he told her he'd stay?

A little bubble of joy floated through his chest. He'd do it. He'd stay. He had to get out there and tell her right away. He knew what he wanted.

He barely felt the snow wetting the hem of his pants, as he ran toward the noisy barn. He grabbed the door handle and slid it sideways, blinking as the light blinded him. Where was Paisley?

Couples danced and chatted among the twinkle lights. The scent of pine mixed with hay. The result was more charming than any dinner party he'd ever attended in the city.

Paisley's laughter floated his way from the dance floor. There she was. In Sam's arms. Though he could see now they were just friends. For St. Nick's sake, the kid was wearing red suspenders and some long, knit version of a Santa Claus hat over the crown of his Stetson. Neither would mind if Josh cut in.

He paused on the side. Not because the dance moves were too complex. He could swing with the best of them. But he wanted to watch her.

She wore a soft, gold dress that revealed curves she usually kept hidden. Her glossy hair had been twisted back, making her look fancy. And her face beamed—radiance more than skin deep. The guests filling the barn may all be enamored with Emily Van Arsdale Lake, but Paisley was the real star.

The music died down. Sam spun her one last time. Her smile flashed Josh's direction. Her eyes caught his and continued to focus on him even as her body turned back around. Her laughter died.

Sam let her go to clap along with the other dancers.

Josh stepped forward. He held out his hand. "May I have the next dance?"

Her lips parted. Her chest rose and fell. "Yes."

Sam noticed him. Lifted his eyebrows in approval . . . until Charlie showed up and pulled him away. But that wasn't Josh's problem.

Pastor Taylor strummed his guitar and crooned the first notes of a love song about God using a broken road to bring a couple together. Josh wrapped her hand in his and slid his other arm around her back. "I got the pond all taken care of," he said.

"Thank you." Her eyes studied his. They even had golden flecks in them as if she'd been born to wear that dress. Born to help refine him with her fire. "I saved you a plate of food. It was so good I was worried there wouldn't be any—"

"I don't care about dinner."

Her fingers tightened against his for a second. Her other hand slipped off his shoulder, but she quickly replaced it. "I . . . uh . . . I didn't want you to miss anything."

"I was hoping you'd say that." He let go of her hand and lifted his palm to cup her face. She stilled in his arms. All except for her heartbeat, which he could feel against his chest. He rubbed a thumb across her satin lips. "May I kiss you?"

She was only a breath away. Her eyes traveled down to his lips then lifted back to meet his. She wanted it as much as he did. "Yes."

He reined in the temptation to crush his mouth to hers with the intensity pent up from all their near misses. He flexed every muscle to keep them under control and slowly bent his neck. Brushing his lips against hers soothed him like the signing of a contract. There was no risk of losing the deal anymore. She was his treasure to be valued.

She returned the kiss, tilting her head to one side and slipping the hand from his shoulder to behind his neck to pull him closer. She tasted like strawberries.

He'd never felt this satisfied before. This was what he'd been looking for ever since kissing the mystery girl at prom. Only this was better. This was Paisley. A woman he knew. A woman he wanted to know better. "Wow."

She pulled away and bit her lip, as if worried the moment wasn't real. And it *did* feel too good to be true. But underneath her hesitation was a smile. "Wow is right." Her nose wrinkled. "What took you so long to do that?"

He reeled back. Because she'd been using Sam as a shield to block his advances. "You've got to be kidding me."

Her eyes sparkled, and she settled into his arms, hands clasping behind his neck. "I am."

Josh relaxed, nuzzling his nose into her flowery-scented hair. He spoke into her ear. "Well I'm willing to make up for lost time if you'd like."

She laughed, and the sound of it warmed his insides like a mug of hot chocolate. He loved that he could make her laugh. And she'd been joking earlier, too. But she still needed to hear the answer to her question about what took him so long to kiss her.

He wrapped both arms around her waist and swayed to the rhythm as the music penetrated his consciousness once again. "The truth is that you were right to push me away before. I wasn't ready for a commitment. But now I know what I want."

She stiffened. But hadn't she been expecting him to say as much? She should have known he'd fallen for her. Or she never would have let him kiss her.

"I want to stay here with you," he finished.

She looked away, and when she finally returned her gaze, it didn't shine with the joy he felt. "You don't have to do that, Josh."

Did she not believe him? "I mean it."

Her hands slid down from his neck. They settled on his biceps as if prepared to push him away again. "Don't ruin the magic by making promises you don't know if you can keep."

Magic? She'd kissed him because attending a ball was like living a fairytale? She thought it would end at the stroke of midnight?

His fingers dug into her lower back. He couldn't let go. "This is real. What I feel is real."

She sighed, the puff of breath warm on his skin. "It's real now. But you're going to have to return to Chicago at some time, even if it's to quit your job and sell your condo. And while you're there, I want you to be free to stay if your feelings change."

Did she not want him to commit? His eyebrows pinched together as he studied her. If she was really in love with him as Sam claimed, why wouldn't she say so?

Her gaze flitted about, never settling on his, but when she did make brief eye contact, it was from behind a glaze of grief. Did she still think a relationship with him was impossible?

"Feelings change all the time, Paisley. But love is about commitment."

She dropped her chin so all he could see were her glittery, gold eyelids and the tops of thick lashes. "I don't want to be an obligation."

"Oh, honey." His belly churned at the idea she didn't think she was worth choosing over his empty life in the big city.

Her eyelids flicked up at his endearment, revealing a flash of fear in the depths of her irises. "Can we not talk about it? I want to enjoy the night."

He wanted to protect her from whatever it was that created such dread. But how could he do that if they didn't talk?

He'd keep dancing with her. He'd hold her hand or wrap his arm around her shoulders. He'd join the line to get their pictures taken with Tracen and Emily. He'd watch her laugh with his family. He'd steal another kiss when nobody was looking. But without knowing he'd have the rest of his life to do so, the actions felt just as empty as his old life. It left a pang in his gut that every moment with her might be his last.

But maybe giving Paisley what she wanted would make her want more. She'd realize one magical night wasn't enough.

So he'd play Prince Charming. And later, after the magic had ended, he'd repeat his promise. Because fairytales had to end happily-ever-after.

CHAPTER TWENTY

Josh trudged through the snow toward the lodge the next morning, formulating a speech in his head. Actually two speeches. There was the one he'd use if Paisley greeted him with a hug, or better yet, a kiss. Then there was the one he'd use if she turned back into the woman who'd once prayed for him to go home to Chicago. The idea of giving that speech made him want to double over and vomit.

He stomped up the stairs and took a deep breath of icy air before turning the doorknob and entering the great room. The room smelled buttery, but Paisley wasn't in the kitchen. Nobody was in the great room at all. Were they all still getting ready for church?

Josh swung the door closed and paused. Did he act like everything was normal and make himself a cup of coffee, or did he track down Paisley and kiss her before she had a chance to speak a word. He'd simply continue their magic from the evening before. He'd keep that magic from ever ending.

Laughter floated down the hallway. He followed the sound and found himself at the top of the stairs. Everybody seemed to be enjoying themselves without him.

"Josh did a great job with your website, Paisley. And the cowboy ball last night was dynamite." Emily's voice. At least they were talking about him. Paisley must have been showing them what he'd been working on.

"You know he's always loved horses." Tracen. "Did you hear about the Christmas where Josh thought Santa brought him a horse?"

Josh waited for Paisley's response.

"Yes," she said. "He said that's what made him want to work on our ranch."

"Really?" Tracen asked. "I didn't know that. I figured he just liked to swagger around wearing a giant belt buckle."

All right . . . enough of that. Josh jogged down the first couple of stairs.

Sam this time. "The girls at school certainly thought he was—"

Josh descended into the daylight basement. "There's no reason to be jealous anymore, Sam. If you want a girlfriend, all you have to do is ask someone out."

Tracen roared in laughter. Sam's cheeks turned pink. Emily sat on the middle of the T-shaped desk, swinging her legs and swiveling her head to watch the conversation bounce around. But Josh only cared about Paisley's reaction.

She looked up from her spot in front of the computer screen, her face washed fresh and her hair still damp from the shower. She was even more beautiful than he remembered. She indulged him with a smile, but he couldn't help thinking that she somehow considered his brothers' statements confirmation he wasn't going to commit to her.

"If I'd wanted a girlfriend," Sam countered, "I would have asked Paisley out a long time ago, and you wouldn't have had a chance, bro."

Paisley's lips curved up, but her eyes remained neutral. She was emotionally preparing for her coach to turn back into a pumpkin.

Tracen rose and slapped Josh on the shoulder. He seemed to be relishing his brothers' relationship problems a little too much. "I'm not sure what you see in this guy, Paisley, but if you don't mind his expensive taste or the way he can err on the arrogant side, then we would love to have you in the family."

Paisley's eyebrows lifted, but there was no humor in her expression.

"In fact, you might be exactly what he needs to—"

Emily rose and placed a hand on Tracen's chest. She looked between Josh and Paisley. The color had drained from Paisley's face. "Let's go check on that puff pancake in the oven, Tracen."

"What? I was . . ." His voice faded as Emily pushed him up the stairs.

Sam jumped to his feet. "I think I'll go eat, unless anyone here needs me for anything." He peeked at Paisley like he thought she might need him to chaperone again.

Had she said something that would make Sam think that? Paisley gave a small shake of her head, and Josh sank into the spot Emily had vacated. Might as well address the awkwardness so they could get to the important stuff.

He rubbed a hand over his face. "It sounds like my family likes you more than they like me."

She slumped in the swivel chair and gave a small smile. That was better than turning toward the computer but not as good as standing and putting her arms around him. "You are blessed to have them."

Josh nudged her seat with his foot. He needed to make a connection somehow. "You could have them, too," he said.

She didn't say anything. Simply looked at him as if there was something she couldn't say. Something he wouldn't understand. Why wouldn't she talk?

She opened her mouth. At last he'd know what was going on inside her head.

The phone rang on the desk. Josh jolted. Was he really that on edge?

Paisley pressed shiny lips together and leaned forward to reach past him and grab the old cordless receiver. "Bright Star Ranch. May I help you?"

Josh propped his hands behind him to lean back and stare at the wooden beams on the ceiling. The call gave him a few minutes to remember what he'd been planning to say on the hike up the hill. He'd always had the right words with women. But not this woman. He needed God's help. Because getting through to her could take divine intervention.

"You want to speak with Josh?"

Josh's spine snapped upright. Only his boss had this number.

"Here he is." Paisley held out the phone, her eyes wide in surprise.

Josh shook his head to communicate that he didn't know what the call was about. Did he lose his job? Was that God's answer to his prayer for intervention? Because then Paisley wouldn't have to feel like she had to compete. He gripped the smooth plastic of the receiver and held it to his ears. "Josh here."

"Josh." His boss paused.

That sounded bad. That sounded like he was being let go. Fear of failure fired up his pulse and drenched his scalp in a cold sweat. Because what if Paisley didn't want to be with a man who couldn't keep a job? If he got terminated for idea theft, might she believe he'd actually been guilty the way Bree had? Did he want her in the room for this?

He reached for her hand resting on the arm of her chair and engulfed her fingers in his. Yes, he wanted her in the room. Always. No matter what Marcus had to say.

"It was Bree," Marcus said.

Josh rocked forward, his hips slid off the edge of the desk, and his feet planted on the ground. He squeezed Paisley's hand tighter. She was his lifeline as thoughts and emotions swirled about him like a whirlpool.

"Bree?" he echoed.

She'd stolen his ideas? But she'd accused him of lying. And she was living in his condo. Had she just wanted him gone so he wouldn't figure it out when she suddenly had millions of dollars to spend?

His mouth hung open. This new information did not compute. Because if she could do that to him, then she'd never loved him in the first place. She didn't reject him. She used him.

Paisley studied him with concern. Did she understand what was going on?

"Yeah. She must have copied your files from your computer then gone to the competition. I'm so sorry."

Marcus was sorry? Josh shook his head even though the other man couldn't see. Josh was the one who should be sorry. He'd let the theft happen. Goodness, he'd proposed to the thief.

No wonder their relationship had been so easy. Bree had made it easy.

"What . . ." What was he asking? Pieces and parts of the puzzle clicked together, creating a picture of his life that wasn't pretty. "What happens now?"

"We are pressing charges against Bree. That part is tough, but I have good news, too. I explained everything to Computex, and they still want to sign with us."

"Oh man." Josh sank back to sit on the desk again. Relief poured from his toes and fingertips. His relationship with Bree hadn't screwed everything up after all. "That's huge."

"Great Christmas gift, huh?" Marcus chuckled. "Can you make it back to sign the contract tomorrow?"

Josh scrunched his eyes closed. He must not have heard that right. Tomorrow was Christmas Eve. The contract could wait a few more days. Besides he wasn't leaving Paisley over the holidays. "No."

"We need you, Josh. The CEO of Computex is headed to New York for New Year's, and we have to get this deal done before he goes."

Josh balled his fists before realizing he still had Paisley's fingers in his hand. He relaxed his grip and ran a thumb over her knuckles. Her eyes didn't reflect any pain from his tight clasp, but she studied him through a narrowed gaze as if trying to follow the one side of the conversation. If only he could cover the mouthpiece and assure her he wasn't leaving.

"Marcus, I'm spending Christmas with family. You sign the contract." His shoulders knotted with tension.

"I wish I could. Seriously, I wish I could. But you are the one who pitched the CEO, and he wants to make sure we are patching things up with you after the misunderstanding and suspension." Marcus clicked his tongue. "Besides, don't you want to get to work right away? This deal is a record breaker, buddy."

Josh let go of Paisley to massage his temples. He hadn't wanted to be fired, but this was almost worse. He had to let a lot of people down to keep his promise to Paisley. His guts clenched. "I'm not going to be working at Synergy anymore. I'm moving to Montana."

Paisley stood in front of him. Was she finally going to step into his embrace? Did she finally understand he wasn't playing her?

She walked around him toward the stairs. What? Why? He stretched for her hand to pull her back. She moved beyond his reach.

"Josh, that's ridiculous. Are you trying to get me back? Because I couldn't be more sorry . . ." Marcus droned on.

Josh spun around on the desk to swing his legs over the other side and block Paisley's path. He needed to get off the phone so he could talk to her. Though he hadn't planned a speech for this.

He stood and set a hand on her shoulder. "Wait," he whispered.

She wouldn't look him in the eye, but she stayed in place.

"Marcus, I'm not trying to get you back. I've just found something else I want to do with my life."

Pause. "A woman? Josh, you're on the rebound. That's not real."

Josh cringed at the possibility Paisley could make out his boss's words.

She turned her head away and covered her mouth. She'd heard.

Josh wanted to throw the phone the way Paisley had thrown her shoe when she hadn't gotten her bank loan. "Marcus, I'm moving to Montana."

"Fine." Big sigh. "But you still have to be here for this deal to go through. Don't let the whole company down, Josh. We can take over from here. In fact, you could work from Montana as our consultant if you want. You wouldn't get as big a share of the money, but you'd still get something. It's the best of both worlds. You must be here tomorrow to make it happen."

Josh shook his head. He didn't want to leave for Christmas, but as Paisley had pointed out, he'd have to return some time to get his stuff and sell his condo. If he went the next day, he could get all that done and come back to Paisley sooner so she wouldn't keep pushing him away. Plus, he'd have the opportunity to make an income through the ad campaign. Then he would actually be able to buy Paisley a ring. She may not understand his decision right away, but eventually she'd realize he'd done it for her.

"Okay. I'll be there." Josh clicked the button to hang up the phone and got rid of it to focus on Paisley.

"Hey." He cupped her soft face in both hands so he could get her to look at him. "Hey."

Her eyelids finally lifted. Wariness hid her emotions, but she wrapped fingers around his wrists as if ready to knock his hold away and bolt. He'd rather she cry and beg him not to leave. At least then he'd be hearing directly from the source how she felt rather than having to rely on Sam.

He tilted his head to beseech her. "I have to fly to Chicago tomorrow morning. But only to sign a deal and put my condo on the market. I told my boss I'm moving here, and I mean it. I want to be with you."

She pulled his hands down. He slid them to lock fingers with her.

Her chest rose as she took a deep breath. "I'm glad you're going home."

His heart stopped. Wasn't he supposed to be prepared for her to do this? But he was being vulnerable, which had left him open for attack.

Did she not care about him at all? Had Sam been wrong? Had he imagined their connection when dancing? "What about last night?"

She rocked away slightly. She swallowed. Her face contorted then returned to its neutral expression. He hated that expression.

"Last night was amazing, but it was one night."

Why wouldn't she want amazing all the time?

"And your boss is right. You're on the rebound."

Gah. Josh squeezed her hands. "A rebound relationship is when someone is trying to fill a void that another person left behind. Bree didn't leave a void. You will."

Would he not leave a void in her life? That didn't seem fair.

Her mask slipped. She looked down again. "Josh, we don't have to do this. Let's just enjoy each other's company while we can. You'll leave tomorrow, and then you have the freedom to look at your life objectively and make decisions from there. I want the best for you."

How could she not see she was the best thing for him? Maybe he'd have to prove it.

"Okay," he said. Because he did want to enjoy his last day with her.

Her eyes peeked up. "Okay?"

He nodded. This might be how it had to happen. This might be how God planned all along. Josh had been vindicated. He got his job back if he wanted it, which meant he'd be able to show Paisley how much she meant to him. Synergy got the big deal. He got to work from Montana. And he'd be able to finalize everything by Christmas. "Okay."

PAISLEY LED CASSIDY AROUND the band stage left in the barn from the ball. She'd let herself be swept away in the moment last night. She knew it was all she was going to get with Josh, so she'd decided to enjoy it, to make some memories, to recreate prom in a way. Only this morning he hadn't forgotten her like he had in high school. He'd practically quit his job to be with her.

She couldn't have that. It was impossible. Which was why she wouldn't let him talk about it anymore. But, oh, it was all she could think about.

Her heart throbbed in her chest as she stood Cass in the grooming station and grabbed a brush. She ran it over the horse's mane like old times when it was just the two of them. Soon it would be the two of them again.

Tracen and Emily had left after church. And Josh was online, buying a plane ticket with his company credit card. She couldn't stay inside with him. She couldn't let herself see if he got a round-trip ticket or not.

What would she do if he did? What would she do if he called to say he was flying back to Montana? She'd have to do something drastic. Like claim she was in love with Sam.

Sam would surely take off if she did that. But then they could all move forward with their own lives, the way it had to be.

She leaned her forehead into Cassidy's velvety hide. Less than twenty-four hours ago, she'd been in Josh's arms in this very barn. She'd let him kiss her. She kissed him back. And it had been one of those moments that changed everything. It had revealed what she was missing out on.

Not being able to have kids was hard enough. But not being able to have Josh . . .

Her bones ached.

At least he'd agreed to enjoy the rest of the day with her. She had that. And there would be no more conversations about a future together. So what would they talk about?

Rollers whirred as the barn door slid open. Josh stood in the golden light of a sinking sun. Underneath a leftover sprig of mistletoe. But it didn't scare her anymore. Her greatest fear had already come true.

"There you are."

"Here I am." She spoke to Josh but continued to face Cassidy.

His footsteps carried him her way. He settled his strong hands on her shoulders. Awareness rippled down her spine. "We got a call from the group that booked tonight's sleigh ride. There's been a small avalanche, and it's blocking Gallatin Road. They can't make it."

"Is everyone all right?" she asked. If so, then she was okay with the cancellation. She didn't feel much like listening to jingle bells, let alone pretending to be "laughing all the way."

"They're fine." Josh massaged. "I was thinking maybe you and I could go for one last trail ride before I leave."

One last ride together. She smiled sadly. "You think you can stay on the horse this time?"

He wrapped his arms around her waist and nibbled on her ear. She shivered.

He whispered. "If you don't keep your smart mouth under control, I'm going to have to find some way to shut you up."

She lifted her hands in surrender, sorrow smothering the tickle of a giggle she'd felt inside at his words. "I apologize. I'm sure Butch will let you lead this time."

"That's better." Josh released her to saddle the other horse.

She mourned the loss of his touch, which did not bode well for his departure the next day. Did he know she was stealing glances at him as he prepared to mount? He looked the part of a cowboy now, hat and all. He looked authentic. What had ever made him want to leave the rugged beauty of nature for a noisy, dirty city?

She'd be better off getting out into that nature rather than speculate about Josh's views of it. Grabbing the horn of Cassidy's saddle, Paisley stuck one foot in a stirrup and swung the other leg up and over. "Ready?"

She didn't wait for an answer but rode outside and along the trail toward the bright moon peaking over the tip of a mountain in the dimming night. Butch's feet plodded after her, telling her Josh wasn't far behind.

She pushed through her legs and leaned forward to climb the hill. Snow-covered evergreen trees dispersed at a clearing. She rode toward the edge of a cliff to look back down at the lodge and barn and pond. So peaceful. Yet soon to be so lonely. Maybe she shouldn't have changed the name after all. Lone Peak Ranch would be more appropriate.

Josh sidled next to her. "Bright Star Ranch is the perfect name."

Paisley startled. Had he read her thoughts? No, he couldn't have. He was disagreeing without realizing it. He had no clue.

She sat back in her saddle. "You think?"

Josh stared toward heaven where one pinprick of light displayed the first star. "You don't see stars like that in Chicago."

Paisley would never make it in Chicago. She could at least be glad he hadn't suggested she move. "Why'd you leave Idaho?" The words snuck out before she had a chance to censor them.

He glanced her way then gave an embarrassed smile. "You want the whole truth?"

Did she? She wasn't willing to give him the whole truth. How could she expect honesty from him? She shrugged. "Only if you want to tell it."

He grunted and ran a gloved hand over Butch's neck. "It's because of a girl I kissed at my senior prom in high school."

Her spine shot rigid. Her collar bone tingled. Her face warmed despite a chilly breeze.

A girl he kissed at senior prom? Was he talking about her? That didn't make sense. She had nothing to do with Chicago. Had he kissed someone else that same night?

Her hand rose to her lips. All that time as a teen she'd hoped his kiss had meant something, when he'd only been practicing on her for someone else. Did he even remember kissing her? If so, how could he tell her about kissing someone else now? Or was that why he was embarrassed?

It was a good thing she'd never said anything. A good thing she didn't make a big deal out of it when he came to her family's ranch the next Monday. That would have been so humiliating. Almost as humiliating as how she felt here.

"I don't even know who it was."

Her breath burned in her lungs. What did he mean he didn't know who he'd kissed? How would that possibly affect his move to Chicago?

"She wore a mask. You know, the kind for masquerades."

Oh no. She'd forgotten about the mask. She'd been pretty out of it with her blood sugar so high.

Did that mean what she thought it meant? He didn't even know he'd kissed her?

"Do you remember that? You must have been a sophomore, so you wouldn't have been there. It was the only year they did a masquerade prom because when a couple of guys spiked the punch, the administration couldn't figure out who it was."

The punch had been spiked? Well no wonder her blood sugar had been a mess. But he'd rescued her. And he was oblivious to that fact.

He looked at her, and she realized he'd asked a question. Masquerade prom? Did she remember it? She wanted to laugh hysterically. She wanted to scream her answer loud enough to echo through the valley below. But she'd hold back. She'd wait to hear the whole story in case such a response could lead to more humiliation. She'd force herself to breathe. "Yes."

"Well . . ." He shook his head at himself. "Promise you won't laugh at me."

Good thing she hadn't given into hysterics. She squeezed her fingers around the reins to hold as still as possible. "I promise."

"It was the most amazing kiss of my young life, but when I went to get her a glass of water, the girl disappeared like Cinderella."

Josh didn't even know she had diabetes, did he? If she'd ever injected insulin in front of him or if Annabel had blabbed, would he have figured out she was the girl from prom? He was talking about her. Yet, he wasn't making any sense. Because how had she influenced his decision to move?

"So why did you move?" Her voice barely carried over the white noise of the wind.

"I was looking for her."

"In Chicago?" Paisley wanted to throw her arms in the air. Because she was right there. In front of him. As she had been the whole time.

Josh rubbed a hand over his face. "First at school. But none of the girls in my class knew what I was talking about."

They wouldn't. Evangeline hadn't even known. How might her life have been different if Paisley had told Evangeline?

"Then I found out prom had been crashed by a group of female hockey players from Boise who were staying at the Sun Valley Lodge the same night. So I attended Boise State to try to find my mystery girl."

Paisley's toes curled in her boots. Kissing her had meant that much to him? What would he do if she reached over and cupped his face the way he'd cupped hers? Would he figure it out? Did she want him to?

"It wasn't any of the Boise State hockey players. I gave up then. But someone mentioned one of the players from the hockey club had transferred to UIC. And when I got offered the job at Synergy Ad Agency, it felt like fate."

She wasn't going to laugh at him. She was going to cry. If she believed in fate, she'd believe it tore them apart. It stole their only chance to be together. Because back then she would have given anything for him to love her. Back then she didn't know how broken her body was.

But she didn't believe in fate. She believed in God. She believed He was in control and that He'd allowed Josh to leave to protect her. To protect them both from the regrets marriage would have burdened them with.

Josh reached for her hand.

Her pulse pounded in her ears, but she allowed him to hook their gloved fingers together. What next?

"Paisley, I've been looking for that girl a long time."

Oh no. He knew. And now it wouldn't only be her getting over him. It would be him getting over her.

His eyes met hers in the moonlight. They radiated confidence. Contentment. "But now for the first time, I've found something better."

It was worse. Because if he would go through all that to find a stranger he'd kissed at the age of eighteen, what would he do to pursue the woman he wanted to spend the rest of his life with?

She couldn't tell him. He could never know. Knowing would only deepen his resolve.

She might even use the story as an excuse for them not to be together. She could say he needed to keep looking for his first love. She could say God had brought that girl into his life for a reason.

Except she wouldn't pull God into this. She needed His help. She needed Him to be her all. She needed His strength and comfort to heal after Josh left.

And Josh was going to leave. He might want to make promises about returning, but the only promise he'd made was the one where they didn't talk about their future. "Josh, you promised."

He studied her. Openly. Honestly. Transparently enough for her to see him for who he was. For who he'd always been.

He was a romantic. Not a player as she'd thought. He wanted to give his all to one woman. And he wanted it to be her.

All along she'd been worried about having her heart broken. But here she was breaking his. Which hurt even more.

"I'm keeping my promise," he said. He lifted her gloved fingers to his lips. "I'm not talking about our future. I'm talking about my feelings. I wouldn't be able to enjoy my time with you today if I didn't tell you how I felt."

She swallowed down the lump and blinked away the tears. She'd cry tomorrow after he left. For now, she had to pretend she didn't feel the same.

CHAPTER TWENTY-ONE

Paisley crunched through the snow toward Big Red in the silver light of morning. The sooner she took Josh back to his Mercedes, the better. But that didn't make her ready to say goodbye. Hopefully Josh was. "Ready?"

Josh looked down at the luggage in his hands rather than toss it into the bed of the pickup. His gaze rose to meet hers. "No."

Wrong answer. Delicious like ice cream but still wrong like Sam eating it in the winter. If the timing had been different, then his words would have been the sweetest treat—say a Big Dipper cone dripping onto sizzling pavement in July. But not now. Now his response chilled her to the bone.

"Maybe I don't have to go."

But he did.

She marched past him and yanked the driver's door open with a squeak. She'd retrieve the brush on the end of her ice scraper and wipe off the windows from the small dusting they'd gotten the night before.

"Paisley."

She turned the red bristles toward the glass. Cold powder sprinkled over her hand. The sting was good. A distraction from Josh's warm voice and searching eyes.

Why did he have to tell her he'd been looking for the girl he kissed at prom? It had been better when she'd believed he was a player.

Why did he have to kiss her again? It had been better when she'd been able to tell herself his arms weren't really as perfect and comforting as she remembered.

His body blocked her path around the front of Big Red. "Hey. Are you mad at me?"

She could pretend to be mad. Like those movies where the kid was mean to the dog to get him to run away and find safety. It would be for his own good.

But she wasn't mad at him. He was wonderful. Too wonderful.

She could go around him. Or she could retreat and get to the other side of the truck around the back. But she didn't.

Her arm dropped to her side. She studied the soft concern in his expression. This gentleness was even more attractive than his confident smile and teasing remarks. How was that possible? "Of course I'm not mad at you. I just think you're too emotional to make a clear decision right now."

How heartless did she sound? Clinical. Judgmental.

His eyes narrowed in confusion. His head tilted. "Emotional?"

He wanted her to spell it out? How could she do that without coming across as condescending? She might have to hurt him to get him to leave after all.

Once he was back in Chicago—back at work in the big city, back to the life he loved—he'd realize how much he would have had to give up for her. All that money. All that power. All that acclaim. All those fancy women in their high heels and salon styles. They were a better match for him.

And maybe Bree hadn't been a good person, but their relationship had been easy because she fit into Josh's life so well. Paisley didn't.

Sure, he thought she'd been his dream girl after prom, but she'd been wearing high heels and had her hair and makeup done by Miss Teen Rodeo Montana. She'd been in disguise.

He never looked twice at the freckled Paisley in cowboy boots.

Until now.

But his feelings for her could still be part of a rebound relationship. Or simply because she was the only woman around. And the truth was, he'd hadn't kissed her until she'd been dressed up for the fancy ball he'd planned.

Those were the things he'd figure out. But there were also things he didn't know. She couldn't explain it all.

"You're here now, Josh. You're in the moment. You're surrounded by a winter wonderland. You're still hurting from your employer's suspicions. You're . . ."

He took a step closer. His gaze dropped to her lips.

Her breath caught. Was she purposefully rocking toward him, or was she simply light-headed from forgetting to breathe? Either way, he was close enough to kiss if she lifted up onto tiptoes.

She didn't. She had to finish her sentence before she forgot it. What was it again?

He was emotional because he was with her . . . Oh yeah. "Don't try to commit to me now. Go home to Chicago. See if you still want to be here then."

His eyes didn't harden. She hadn't hurt him. She hadn't shoved hard enough.

He lifted a hand to her cheek then slid his fingers into the hair at the nape of her neck, his thumb stroking her cheekbone.

This was not her plan. It was better. She rocked forward again.

Oh, wait. She was supposed to be pushing him away.

"Are you afraid?" he asked.

Her pulse skidded to a stop. How did he know? Had Sam told him?

"Are you afraid of being second place?"

Her pulse thumped back to life in her ears. She exhaled. He didn't know. He thought she was afraid he only wanted to be with her because the life he'd originally planned for himself hadn't worked out. He thought she was afraid he might resent her for keeping him from the career success he'd achieved.

That wasn't why he'd resent her if he stayed. But she'd go with it.

"Maybe," she said, his caress still threatening to lull her into dreaming with him. But their dreams could never be complete. "You've worked so hard. I don't want the reward of all your hard work to be destroyed by an impulsive whim."

Josh didn't really want to muck stalls and shovel snow and chop wood. And even if he did, even if he saw his happily-ever-after on a ranch with Paisley, his fairytale would surely include a Josh Jr.

"A whim?" He shook his head. "You're not a whim. This isn't a whim."

His lips brushed over hers—soft, promising. He pulled away before she could make the mistake of kissing back. Or was it a mistake?

She stuffed her free hand into her jacket pockets to keep from reaching for him. Though she didn't move away.

"Paisley, the idea of staying here makes more sense than anything I've ever done. I've got the money to invest in the ranch now. I've got the marketing experience to bring in all the campers and tourists you need. And I'm so at peace. I don't have to go back to Chicago to know there's nowhere else I'd rather be."

"Really?" She'd never imagined she'd hear such words. She wanted to reach out and accept all he offered. It sounded so good. But she knew it was too good to be true. Wasn't it? She balled her hand and pushed it deeper into her jacket, stretching the material tight on her shoulders.

His duffle dropped into a snowdrift. His other hand joined the first one, framing her face. He leaned down slower than before. He'd kiss her longer this time. Long enough for her to have to choose whether to kiss him back or not.

Her lips parted. But he remained a breath away.

"I love the horses. I love the land. I love—"

You. He'd been about to say *you.* Why had he stopped? If he said the words, she'd have to tell him her secret. She hadn't told Nick, but she'd tell Josh. She'd tell him she loved him, too. Loved him so much she couldn't keep him from having a family.

She wanted to tell him. She didn't want to hide anything anymore. He might not understand. But at least he'd go back to Chicago knowing he was loved. Knowing the difference between a relationship that looked good and one that *was* good. He wouldn't settle next time.

And selfishly, telling him she loved him would also mean he'd kiss her again. She couldn't have children. She couldn't marry. But she'd always have this memory.

What was taking him so long?

His eyes focused past her. The sounds interrupting their silence filtered into her brain. Tires slurping snow. A door slamming. Footsteps crunching.

Pastor Taylor? Dot and Annabel? Whoever it was had terrible timing. She wished the trespasser would continue on up to the cabin, but as it was her ranch, they were probably there to see her. She'd have to step away from Josh, breaking their connection. She might not get another chance to connect with him again. If she was honest, she knew it was for the best. God was giving her what she needed, not what she wanted.

"Paisley Therese Sheridan."

Dad? No. He wasn't what she needed. He'd never been what she needed.

She turned his way and covered her mouth as if watching a car crash.

"I want to talk to you," he barked.

She'd avoided his phone calls to avoid the scorn, yet here it was in person. Should she run? That would be her only way of preventing him from exploding in front of Josh. Because he wasn't the type of man to be convinced to have a conversation privately. He wasn't the type of man to respect anything she said.

Josh's hand squeezed her shoulder. He stepped forward between her and her father.

Josh had always liked her dad. Was he going to greet the man in friendship or had he seen the fear in her eyes? Was he protecting her?

"Mr. Sheridan." He extended his arm. "What a nice surprise."

Dad paused. He sized up the younger man. His face broke into a giant grin. He had a great smile. Which was why people liked him. They didn't know he took it off along with his hat and coat when walking in the door of his house.

Dad gripped Josh's hand and clamped his other hand over Josh's elbow as if to ally them together. "Joshua Lake?" He grinned past Josh at Paisley. "It all makes sense now."

Paisley's spine stiffened. It made sense that Dad was happier to see Josh than her, but that wasn't what he was talking about.

"I am so relieved." Dad wiped a hand across his brow. "So this is why you broke things off with Nick, huh, Paisley?"

Paisley gripped the snow scraper. If her father was relieved to think she ended her relationship with Nick to be with Josh, then he must have been worried there was another reason.

"I have to say I approve," her father continued. "Nick may have been a good vet, but he wasn't a man's man. As for Josh . . ." Dad motioned toward the man she loved. "Son, I read in the paper that you're making some huge deal with a computer company. You've got to be riding high. Yet, of all the places you could be, you're here on a ranch. I knew I liked you for a reason."

Josh rubbed at the scruff on his jaw. He had to be a little confused. Sure, it would be flattering to have Paisley's dad prefer him over Paisley's ex, but would he be suspicious as to why Mr. Sheridan drove all the way up to Montana to find out what was going on in the first place?

"Sir?" Oh no. Josh was going to explain their situation. "Paisley didn't break up with her ex for me. I was driving home to Sun Valley at the beginning of the month when I ran into her in town at a coffee shop."

Paisley's breath puffed out into a little cloud. She wished she could pull some kind of ninja move where she disappeared before the cloud did. Her stomach knotted with dread because she couldn't. There was no way to avoid the confrontation that was coming.

Dad stiffened. His eyes darkened. He turned his head her way. "Paisley?" Her name came out slow, as if a warning. She was in trouble. "Doc Matthews is boarding his horse at my ranch, and I had an interesting conversation with him the other day."

Josh's head swiveled toward her, his eyebrows drawn together as he tried to read her expression. He would have no idea what Dad was talking about. She wished she could keep it that way. Because if anybody was going to tell Josh about her condition, it should be her.

Dad stepped past Josh.

She took a step backward, though with the way her heart pounded, she might as well have taken off at a run. What was she more afraid of—Dad's disgust or Josh's reaction?

"Doc asked how you were doing." Gone was the charming smile. But she was used to having him looking at her like he wanted to spit. "He said he was worried your engagement might have ended because of his recent warning to you."

Her throat tightened as if in refusal to let out the words she'd dreaded to speak. It didn't even want to let her swallow.

"What?" Josh joined their little circle, most likely unsure if he needed to step between them. It was a nice gesture but pointless. Dad's next words would reach both of their ears whether Josh blocked his path or not.

Dad continued as if Josh had disappeared. "I asked Doc what warning he was referring to then he wouldn't say anything else. Obviously he was surprised you hadn't talked to me about something."

Dad made it sound like she was a bad child. As if she were the one keeping the two of them from having a loving father/daughter relationship. As if Mom hadn't slept on the couch facing the door whenever Dad was out drinking so that when he returned, she'd be able to protect Paisley from his rage.

Paisley wasn't afraid of him hurting her physically now, but there were many forms of abuse. And they all hurt.

"What kind of warning might a doctor have given you that would keep you from marrying Nick?" His eyes radiated contempt.

He'd only ever considered her good for one thing. And if that one thing wasn't possible anymore, then she was worthless to him. She was garbage. She was a waste of time.

Well, she didn't need to waste any more of his time. She lifted her chin so she didn't have to look him in the eye. She focused past him. Past Josh. At the ranch Grandpa had willed her. At her chance to make a difference in the world. She was going to create a camp where kids could be free from the demands of dysfunctional families. Where she could love them like the parent she would never get to be.

"Doctor Matthews warned me I shouldn't get pregnant."

PAISLEY'S WORDS DREW ALL Josh's attention despite the way her father glowered. His body grew heavy for the burden she had to bear. She couldn't have kids? That would be life-changing. Was that really why her ex had left her? Well then the guy was as bad as her father. No wonder she'd had a hard time opening up to Josh.

"Nick was smart to leave you." Mr. Sheridan spat out the words. "You're worse than your mother."

Josh balled his fists. He'd never punched anyone before, but Mr. Sheridan was asking for it.

"I'm worse? How so?" Paisley's arms flew wide. "Because I'm not willing to risk my life to give birth to an heir the way you forced Mom to?"

Risk her life? Like her mother had? Josh knew Mrs. Sheridan had died in childbirth years ago, but he'd just assumed that made Paisley's dad a grieving widower. The man had always been a monster. Josh had simply held up a mask in front of his face.

Paisley's dad scuffed his foot in the snow with all the energy of a raging bull. "You better be willing." He turned toward Josh. "She could still give you a child. Madeline made it through one pregnancy. Paisley could, too."

Fury surged. The heat of it singing his thoughts and preventing him from responding. If he opened his mouth, if he unlocked his limbs, he'd unleash the kind of anger he'd never felt before. Being accused of plagiarism in advertising didn't compare. Being dumped by the fiancée who'd claimed to love him didn't compare. Even finding out Bree had only claimed to love him to steal his ideas didn't compare. Because he'd always had his family there for him. He'd always known he was wanted by the people who mattered most.

Family wasn't about heirs. Family wasn't about having your name carried on. Family was about loving unconditionally and accepting others for who they were. In fact, his own mother wanted a daughter, yet she still treated each of her five sons as if they were her favorite child. How was it possible for Paisley's father to be willing to let her die so he could have a grandson? And even worse, he seemed to think Josh might agree with him.

"Josh is going back to Chicago," Paisley said into the silence.

But no. He wasn't. He was going to marry her. She may not have a mother anymore, and she certainly didn't have a father, but she was going to be a daughter-in-law. She was going to finally have the relationships she should have been born with. He reached for her hand to unite them against the enemy. Her cold fingers trembled in his grasp. Though it wasn't only her hands, was it? Her whole body trembled. She feared her father.

"I'm staying," Josh said. "But you need to leave, sir." Before Josh lost all pretense of respect.

Sheridan stepped away and raised his hands. A sneer twisted his lips. How had Josh ever thought he had a contagious smile? "You're kidding me, right? She owes me. Paisley owes me. After all those years of medical expenses. Do you know how much insulin costs? It's not cheap, son. Being self-employed, I had to pay for the insurance myself. And now this?"

And now what? Paisley didn't owe him anything. He was talking like a horse-breeder, not a parent.

"You think she owes you a grandchild?" Speaking the words out loud made Josh even angrier. "You think you deserve to be a grandfather when you haven't even been a father?"

Mr. Sheridan stilled. His head tilted to face Josh. His gaze, razor sharp. "Is that what she told you?" he hissed.

Josh let go of Paisley's hand to step in front of her. He crossed his arms. "She didn't have to."

The man slammed the side of his fist against Big Red. "Well, I'm not her father anymore. I'm disowning her." He raised his voice. "Do you hear me, Paisley Therese? That's a stupid name, anyway. Therese. I never liked the Norwegian in your blood. But now it's all you can claim, because I'm disowning you."

Josh stepped one foot forward with the intention of shutting the man up. The ice scraper dropped to the snow beside his feet and two hands bunched in the back of his jacket to hold him in place. Was Paisley protecting herself or protecting him? It didn't matter. If she felt safer with him standing there, he'd stay put.

"You know what?" Sheridan pulled his keys from his pocket and walked backwards as he spoke, though Josh couldn't be sure whether the man was talking to himself or them. "I can still have a son. It's not too late for me. I'll remarry. I don't know why I haven't done this before. Probably because I didn't want another woman to take care of." His eyes connected with Josh, and he spoke louder. "But no woman could be as much of a letdown as Paisley."

The tension on Josh's jacket slackened, but any thoughts of chasing away Sheridan vanished as the small body behind him leaned against him for support. Going after the raving lunatic would mean leaving Paisley alone. Her father would be gone soon. While Josh was there for good.

He turned to wrap his arms around her. She continued to shake. He rubbed his gloved palms up and down her arms, though he should really get her back inside in front of the fire. Eventually thoughts of her father would fade.

A truck door slammed behind him and an engine revved. About time.

He kissed her damp forehead then closed his eyes and held her to him. He wouldn't ever let her go through this again.

His heart lurched as the 4x4 rumbled away. How had Paisley put up with that man? How had Josh ever admired him? All the while Sheridan had charmed strangers and impressed them with his beautiful ranch and knowledge of horses, he'd treated his wife and child worse than the animals. It was as if the man would have rather spent money on a vet than pay doctor bills for his own daughter.

Josh's eyes flew open with a thought. Insurance. For insulin. She must have been diabetic. Is that why she couldn't have children? Is that why she'd been sick the other day?

His stomach knotted.

If he'd known she was diabetic, he might have given more credence to Sam's suggestion that she was the girl he'd kissed at prom. But she couldn't have been. Because he'd told her that story the night before, and she hadn't said a word.

His heart thumped in his chest. Or was that her heartbeat he felt?

He had to know for sure. Not about the heartbeat, but about the girl. The one he'd been looking for all these years. If she was Paisley . . .

He lifted his hands to her shoulders and pulled away to look her in the eyes. Her gaze darted down, sideways, down again, finally at him. There was no relief her father was gone. There was no brokenness from the way he'd treated her. Sure, she couldn't have been as shocked by her father's behavior as Josh had been, but that wouldn't give her a reason to veil her expression. The only reason for the wariness in her eyes was if she was afraid he'd found out something she hadn't wanted him to know.

Those eyes. Those amber eyes. He pictured them behind a lacy, feather-embellished, royal blue mask. "It was you."

CHAPTER TWENTY-TWO

She licked her dry lips rather than respond. Where was her lip gloss?

He'd put the pieces together like she knew he would, but the confusion in his eyes told her he still didn't understand. Would he be hurt? Angry? Relieved to know she couldn't have children before he made the mistake of telling her he loved her?

Because he didn't really love her. And even if he did, loving her wouldn't be enough.

He waited quietly for her to admit it, though his countenance spoke volumes. He wasn't going to drop the subject. She had to confess.

"Yes," she whispered.

His hands rose to frame her face again. Though he wasn't leaning forward to kiss her this time. He was studying her to figure out how reality fit with memories.

She almost asked if he was disappointed. Almost. But she couldn't bear to hear it from his mouth. Not after the way her father berated her.

Sure, he'd stood up for her when dear old Dad was doing the criticizing, but if he stayed, he'd someday feel the same way. Mom always told the story of the day she'd met Dad. He'd swept her off her feet. He romanced her like no other.

Paisley knew Mom only told that story to remind herself how she had once loved the man. He'd made her feel so cherished that she'd ignored the advice of family and friends. She'd refused to listen to Grandpa Johan's warnings. More than anything, Mom had wanted to feel cherished again. So she kept getting pregnant. Kept miscarrying. Kept making herself sicker and sicker. Until she'd gone into diabetic ketoacidosis and never recovered.

Josh's gaze warmed her. Her cheeks almost burned from it. Or maybe that was from the shame of him knowing.

"Why didn't you tell me?" he asked.

Because it would pop the bubble of hope he'd felt at having a mystery woman to believe in. Because she didn't want to see the disappointment in his eyes when she didn't live up to his hopes. And because it wouldn't change anything.

She rocked back on her heels to keep from leaning into him. "In . . . in high school, I thought you knew. I thought you kissed all the girls the way you kissed me. And when you came back to work on the ranch after prom and acted like nothing had happened between us, I figured you ignored them afterward the same way."

His lips parted. The sheen of pain over his eyes turned to awareness. "That's why you were always so snotty." One side of his lips turned up.

She felt his smile. It made her want to smile. It made her want to laugh. In this crazy moment after having her father disown her and having the man she loved realize she'd been hiding her feelings for a decade—when she should have been running away toward the cabin or at least rebuilding the wall around her heart—he made her want to laugh. "I was *not* snotty."

Now both sides of his mouth curved deliciously. "Not to anybody else, but you were to me."

She didn't want to like him so much. Not then. Not now. But not now for a whole different reason. Not now because he was a good man, and he did care about her. And she could never be with him. "I figured you could handle it."

He shook his head, scrutinizing her but probably seeing all their past connections and misconnections. "I never would have gone to Boise State or Chicago. I would have stayed and taken over my parent's Christmas tree farm to be close to you."

Now he was being ridiculous. Playing a game she couldn't join. She pulled his hands down from her face and stepped back. "You hated Santa. And you hated taking care of trees. Sam told me you couldn't even keep a cactus alive."

He shrugged a shoulder, but the intensity in his eyes told her he would have made the sacrifice to be with her. It told her nothing else in his life mattered if he had her.

But that intensity wouldn't last. Couldn't last. Eventually she wouldn't be enough. And he'd be stuck with her. Stuck with regrets.

She buried her own regret deep inside, deep enough that it couldn't tempt her to make a terrible choice. "You don't want to stay with me, Josh."

He looked at her like she was crazy. It would have been funny if it weren't so sad. "I've never wanted anything more."

She choked out a laugh. The kind that sounded condescending. The kind that would echo in her nightmares. "Just because you found out I'm the girl you kissed in high school? Grow up."

He jerked like she'd slapped him. "I was going to tell you I loved you before I knew about prom. I fell in love with you as a woman, Paisley."

He had. And he was. And she'd been about to tell him she loved him, too. But she couldn't now. Not when he thought she was everything he'd always wanted. Not when he was about to give up his whole life for a fantasy. Not when she was stinging from the reminder of her failure as a woman. He deserved more than that.

"Goodbye, Josh." The words rang in her mind. Echoed through the emptiness inside.

"What? What are you doing, Paisley?"

She couldn't stay there and face off with him anymore. She had to get away. "Sam can drive you to The Coffee Cottage."

"No. I'm not leaving."

Then she would. Blood pounded through her veins as she turned and ran. The snow slowed her pace, but at least it would slow his, too. She listened for his footsteps. Would he chase her? Did she want him to?

He'd catch her. Spin her. Kiss her. Melt her resolve like ice in sunshine.

She charged faster, legs pumping against gravity, oxygen burning her lungs. Wind bit at her face, drying her tears. She'd had her last kiss with Josh. And she should thank her dad for preventing any more.

Preventing her from trapping Josh in a relationship he would later regret no matter how he felt in the moment.

"Paisley," he called. He sounded too close.

She refused to look back. She'd beat him inside. Use Sam as her shield. Lock herself in her room.

She pounded up the steps and flung the lodge door open. She dug in her pocket for the sharp, metal truck keys.

"I knew Josh wouldn't leave." Sam stepped out of the kitchen holding a bowl and spoon, but the triumphant gleam in his eye faded as he watched her fly across the room. "What's wrong?"

Paisley tossed the keys. They'd be hard for him to catch with his hands full, but he had more time to retrieve them than she did. "You're driving Josh to his car."

"Um . . . why?"

She didn't answer but picked up speed, her wet boots screeching against hard wood as she headed down the hallway. Sprinting inside, she slammed the door and fumbled with the lock in slow motion the way she'd only experienced in nightmares. But she'd never dreamed of this. Never dreamed she'd be running from the man she loved—the man who claimed to love her. No, she'd never been so scared.

Footsteps pounded in the great room. Josh or Sam? It didn't matter. She had to get that lock twisted.

The thing finally budged in her numb fingers. Twisted. Locked. She leaned against the door and tried to listen over the sound of her panting.

WHAT WAS SHE RUNNING from? Josh had dated a lot of girls in his life but never had one snuggling in his arms one second then sprinting away the moment he told her he loved her and wanted to be with her. It was usually the other way around.

Now that everything was out in the open, there should have been nothing standing in the way of a relationship. He knew she was the girl he'd kissed as a teenager. He knew she had diabetes. He knew she couldn't have kids.

That one was rough, but there was always adoption. And really, with the childhood she'd had, she should see the value in rescuing kids from abusive or neglectful environments.

Oh. Her ranch. That's why she was turning it into a camp. She wanted to save kids.

Did she think she had to do it on her own? Had that Nick fellow been as much of a dud as her dad? Had he dumped her when he found out he'd have no offspring?

Josh ground his teeth and added Paisley's ex to the growing list of people whose faces he'd like to smash for hurting her. Of course, he'd hurt her once, too. But he hadn't meant to. And as soon as he told her he wasn't going to leave her the way Nick had, she'd let him fix all that. But first he had to catch her.

He rushed through the cabin door she'd left open. Sam stood by the kitchen counter, retrieving keys from a bowl of ice cream. Which was weirder—that Sam served himself a bowl of ice cream at nine in the morning or that Paisley had tossed her keys in it? It didn't matter.

"Where's Paisley?"

Sam pointed toward the hallway. "What'd you do to her?"

He followed Sam's directions and shouted over his shoulder. "I told her I loved her."

"Dude," Sam called after him. Probably every bit as confused.

Her door was shut. Did she think he'd simply get in Big Red and ride away? Did she know him at all?

He rapped his knuckles against smooth wooden planks. "Paisley, what's going on?"

She sniffed. Right on the other side of the door. Why was she crying? Delayed shock over her dad's disownment?

"Honey, you don't have to be alone anymore." Alone. The word haunted him. He'd felt alone when he'd lost his job but never like this. Never in the way that every member of his family had either died or disowned him. Never in the way he'd never have another living blood relative.

Sam appeared at the end of the hallway, a dish towel in his hands. They looked at each other, awaiting Paisley's response.

Her voice squeaked a couple times before the words came out. "I have to be alone."

His heart hiccupped. Had he heard right? Why would she think that? "Hon, just because your fiancé was an idiot—"

"He wasn't." Her words held no hesitation this time.

Why was she defending her ex? She was alone because of him.

He looked to Sam. Sam shook his head.

"I don't understand." Josh frowned at the door between them. They needed to be having the conversation face to face. She needed it as much as he did. So she could see the sincerity in his eyes. See his compassion. His adoration. See he was nothing like the schmuck who broke her heart.

She sniffled. And for a moment it didn't sound like she was going to respond. "I ended the engagement, not him."

Josh reeled at the news. What had the man done to make her end it with him? She'd said Nick wasn't an idiot, so it couldn't have been that bad. Maybe it was because he wasn't the right man for her. Maybe it was because she'd loved Josh all this time and couldn't marry someone else.

Right. Josh was dreaming again. Only this time he had a face to go with his dream. It wasn't pretend anymore. It was real life. He knew exactly who he wanted to spend that life with. And he'd known before he even realized she was his dream come true.

His dream would come true. He was good at this. Good at selling things. Good at persuading others to want what he wanted. Good at getting the girl.

But he had to figure out what was in his way. At the moment it had something to do with Nick.

"Why did you end your engagement?" He wasn't going to say Nick's name. It was always better to act as though he didn't have a competitor, as though his choice was the only choice.

"For the same reason I can't be with you."

The oxygen caught in his lungs. Because it was impossible to sell to someone who wasn't buying. He had to figure out why. He had to know her argument. Had she even discussed her infertility with her fiancé? Or had she made the decision for him?

If only Josh could knock down the door and kiss her. She couldn't argue at all when she was kissing.

He laid a palm against the door. Leaned his forehead against the slick wood. "Why is that?"

"I can't give you a family."

"I want *you* to be my family."

Her sob shook the door. Shook him. Made a lump form in his throat.

"I'm . . ." Her words were thick and probably as hard for her to say as they were for him to understand. "I'm not enough."

"Paisley." His heart ached for her. Tears rained down. He hadn't cried at all when Bree broke up with him, but these weren't tears for himself. They were tears for her. He only wanted to love her, and she wouldn't accept it. She had to let him in. Or she really would be alone the rest of her life. "Please let me in."

"I can't," she choked out in a way that told him she really believed it.

"Yes, you can."

"I'm not coming out until you leave."

"I'm not leaving until you come out."

Were they going to do this all day? All week? All month? She had to come out sometime.

Maybe she'd come out sooner if he soothed her fears. "Hon, I'm not like your dad. The man doesn't know what love is."

No response.

If she was listening, he'd keep talking. "*My* parents know about love. They have a happy marriage. They aren't perfect, and they could easily hold each other's imperfections against one another—blame the other for not giving them everything they want. Heck, they drive me crazy sometimes."

Sam chuckled. Josh sent him a warning look. He didn't want Paisley thinking she was being laughed at. He wanted to lure her out, and he refused to let anything scare her into staying hidden.

So he continued. "But when it comes to marriage, both my parents think they got the better end of the deal. They both value one another above themselves."

He could hear her breathing. As if recovering from a jog. Or working up the nerve to paraglide off Bald Mountain. Was she working up the courage to open the door?

"I value you, Paisley. Not because of what I want from you. But for who you are. You don't have to do anything to have value." Did she understand that? Had anyone ever shown her that before? "You could run away from me and lock yourself in another room, and you'd still have value."

She giggled then. A sad little giggle. One that bubbled and popped with thick saliva and tears. But it was something.

He smiled at the door. Imagined he could feel her body heat through it. She was closer now somehow.

"Do you value me?" he asked.

He never would have asked in the beginning. Not when he was already feeling worthless. Not when she'd seemed so put out by his presence. Not when she made snarky remarks about his possessions and track record with women. But something had changed. And it wasn't only getting his job back. Paisley had been the one to show him he didn't need all that stuff, and he didn't need to be liked to be worth something.

He held his hand above the doorknob, ready to rush in the moment she admitted her feelings and unlocked the door.

"Yes," she said.

He closed his eyes in relief. Even though he knew she'd say yes, it was still a risk to be so vulnerable. Tension drained from his limbs, out his fingertips and toes. In a moment he'd be able to wrap his arms around her and know he'd finally found a home.

"I love you too much to let you stay here with me."

CHAPTER TWENTY-THREE

HER WORDS RIPPED THROUGH HIS GUT, clawed his peace, and knifed his hope. He looked at Sam in disbelief. She wanted him to leave because she loved him?

Sam's shoulders slumped. He held out an arm as if to say, *what can you do?*

Well, he wouldn't give up. He never did. That's what made him so successful in business.

He lifted his hand to slam it against the door in frustration, but he caught himself. If she was going to be reasoned with, he'd have to use words. "That's not fair, Paisley. I should get some say in this."

"You did."

"What?" She obviously hadn't been listening.

"You explained love to me." How could she sound so calm? It was like she threw a grenade in his camp then sauntered away unharmed. She wasn't conflicted anymore. She was decisive. "It means putting the other person first. I'm putting you first. I'm refusing to let you sacrifice a family."

"You're kidding." She'd completely missed his message.

"You're a Lake. You're surrounded by family. All your brothers will have kids." She paused. "Even Sam someday."

Sam cleared his throat. "I'm not having kids."

Josh glared at him. "Go away, Sam." Not only was his brother not helping the situation, but he just reminded Josh of how he'd originally thought Sam and Paisley were perfect for each other. And now he was finding out Sam didn't want to have kids and she couldn't have kids. If Josh left, maybe the two would end up together after all. The image scraped his soul, jagged and sharp. "We'll discuss your issues later, bro."

"Anyway," Paisley continued, in a voice as light as it was fake. "I'm not going to take that away from you."

Did she hear herself? This was like that Christmas story—*The Gift of the Magi*, except worse. At least in the story when the woman cut off her hair to buy the man a chain for his pocket watch and the man sold his pocket watch to buy the woman hair combs, they had each other in the end.

But was her sacrifice really about Josh? Or was she still afraid she wouldn't be enough? Afraid he'd treat her with contempt because she couldn't give him a son? Afraid she'd risk her life in pregnancy and end up dying like her mother?

He'd never do that. No loving person would do that. How did he make her understand?

"Honey."

"Stop calling me that." Her voice cracked.

He'd keep calling her that if it would break her. "Honey is an endearment. It's a term used when you care about someone very much. Like how your grandpa called you his treasure. Why wouldn't I use it?"

"Because I'm not yours."

So cold. So distant. It couldn't be what she wanted. "You could be."

Nothing. Not even the heavy breathing anymore. She was locking off her heart the way she'd locked off her room.

Sam scuffed his slipper.

Josh slanted his gaze and tilted his head a couple times to tell his brother to get lost.

Sam waved him over.

Josh bulged his eyes. This wasn't the time.

Sam motioned him away from the door again.

Josh couldn't leave Paisley now. Not when she was so recently wounded. She shouldn't be alone.

Sam stuck one hand on his hip and jutted his chin.

Fine. He'd see what was up. But then he'd come right back. He ran his hand down the plank. He didn't want to leave it. He didn't want Paisley to have second thoughts and open the door to find him gone.

She might feel abandoned all over again because he wasn't there and shut herself away a second time. "I'll be right back, Paisley."

His chest expanded as he held his breath. No response. His lungs deflated. He trudged down the hall.

Sam disappeared around the corner. Probably out of hearing range. The kid had military experience. Maybe he knew some tactic to get into her room. They could unscrew the doorknob. Or take off the hinges.

Josh couldn't keep the impatience from ringing through his voice. "What?"

"Give her some space," Sam whispered.

"Space?"

You didn't give a potential customer space. You didn't give them a chance to turn you down. You asked questions that only gave them the opportunity to answer how you wanted them to answer. For example: Do you want to get married in the summer or winter?

Paisley would choose winter. It suited her.

"She's got a lot to process."

"Well, yeah, but I'm here for her. We should be processing as a team."

"You're not a team."

Ouch. Couldn't Josh choose a wife the way he picked teammates in elementary school P.E.? Or at least the way he pitched himself to clients?

"You made a good pitch," Sam said as if reading his mind. "I loved the whole thing about Mom and Dad. It almost had me wanting to get married."

"This isn't funny, Sam." Time to get back to the door. Time to show Paisley exactly how long he'd wait for her.

"You're right." The humor faded from Sam's brown eyes. "It's pretty sad to see my big brother groveling."

Josh crossed his arms and glared. Sam had never been in love. He'd never slowed down enough to date anyone for longer than a few weeks. And he hadn't seen Paisley's dad come down on her. He wasn't aware of the cruelty she'd endured. "You don't know what you're talking about, Sam."

Sam twisted his lips as if to admit he wasn't the best person to give advice. "You're right. I'm not the one you should be talking to, Josh. You need to pray about this. Pray for Paisley. Then maybe read what the Bible has to say about love."

Gah. Memory verses assaulted him. Stuff about love being patient. Love having trust. Love having hope. Nothing about love being controlling. Nothing about forcing its way. Even if it was the best way.

God didn't do that. God didn't demand he make the right choices. God gave him free will and promised to still be there when he messed up.

But . . . but . . .

He leaned back against the cool wall and closed his eyes. This couldn't be God's will. God wouldn't bring Paisley into Josh's life only for her to push him away. God wouldn't finally reveal the girl Josh had been looking for since he was eighteen only to have her be out of his reach.

That experience had to be more like the prophecy that told the magi to look for the star. He'd been on a journey. And he couldn't stop here, could he?

Pressure formed in his chest. What if he was supposed to stop like the magi stopped at King Herod's? It took God's revelation to both the magi and the Israelites for the magi to be able to use their gifts for God's glory.

Would any of the Jews have believed Jesus to be their savior if they hadn't discovered it for themselves? If God hadn't given them direction, as well? Would Paisley's decision to let down her walls have to be more about hearing from God than being persuaded by Josh?

"Why, Lord?"

Josh didn't want to have to trust God to give him what he wanted. He didn't want to have to wait for God's timing with an ache inside that only washed away when the waves of God's love rolled in. He wanted the girl. He had to convince her she was enough.

But maybe it wasn't about *her* being enough. Maybe it was about God being enough.

Josh had a lot. He would be who Jesus was referring to when he talked about the rich. But the money wasn't enough. The career wasn't enough. A fiancée wasn't enough. It never had been. Maybe Paisley was right to worry she wouldn't be enough for him.

He tried to shake the thought away. Josh wasn't like her dad. Was he?

He had a chance to prove it. But that meant being satisfied even when he didn't get his way. It meant letting her go.

He had to overcome his own fear to allow her to overcome hers. The fear didn't want to be overcome. It knotted inside him. It curled his hands into fists. It threatened to strangle him.

But what was love without free will?

Josh's love life hadn't had much to do with free will. He'd chased a dream girl. He made the mistake of proposing to a woman who chased *him*. And now he found the one he wanted to be with, but she'd locked herself in her room.

On Christmas Eve.

Josh shook his head. Christmas wasn't supposed to be like this. But what was it supposed to be like? It started with Jesus being born into a world that would reject Him. Jesus was willing to give up His life for people who hated Him. He loved them despite the way they used their free will against Him.

Could Josh love Paisley that much? He had to. He had to love her enough to let her go.

He ran a hand over his face and opened his eyes with a cringe.

Sam stood there, looking down at him. He held out a small box wrapped in shiny blue paper with silver snowflakes. The necklace.

"I'm afraid." He was afraid she would never open it. He was afraid she would never wear it. And he was afraid she'd never allow herself to accept his love the way she wouldn't accept the gift.

The partnership that turned into friendship that turned into chemistry that could have turned into happily ever after. Was he going to walk away from it? Could it all be for nothing? She'd moved on without him before. There was a high possibility she'd do so again.

But it was a risk worth taking. Because even if she didn't choose him, his love could help bring her healing. That's what perfect love did.

PAISLEY LISTENED AT THE door. Was he gone? Had he left without saying goodbye? Isn't that what she wanted?

She reached for the handle to check. But maybe that's what he hoped she'd do. And he was waiting quietly on the other side. If she saw him, she'd crumble, and she couldn't crumble.

She was calm now. Confident in her choice. Strong enough to keep going without him. Or maybe she was numb. Running on cruise control.

She strode to the window to see if Big Red had moved yet. It hadn't, though Dad was gone. If only he'd never come.

She kicked off her boots with the intensity of kicking them at her father. Immature, but it was hard to stay calm with all the anger trapped inside. She shrugged out of her jacket. Maybe she was just uncomfortable because she was warm. Or maybe because she'd been sobbing on the floor as Josh professed to love her. As she'd professed to love him. That had been weak of her. But she always felt week whenever Dad came around.

Not that Scott Sheridan was her father anymore. He'd disowned her.

She huffed. She was finally free of him. Though free could be a lonely place.

She wiped at the grit under her eyes and checked the mirror to see if she looked like she'd been crying. Pink, puffy eyes stared back, more empty and anxious than she wanted to admit.

She pressed her hands to her cheeks the way Josh had been holding her less than an hour ago. How had she let herself get into this mess? She'd known he couldn't stay with her. She'd known there was no future together. Had she led him on? Or had she fallen for him and he'd caught her? That seemed to be her M.O.

"Paisley?" Josh.

Her traitorous heart expanded with joy. Her hands slid down to her chest to press it back into place, but they couldn't keep her lungs from rising and falling hard with each hiss of breath. What did he want? Well, she knew what he wanted . . . or what he thought he wanted. The real question was what did she have to do to get him to give up?

Part of her hoped he wouldn't give up. That he'd come around and bust through the window like Indiana Jones swinging from his whip and . . . and . . . and what? Bring her the Holy Grail to restore her health?

No. He had to go. Better now than after she'd become so addicted to his affection that she couldn't survive without it.

"Paisley, I hope you're listening."

She was. With eyes on the door and fingernails dug into palms. And the heaviness of despair.

"I'm going to go."

He was? He must have realized the logic in her argument. He must have agreed a relationship would never last. He wanted a family the way she knew he would.

She'd known it. But that hadn't prepared her to hear it. To picture him with a baby in his arms. A toddler climbing on him like a jungle gym. A preschooler dressed for the first day of class, clinging to his hand as they walked down a linoleum hallway that would be filled with paint-scented art projects every time Josh arrived to pick him up.

The energy drained out her toes. She wilted onto Grandpa's old plaid bedspread and fell over to her side, hugging her knees to her chest.

She wanted all that for him. She wanted it for her, too. She wanted it more than her dad had wanted it. She wanted to be part of the miracle of birth. But even more, she wanted to share it with Josh.

How ironic the Christmas story was about a woman whose pregnancy could have messed up her marriage. Had this been what Mary felt like when God's plans had not been her own? What had Mary said? *May your word to me be fulfilled.* That would have to be Paisley's prayer, too.

"I'm leaving you a gift."

Josh had bought her a gift. Sam had loaned him money when they went shopping. He still wanted to give it to her? Even knowing nothing could come of it?

She'd open the door after he left. Then open his gift—what would be a precious reminder of the time they shared.

"I have something to ask in return, Paisley."

She stilled. Waited. Dreaded what he might ask. She had nothing left to give.

"Imagine our places are reversed."

Imagine she was outside the door, and he'd locked himself in a room and was crying on the bed in a fetal position? That couldn't be what he meant.

"Imagine I was the one who couldn't have kids."

Her hand rose to cover her mouth. Why would he suggest such a thing?

"Imagine you loved me, but I wouldn't even talk to you because I didn't want you to sacrifice pregnancy to be with me."

Her gaze bounced around the room in confusion. Did the idea change everything? Or did it change nothing? It almost made her fear seem silly. Almost.

But she had a right to be afraid. Her mom should have been afraid.

"Would you still want to be with me if I was the one who couldn't have kids?"

She rolled onto her back, clutched her churning stomach, and stared at the exposed beams on the ceiling. Of course she would choose to be with him. She would make sacrifices for him.

She *was* making a sacrifice for him. But was it because she loved him or because she didn't think she was worth making a sacrifice for?

It didn't matter. She was doing the right thing. He could thank her later on when his son wore a bathrobe to play a shepherd in the living nativity or his daughter put on a tutu to perform in *The Nutcracker*.

"If you would still choose to be with me, then I ask you to give me the same opportunity."

If only it were that easy.

"I choose you, Paisley. Above all others, I choose you."

She couldn't let the words seep in no matter how she'd longed to hear them. They were like the scent of chocolate cake baking in the oven to a woman on a diet. Reveling in the moment would destroy all her hard work and the goals she'd set for herself.

Being in love was worse than dieting, though. Ask her mom. Paisley sank deeper into the mattress because she didn't have a mom around to ask anymore.

Silence. Then footsteps. Two sets. A door thumped shut.

Her body tingled back to life, though standing up and walking to the window felt more like a dream than reality. She watched Josh pick up his duffle from where he'd dropped it in the snow earlier and toss it into the bed of the pickup. He looked back at the lodge before climbing into the passenger seat next to Sam.

She didn't hide behind the curtains. He probably couldn't see her anyway. And if he did, it would be the last time he ever saw her. She hoped he would remember her. Even as he went back to his career and hung out with friends and fell in love with someone else, she hoped he would always have a place in his heart for her—the way you did a first love. Even if it took him years to find out who his first love was.

The engine revved and died. Her heart did the same.

If the truck didn't start, she might have to go out there after all. She closed her eyes and leaned her forehead against the cool, smooth pane of glass. It was too fitting. Too tragic. Yet ironic enough to wrench a laugh out of her.

"Why, Lord?" She'd prayed for His word to be fulfilled. Like the prophecies that led the magi to baby Jesus. Wasn't it God's will for Josh to leave? What if it wasn't? What if Big Red's engine issues were a sign, the way the Christmas star was a sign?

The engine clicked again then died, replaced by the stillness of a Montana winter. She normally enjoyed the quiet, but not when it was this thick and suffocating. What was God trying to tell her?

She'd also prayed for God to send her a friend the same day Josh arrived. She hadn't made the connection before because she'd considered Josh more of a foe at first. But they'd become friends. More than friends. And now she was sending him away. Like a gift being returned for store credit.

She bit her lip as she watched Josh through the window. Her temples throbbed. Was he out there feeling the same way? Perhaps he was praying the engine wouldn't start. How would he react if she ran to him? If she gave him that chance he'd asked for?

But she wouldn't do it unless he really was a gift from God. Could God love her that much?

The ignition turned over. Caught. Rumbled to life.

Big Red rolled away.

Paisley's exhale fogged the window. She pulled a hand inside the sleeve of her sweater to use the material like an eraser. To see if Josh was really leaving her. To see if God really allowed him to leave.

The scene that reappeared before her was a familiar one. Snow. The fence. The barn. Trees. Mountains. Blue sky. A lot of blue sky. But no truck. No Josh.

Her eyes welled. She closed them, her lids forcing tears to roll down her cheeks. But that was stupid. She'd been stupid to get her hopes up. She wiped at her face with her sweater, though it didn't dry her skin very well as the material was already wet from the window pane.

Josh wasn't her gift. God had already given her the ranch as a gift.

Gifts . . . Josh had given her a gift, too. She left the window to unlock her door and dig under the tree. But she didn't have to go that far. There in the hallway sat a little box with a silver bow on top.

Why did it have to be the size of a ring box? Her belly warmed. But it couldn't be a ring. They hadn't been at a jewelry store when he bought it. And he'd never spoken about marriage. He said he wanted to stay with her, but he never mentioned marriage. Except the one time when he said she might get married at Big Sky Chapel. Her stomach churned.

She bent over and retrieved the package. She held it in front of her and looked back toward the window. Would he know she'd be opening it right now? Would he be looking out the window as Big Red rumbled down the dirt road picturing her tearing into the paper?

What would she find when she did?

As a kid, Mom always let her open one present on Christmas Eve. This would be her one present. She'd pretend Mom was looking down from heaven. She'd pretend she wasn't alone.

She turned over the box and slid a finger underneath the paper to peel away the tape. She retrieved the leather box with a hinge. It wasn't the velvet kind that held a diamond solitaire. It was rugged and earthy. It was perfect.

She smiled at the box. She didn't even know what was inside, yet she already understood it wasn't going to be a meaningless trinket. It came from Josh's heart. He now had the money to buy her a matching Mercedes if he wanted to, but it wouldn't matter as much as this—as much as a gift he'd had to borrow money from Sam to buy. A gift that he wanted to give her even when he thought she had feelings for Sam.

Now that was love.

She clasped the top half of the box and pinched to lift it. There, nestled against recycled cardboard, lay a silver pendant—the outline in the shape of Montana with a star dangling in the center. The Bright Star Ranch logo.

She fingered the handmade necklace. It was her. But it was also him. His design of her home. A home that was lonely without him.

She carried the box to the dresser. She set it down with shaky hands and lifted the thin chain to clasp it behind her neck. Then she stared at the reflection.

Someday the ranch would feel more like home. She'd have her own kids. The ones who'd arrive on Monday and leave on Friday, but come back year after year. They'd ride horses, hike to pick huckleberries. and swim in the pond during the day. They'd sing around the campfire at night. And over s'mores they might ask, "You don't have any kids?" She'd say, "You're all my kids." And she'd clutch this necklace and remember how the star led the wise men to Jesus, and how Josh's star led all her children to her. That would be her gift.

CHAPTER TWENTY-FOUR

"You're doing the right thing," Sam told him for the third time, as he turned out onto the highway.

How would Sam know? Simply because he gave Tracen good advice about Emily earlier that year didn't make him a relationship guru. "Are you going to get Paisley to change her mind? Are you going to put a plane ticket to Chicago in her stocking?"

"You don't want that."

"Yes, I do." He wanted somebody to do something to keep Paisley from throwing away what they could have together.

"You don't want anybody to make Paisley do anything. That's manipulation. That's what you told me her father did to her mother."

Thinking about Paisley's father made Josh growl. "That man has messed up everything." Not only Josh's relationship with Paisley, but Paisley's relationship with herself.

"No, he hasn't. You're giving him too much power."

"*Paisley* is giving him too much power."

"Which is why she has to be the one to take her power back."

What if she didn't? Or what if she thought taking her power back meant never letting anyone else in again? "She needs me to be there for her."

"She knows you're there. She just doesn't know she wants you to be there yet." Sam slowed to round a bend. He spoke slowly, too. How could he be so calm? Probably because he'd never been in love. He didn't know the sensation of drowning that came after having a woman tie his hands behind his back and walk him off the plank.

What did Sam think would happen? She'd call? Apologize? Invite him to return to the ranch? Not the Paisley he knew. She was as stubborn as she was independent.

"I should have been there for her all along." He leaned against the seatbelt to rest his head in his hands. "She's the girl I kissed in high school."

"I know."

Josh froze. His gut twisted. He sat up and stared. What was wrong with his brother? This was the guy giving him guidance? And Josh was *listening*? "You knew?" He threw arms to the sides. "You *knew*? What else aren't you telling me?"

Sam flipped on his blinker to turn into The Coffee Cottage. "I tried to tell you."

Bah. Sam had made the suggestion then let Josh dismiss it. "You should have tried harder."

Sam shot him a quick glance before turning off the road. He lifted a brow. "She didn't want me to tell you."

The words rammed into Josh's stomach like a fist. Paisley was walling off her heart from him—him, the one person above all who wanted to protect it. And the more he tried to scale those walls, the more she'd believe him to be the enemy.

"I'm sorry, bro." Sam shifted to park and shut off the engine.

Josh was back where he first ran into Paisley. Where she'd almost refused to help him out. Where she'd made fun of his car. And where Big Red had trouble starting.

Why did the truck have to start today? Sam should have given up on the second try. Then Josh would still be at the ranch. Close enough that Paisley couldn't push him out of her mind. Close enough that he'd know if she'd opened up the gift he gave her. Close enough for her to watch him through the window.

She *had* been watching through the window. He'd seen her silhouette. Hoped it would disappear for a moment before she came running out through the snow to stop him. But it was too late. Now he had no choice but to drive away.

The Mercedes sat in front of him, reindeer antlers and all. His sleigh awaited. Ho, ho, ho. What kind of Christmas was this?

"I'll buy you a coffee to keep you awake," Sam offered.

Josh wouldn't need the caffeine to stay awake. He'd more likely need something to help him sleep when he got back to his condo. But he'd accept the coffee because it was one more delay. One more chance for Paisley to jump on Sam's rented snowmobile and block his exit. He climbed out of Big Red's heavy door and slammed it to make sure it closed properly.

Sam followed. "You sure you don't want to spend the holidays with Tracen and Emily in Sun Valley?"

And have to watch a couple of newlyweds kissing under mistletoe every time he turned around? "No thanks."

"What about flying to Florida to hang with Mom and Dad?"

"No time. I'm supposed to sign the contract with the computer company today." Not that he cared about the contract anymore. He cared more about family, but he'd see them at the Sundance Film Festival at the end of January. For now, he wanted to be alone. Alone with his thoughts. Reliving the last month. Imagining what Christmas could have been like if Paisley hadn't insisted he leave Bright Star. What Christmas *should* have been like.

Sam stepped ahead of him and pulled open the red door to the cottage. The rich scent of coffee beans floated out, along with excited chatter. Saying goodbye to the coffee shop owners was more important than actually getting a cup of joe.

Dot spun from where she was standing in front of a mirror, adjusting what might pass as a knit headband over her ears in a way that made her silver spikes stand up even wilder. She clapped her hands. "What do you think?"

About what? The headband? Josh eyed it closer. What was he supposed to think? "Nice."

"I made it myself. It's red, black, and white because I'm going to the Icedogs' game tonight in Bozeman." She leaned forward and cupped a hand around her mouth before stage whispering, "I'm going with Snake, but don't tell Sam. I don't want him to get jealous."

"I heard." Sam crossed his arms and smirked. "Lucky guy."

Dot giggled as if she were sixty years younger.

Good for her. Though thinking about someone else in a happy relationship made Josh itchy and uncomfortable, like the time he mistakenly gathered a bouquet of flowers and Poison Ivy for Mom on

Mother's Day. He'd think about Icedogs. What sport was that? "Hockey?" he guessed.

"Yep." She wove through the maze of tables and chairs to join them. "I've never been to a hockey game before, but I heard there's lots of punching." She swung her little fists around the air.

Josh couldn't help but smile. If he had to spend Christmas with someone besides Paisley, he would choose Dot. She'd cheer him up. Too bad he couldn't take *her* to Illinois. "Dot, if you ever come to Chicago, I'll take you to a Blackhawks' game."

Her arms fell by her sides.

What?

Annabel stepped out of the kitchen carrying a tray of yeasty-scented pastries. "Chicago? Why would you go back to Chicago? Don't you like it here?"

Her words rubbed at the fresh scab on his heart. "I love it here."

"You love Paisley," she corrected, no doubt in her tone.

He couldn't argue. He'd have to learn to hide his heartbreak better, or the whole world would look at him with the kind of pity he'd left Chicago to escape. "What gave me away?"

She sat the tray on the glass counter. "You kissed her back in high school, and you've been looking for her ever since."

His chin jutted forward. How did she know that?

Dot patted his arm. This apparently wasn't news to her, either.

He held out his hands and glared at Sam. "Am I the last to know this?"

Sam's eyebrows arched toward his hairline. All innocence. "I didn't tell them."

Annabel clomped across the floor. "The important thing is that you know now. And that you tell her how you feel."

Josh stuffed his hands in his jacket pockets and shook his head. "I told her I love her. She told me to leave."

Dot clicked her tongue. "I was afraid of that."

Josh narrowed his eyes. What else did these ladies know?

Annabel looked out the window. "I have to talk to her."

Josh studied the sweet redhead. He wanted to believe she could say something to make a difference, but he'd already tried. And Sam warned that Paisley needed to find healing for herself if she was ever going to be in a healthy relationship. "She's not going to let you tell her what to do."

Annabel marched to a basket full of yarn and knitting needles. She pulled out a poorly knit beanie and mittens. "I'm not going to tell her what to do. I'm going to tell her what I should have done."

Josh didn't know what that meant, but he couldn't imagine it would change anything. Annabel wasn't only single, she was old and single. Her life would be an example to Paisley of how one could live happily alone.

"I appreciate it, but—"

Annabel silenced him with a determined glare.

He blinked. The lady had a fiery side. And all this time, he'd thought her bright hair was a dye job.

"You need to get gas in town before you leave, right?" she asked.

Why? What tricks did she have up her sleeve? "Yes . . ." he answered cautiously.

She nodded, wrapped a holey scarf around her neck, and sailed under Josh's nose to grab her parka off the wall. "Sam, you hold down the shop. Dot, you're taking me for a snowmobile ride."

PAISLEY PULLED HER JACKET and boots back on. The horses probably didn't need to be fed yet, but she needed something to do. She stopped on the way to the barn to watch the skaters. Two giggly teenagers who kept falling down, a mother pulling her son along, and a couple skating hand in hand as if they were posing for the cover of a Christmas card. She hadn't thought about having to deal with cozy couples when she'd decided to follow Grandpa's plans for the skating rink. Though it wouldn't have bothered her then as much as it did now.

She'd kind of skated with Josh. Not because they were a couple, but because he was fun to skate with. He was fun to *be* with. His smile made her happy. His arms kept her warm. And his kiss . . .

She groaned and refocused on heading to the barn. She didn't want to think about it. But that didn't mean his kiss hadn't been better than she'd remembered.

Maybe it was only that good because she couldn't have him. Because she'd spent so much time trying to forget him that he was always at the forefront of her mind. Because it was a goodbye kiss.

Though kissing Nick goodbye hadn't been any big deal. It wasn't about Nick so much as it had been about leaving the kind of life she'd planned for herself.

Josh was not in the life she'd planned for herself, yet he'd shown up anyway. At least there were no more secrets between them. He knew why she couldn't be with him. And he'd eventually be able to accept the fact they couldn't have a happily-ever-after the same way he'd have to accept that he didn't need to keep looking for his dream girl. No such thing existed.

Though finding out how much their kiss at prom had meant to him had affected everything. It was like a drop of peppermint in a cup of hot cocoa. Life tasted sweeter somehow. More refreshing. More merry.

She slid the barn door to one side and welcomed the scent of hay and manure. This was her life.

Cassidy neighed. Paisley's eyes adjusted to the darker interior enough to see her favorite horse press her body against the stall to get closer.

It was nice to be loved. It was even nicer to be able to love back. She pulled her gloves off her hands to feel Cassidy's soft coat, as she brushed her hands along the hair. Cass nudged her with her nose, and Paisley held her hands beyond the mare's nostrils to heat her frozen fingers.

Paisley wasn't alone. She had Cassidy and Butch and Sundance.

"God gave me you," she said. Whereas Josh had been more like the horse he "received" at Christmas as a child.

The memory brought a smile to her lips. Why was it that some people got horses when other people really wanted them? Why was it that some people got babies when other people really wanted them? Why was it that some people got to fall in love and marry when other people really wanted to? Other people being her. She wanted that life. With Josh.

She fingered the necklace. "Josh gave me this," she told her horse.

Cassidy nudged her to get her to keep petting.

She sighed and reached her arms around Cassidy's neck. "You liked him, too, didn't you, girl?"

An engine revved outside. Not a car engine. More like a snow blower. Or a snowmobile. Sam's snowmobile sat outside, so it couldn't be Josh coming back for her. Probably more skaters.

"We've got a good thing going here, don't we?" She asked the horse. "It may not seem like much, but it will be. Bright Star Ranch will bring joy to lots of people."

Joy. Hard to imagine she could bring people joy when she felt so miserable. Why did she think she could do this again? Who was she to offer a camp for kids when she didn't know how to raise them? Who was she to offer a Christian retreat center when she didn't even want to celebrate Christmas?

She wasn't enough. Her own father didn't want her.

She buried her face against Cassidy's coat exactly as she had when her father called her mother worthless. She'd run out of their house. Cried. Asked her old horse Ranger for help.

Josh had overheard her that one time. She'd been so embarrassed. He'd asked if she was okay, and she'd rewound her words to consider them from his perspective. She hadn't really said much more than, "It isn't fair. It isn't fair." He hadn't known she'd been talking about another one of her mom's miscarriages. She'd tried to laugh at herself and claimed she liked to talk to her horses about her problems. That's when he suggested talking to God instead. Because God understood.

She needed someone to understand now, too. She needed her heavenly father. How amazing was it that Josh led her to Christ, and he didn't even know? He'd never know how much his life had touched hers.

"Father God?" She choked on the words. How could the creator of the universe love her as His child when her own father couldn't? Josh had said God understood. Could that be because God had been rejected before, too? He hadn't only been a father; He'd been a child in a manger, vulnerable and needy. He knew how she felt, and He knew what would heal her heart. "What do I do? I'm lost without You."

"Paisley."

Paisley jumped. Had she really heard a voice? Female. Older. Distant. But it sounded like it called her name.

Paisley turned toward the door. Who was looking for her? And why?

"Paisley," the voice called again. Stronger this time.

"In here."

A lone silhouette appeared in the doorway. Annabel? Where was Dot?

Paisley wiped up her tears before the woman noticed them. "Are you here to skate?" She hoped her voice sounded at least a little cheerful.

Annabel shook her head, her hair flying underneath a crooked beanie. She stepped into the darkness of the barn, moving slowly as if her eyes hadn't yet adjusted. "Dot is skating. But I'm here to tell you about your skating rink."

Paisley sniffed away the stuffiness left over from crying. Was her ice not up to Annabel's standards? Was that why she hadn't come out to use it yet? "What's wrong with it? Are people talking about it in town?"

"No, it's . . . it's wonderful."

Okay . . . Paisley scratched her head. Of all the times for Annabel to show up and play guessing games, why did it have to be today? It was Christmas Eve. Shouldn't the woman be hosting a white elephant gift exchange or dressing up like Mrs. Claus or something? "Do you need new skates? I was wanting to get you cowboy boots for Christmas, but if you prefer skates instead . . ."

"That's so sweet of you." Annabel wrung her hands together. "Your grandpa was sweet to me, too."

Grandpa? Grandpa Johan and Annabel? Paisley turned completely from Cassidy to study the woman more closely.

She was about Grandpa's age. And Grandma had been gone for a while by the time Annabel and Dot opened shop. Come to think of it, Grandpa had never gone out for coffee before The Coffee Cottage arrived. He'd used an old green percolator that he'd accidentally dropped and refused to replace with one of the "new-fangled" Keurigs. Maybe it hadn't been an accident after all.

But was that what Annabel was talking about? Was she the woman Grandpa had been dating? "What do you mean?"

Annabel took another couple of steps forward. "I mean he was going to build the ice skating rink for me. To get me out to the ranch more."

Oh. That *was* sweet. Grandpa Johan had loved spending time with her. "Oh, Annabel, I had no idea."

Maybe she should have suspected. By the way Annabel had called Paisley a "treasure" exactly like Grandpa had.

But not only was the story as sweet as a Nicholas Sparks novel. It was as tragic. Paisley spoke the tragedy aloud. "Grandpa died before he could get the skating rink going for you."

How had Annabel hidden such grief? How had she endured the loss? Paisley knew a fraction of what it felt like to lose a man she loved. But Josh hadn't died. He was simply going to live elsewhere.

"No." Annabel leaned her head to one side. "Johan had time to build me the rink, but I told him not to."

"Why?" Annabel didn't love Grandpa in return?

Annabel looked down. Then she looked up and stepped forward. Close enough to wrap one of her mittened hands around Paisley's icy fingers. Her eyes peered clearly into Paisley's. "I was afraid to love your grandfather. I'd decided not to love again after my husband died. I thought it would hurt too much if I outlived another spouse."

"Oh, Annabel." Paisley reached out and engulfed the woman's frail shoulders. If Annabel had taken that risk, she'd be Paisley's grandmother. Paisley would have family. Annabel would have family. Maybe they could still be each other's family.

Annabel rubbed her hands up and down Paisley's back. She smelled like a chocolate covered coffee bean. Paisley closed her eyes. She'd been praying for a friend, and now she had more than that. The woman would help her get over Josh.

Annabel pulled away but only far enough to grab both Paisley's hands and look up into her eyes again. "I missed out on a beautiful relationship because I was afraid. I protected myself so I wouldn't be hurt. But it still hurt when Johan died. I didn't prevent the pain. I only prevented the joy."

Paisley's heart burned in her chest, similar to the feeling of stepping into a hot springs after hiking through the snow. The thawing stung. It would be easier to remain frozen. But Annabel's words bubbled around her like the jets of a Jacuzzi. She hadn't come over to talk about the skating rink. She came because she knew Paisley made the same choice she'd made.

"Did Josh stop at The Coffee Cottage?" Paisley asked.

Annabel nodded.

"Did he ask you to come by and tell me this story?"

It was good. It was too good. It was the kind of thing an advertising designer might come up with.

Annabel shook her head. "Nobody knows this story but me. Dot doesn't even know."

The confession knocked another chunk of ice away. Annabel was really there on her own. Because she didn't want Paisley to go through the same kind of pain. But the older woman's life had worked out. Annabel had Dot. God would bring Paisley someone else. It could even be down the road when she was Annabel's age. Maybe she could marry a widower then. Because he would have already had children. The thought brought no relief.

Annabel squeezed her hands. "You can still have a happy ending."

Could she? She pressed her lips together and looked away. She wanted to believe. Oh, how she wanted to believe. But there was the echo of Dad's demands that if Mom loved him, she'd give him a son. There was the image of Mom lifeless in a hospital bed. "What if you're wrong?"

Annabel lifted a hand to Paisley's cheek and wiped away the tear she hadn't realized escaped. "I could be wrong. There are no guarantees in this life."

Paisley's shoulders slumped. She looked away. Why couldn't the woman lie to her and tell her everything would work out? That Josh's love would fill her every hole. That she would finally be complete.

"As the woman who could have been your grandmother, I'm going to tell you something your parents should have told you." Annabel's voice deepened in conviction. "You are fearfully and wonderfully made."

Paisley knew the Bible said that. But she didn't feel it. In fact, to have Annabel say it felt like a lie. "The fearful part fits." She laughed to keep from crying at the sad joke.

Annabel's gaze softened. "Well, I'm not God, but I think you're wonderful. You're strong. You're beautiful. You're smart. You're hard-working."

Each compliment struck at her heart with the force of an icepick. If she let Annabel keep going, there'd be nothing left but raw flesh, vulnerable to pain.

She added to the older woman's list. "I'm diabetic . . ."

"You're treasured."

Paisley looked down. She wanted to believe it, but—

Annabel's hand blocked her view. The woman's finger extended to reach under Paisley's chin. She lifted until Paisley was forced to look into her wise eyes, but she didn't stop there. She kept tilting until Paisley was staring at the rafters Josh had decorated with twinkle lights.

"Lift up your eyes and look to the heavens." Annabel released her hold, but kept her captured with a quote that sounded like scripture. "Who created all these?"

All these?

"He who brings out the starry host one by one and calls forth each of them by name. Because of His great power and mighty strength, not one of them is missing."

Stars. Again.

"Don't you think if God calls the stars by names, He cares for you too, Paisley? He treasures you?"

Paisley's tears rained down harder. "If anybody is a treasure it's you, Annabel."

Annabel's eyes glistened. "I'm okay. I survived another loss, and God is still here for me." She reached up to smooth a strand of Paisley's hair away from her wet face. "You'll be okay, too. If you decide to continue your life as a single woman, you'll be okay. You're going to make this ranch run. You've got what it takes. You're enough."

Paisley nodded. She took a deep breath. No more heart thawing, just a good old fashioned pep talk. God had blessed her with friends, a beautiful home, and a purpose. She had all she needed.

Annabel opened her arms wide like Vanna White revealing the prize on a gameshow. "But is this all you want, Paisley?"

The rest of the shell around her heart broke off like an iceberg. She crashed into the truth with the impact of Titanic.

She wanted more. Her throat constricted, but she choked out the word, "No." She shook her head. No, this wasn't all she wanted. She may have to deal with a disease that wouldn't let her have children. But God hadn't left her to deal with it alone. He'd given her a man who wanted to be there for her through it. God had given her more than she'd dared hope for. He'd led Josh to her ranch, and she'd almost missed it. "I want to share all this with Josh."

CHAPTER TWENTY-FIVE

"Joshua is heading into town for gas. Hop on the back of the snowmobile with Dot, and she'll beat him to Highway 64."

Highway 64? They might beat him taking snowmobile trails, but Paisley would have a better chance if she rode through the trees. "I appreciate your offer, Annabel, but I have another idea."

Paisley grabbed a saddle. Cassidy neighed. But she wasn't taking Cass out this time. She'd take Butch. Not only was he faster, but he was the horse Josh rode. And Josh had been wanting his own horse for Christmas for a very long time.

A smile started within and grew until her cheeks burned with it as she bridled and saddled the magnificent animal. This was what it was like to love. And it felt a whole lot different from locking herself in a room, pretending to protect someone else when she was the scared one.

Josh was right that her parents never taught her about love. Annabel had taught her more about it in one moment than her parents had taught her in a lifetime. She'd taught Paisley that in order to fly, she might have to crash a few times.

Paisley was created to spread her wings. To soar. To rise above.

A rush of adrenaline surged through her veins as she stepped a foot into the stirrups and mounted. She gripped the reins and sat tall.

"Pray for me, Annabel."

Annabel held a hand to her heart. "I've been praying for you since before we met."

Where would Paisley be without the woman? More tears welled up. Paisley had thought she was alone, yet God had never left her. He'd provided someone to step into the shoes Grandpa left behind. He'd known what she'd needed before she did.

"All this time you and Grandpa called me a treasure." Paisley turned the horse in a circle to keep him from trotting out the barn door. "For the first time, I feel valuable."

Annabel stepped away from the horse's impatient hooves. "Your value doesn't come from me or Johan. It doesn't come from Josh. It comes from God, and you have to accept it from Him before you can accept it from anyone else. Then you can accept He has good things planned for your life."

Paisley reached for the pendant resting against her chest. The star was a symbol the magi followed to bring treasure to baby Jesus. They honored Him for loving them enough to come into the world and meet them where they were at. Jesus would meet anyone where they were at. That was the real treasure.

"I accept." Too bad she hadn't been ready to accept the meaning of God's gift before Josh left. Before she had to ride after him. But nothing would stop her now.

Annabel patted her leg. "Go get 'em, treasured one."

Paisley squeezed her legs together to signal Butch she was ready. As they trotted through the barn door, she pushed to an almost standing position and leaned forward along Butch's mane to duck out of the wind.. Butch seemed to sense her urgency. They glided together across the snow, hoof beats racing her heart beat.

She was doing this. She was really doing this. She was chasing down the man she'd always been afraid to love.

He'd said he loved her. He said he wanted to spend the rest of his life with her. He said it was okay if she couldn't have kids. It was still scary, but scary in a good way. Scary in the way that even if he didn't catch her when she fell next time, she knew God would.

But then there was also a part of her that felt safe. A part that knew she could trust Josh. A part that knew he was a better man than her father. And if he didn't drop her, if he didn't let her down the way she'd feared, life was going to be better than she'd ever imagined it could be.

Josh had said he wanted her to be his family.

She pinched her lips together to keep from sobbing as the possibilities washed over her. The possibility of having in-laws.

Sam had always felt like a brother. Now he was actually going to *be* a brother.

And Josh's older siblings already had kids. That meant she was going to be an aunt.

And Josh's parents were going to be her mother-in-law and father-in-law. A couple who loved each other in spite of each other.

And then there was the famous sister-in-law. The one who'd changed her holiday plans to help Paisley raise money for the ranch before they'd even met. Would Paisley be invited to the Sundance Film Festival in Utah? She knew if it was up to Emily, she would be.

What were the odds? An hour ago she wouldn't have even considered it.

The tiny speck of a town grew in the distance. She had to make it. She had to catch Josh before Butch ran out of energy.

Her ragged breaths puffed into the frigid air, but she wasn't cold anymore. Her thighs burned and sweat beaded on her brow.

Butch continued to climb through the snow, his muscles rippling under her touch. "You can do this, Butch. You can do this."

What if they didn't make it? She could try to call Josh, but coverage would be spotty. She might not get hold of him before he boarded his plane.

She'd ride to The Coffee Cottage. She'd have Sam drive her to the airport in Bozeman. If she missed him, she'd get the first flight to Chicago. Because if she didn't have to be alone anymore, why would she choose to be alone on Christmas?

Sam wouldn't mind. He'd watch the ranch for her. And she'd make sure Dot and Annabel took him pastries for breakfast. She'd promise to buy him lots of ice cream when she returned.

She laughed at the idea. Sam was like a big kid, and she needed to know how to take care of kids when her camp started.

Her joy turned poignant. She could have kids now. No, not biologically. But she and Josh could adopt. She'd have the stability and family to offer a child. An unwanted child. Like she had been.

The lure of doubt wiggled inside her as if she'd swallowed a worm on a hook, but she wasn't going to be caught by fear again that easily. She didn't know what the future held, but she knew God treasured her. And a little insecurity couldn't keep her from opening the gift He'd prepared for her that day.

The gift came in the form of a silver Mercedes with antlers pulling out of the gas station ahead. Josh had left the antlers on. That had to mean *something*.

Her pulse throbbed in her temples. She leaned forward farther and straightened out her spine even more as if it would get her across the field to the street sooner.

"Come on, Butch. Almost there."

She had to get Josh to see her before he disappeared around the bend in the road. She willed Josh to look over his left shoulder.

The little sports car handled the snow pretty well. Too well. She'd been gaining on him, but now that he was headed out of town, he was able to pick up speed.

"No." She panted. "Help, Lord. Please help me catch him."

But it was too late. The coupe slowed long enough to round the corner toward The Coffee Cottage. Then it shot out of sight.

JOSH JAMMED HIS FINGER against the power button for the radio. On his way to Big Sky from Chicago, he'd wanted to listen to songs like "Blue Christmas." Now he didn't want to listen to anything.

Annabel had acted like The *Miracle on 34th Street* was going to become *The Miracle on 64* when she'd left to talk to Paisley. He'd been absurd to hope. He couldn't put his hope in anything but God. So he'd spend the flight home in prayer. He had some making up to do for all the years he'd been going his own way.

"What now, Lord?" He'd heard once that it was hard to listen to God when you weren't at wit's end, because you had so many other options. Josh had no other options now. He wanted God's will for his life. Nothing else. "I need direction."

He stepped on the gas to blow past The Coffee Cottage. So many good memories there. It hurt to think what he was leaving behind.

A snowmobile darted from the trees toward the coffee shop, but it stopped in the middle of the dry road. Red hair flew underneath the helmet of the second rider. Annabel? And . . . ?

Josh slammed on the brakes to slow. But even as he gripped the steering wheel tighter, his palms itched with excitement. Was Paisley with her? Had the coffee store owner succeeded where he'd failed?

The front rider pulled off her helmet. Spiky, silver hair stood on end. Dot.

Josh waved the women out of his way. Annabel stood. Climbed off the machine.

He'd have to go around them. There was nothing more they could do for him.

Motion to his right caught his eye.

Sam?

What was the kid doing? Running towards the road, waving his arms? He was going to get himself hurt.

Fine. Josh would stop. Until he could get the fruitcakes to go back into the nut house.

Then he'd head home for Christmas. Though Chicago didn't feel like home anymore.

He rolled to a stop on the highway and shifted to park. That's when he heard it.

Horse hooves. They weren't just clopping along like when pulling a sleigh. They were pounding the road like in a Western movie. He could almost hear the theme song to *The Lone Ranger*.

Did Josh dare look in the rearview mirror? Was God really going to answer his prayers in the form of a woman riding a horse after him? Or was he still dreaming?

He held his breath and flicked his gaze to the rearview mirror. Sure enough. Paisley's tiny figure rocked above the image of Butch slowly cantering his way.

He dropped his head against the heated leather headrest that had once seemed so important to his happiness. The old Josh had worked hard to prove himself. The new Josh had found everything he'd ever wanted simply by being still. Now all he had to do was open his door and embrace the best Christmas gift he'd ever received. He couldn't keep from grinning all the way to the toes of his ridiculously expensive boots.

Sam, Dot, and Paisley stood in front of his windshield, their smiles every bit as wide.

The horse hooves slowed.

Josh gripped the handle. He swung the door wide and stepped into the road. Good thing traffic was light for the holidays.

He bolted out of the car and pivoted to face the woman on the horse. He didn't know what had changed her mind. But one thing was for sure, they'd come a long way since they'd met at the coffee shop the week after Thanksgiving.

"Paisley Sheridan. What are you doing here? Aren't you supposed to be on top of a Christmas tree this time of year?"

Her pink cheeks flushed even darker. She bit her lip as she pulled on Butch's reins to halt a few feet away. She swung one leg over the saddle and joined him in the middle of the road, then reached over to stroke the heaving horse's neck. "Good boy, Butch. You did it." Her head tilted his way and her eyes narrowed. "I've heard that line before. You're going to have to do better."

Oh-ho. Josh lifted his eyebrows. Even after she'd chased him down on her horse, she was still going to act all sassy. He loved her for it.

He looked over his shoulder at Sam and the gang. If they wanted a show, they were going to get a show.

Josh stepped forward, bent down on one knee, and took Paisley's hand.

Her eyes flooded but continued to sparkle. She squeezed her fuzzy mittens against his fingers.

Sam whooped. Dot clapped. Annabel giggled.

Josh took a deep breath of crisp air. He used to be so suave. He used to charm. He used to make people feel good about themselves so they would like being around him. But that was before he realized that the only people whose love mattered were those who accepted him for himself.

Paisley liked to tease him for his quirks. She liked to laugh at his eccentricities. And he loved listening to her laugh. With as long as it had taken them to get to this place, they'd either have to laugh or cry.

Her head bowed to focus on him. Her lips curved up. Her eyes sought his but not with uncertainty or longing. They flashed with satisfaction.

He felt it, too. There they were in the middle of a Montana road. His car dressed like Rudolph. His brother and fan club cheering him on. Yet there was nowhere else he'd rather be. And there was nothing else he could think to say except . . . "Is your name Christmas? Because I want to merry you."

She threw her head back, her laughter ringing like bells through the clear blue sky. An actual answer to his question wouldn't have been any sweeter.

He rose to join her and wrap his arms around her back. And he couldn't help but brush his lips across hers once. Twice. A taste of forever.

Sam and Company cheered. A car horn honked.

He ignored it all to lean his forehead against hers. "I'll propose again for real after we pick out rings. I just want you to know I'm serious about staying here in Big Sky. I'm serious about you."

She grinned up at him. "I was hoping you'd still say you were serious about me, though I wasn't expecting a proposal today."

"No?" He'd propose every day for the rest of his life if it meant holding her like this. But this had to be a once in a lifetime moment. She'd ridden after him on horseback, for St. Nick's sake. "What changed your mind? What had you chasing me down?"

"I realized that truly loving someone means giving to someone even when you don't know if you're going to get anything in return."

Walking away from Paisley had been the hardest lesson of Josh's life. He would have preferred for love to be a sales pitch. He would have preferred a money-back guarantee. But then he would have missed out on the joy of receiving it as a gift.

She leaned away, and his heart throbbed at the loss of intimacy until she lifted a hand between them and pulled her Bright Star necklace from inside her jacket. "Thank you."

It looked perfect on her. Not only did the size of the charm and the length of the chain hang around her neck as if it was made for her, which it had been, but it symbolized who she was created to be. She was beautiful, wild, and tough like the state of Montana. And her determination and passion for life shined brightly like a star.

The piece had cost more than he'd been able to afford at the time, but it had been worth every penny. And now, it was only the beginning of the gifts he would love to lavish on her. "Do you like it?"

She relaxed back into his embrace, her face softening, her eyes radiating with a wonder he doubted would ever get old. "You couldn't have gotten me anything better."

He hugged her tight, promising to outdo himself next year.

She pushed against his chest. He didn't want to let her go, but they'd have to get out of the middle of the highway sometime. He'd follow her lead.

She reached for Butch's reins. "I have something for you."

"You do?" She hadn't put a package with his name on it under the tree. He knew because he'd checked before he left. It had hurt to think she hadn't cared enough to want to give him something for Christmas, even though what he'd really wanted was her heart.

"I do." She held the reins out to him.

Did she need him to hold Butch while she dug a package from the saddle bags? He gripped the leather straps in one hand and watched and waited.

She stood there, watching him as well.

He gave a confused smile. He didn't mind staring at each other, but he got the feeling he was missing something.

She held a hand over her mouth.

Laughter burst from behind him. Though with Sam, it sounded more like a guffaw.

Josh twisted around to quiz his brother with a look.

Sam shook his head in disappointment. "She's giving you the horse, dum-dum. She's giving you what you've wanted ever since that Christmas I was in kindergarten."

She was giving him Butch? Sure, Josh had told Paisley that story, but he'd never imagined . . . In fact, he was more shocked now than he had been to wake up at age seven to find a horse in his front yard. He spun to face Paisley and confirm Sam's words.

She beamed up at him, her warmth as inviting as the huge stone fireplace at the lodge. It was like he was a kid again, running to retrieve his stocking on Christmas morning. Though Paisley was giving him something Santa never had.

Josh looked at the Fjord in a new light. He swallowed over the lump forming in his throat. "You're giving me Butch?"

She stepped forward and wrapped her arms around his waist. "I'm giving you everything."

More squealing and cheering from their audience as he cupped her face like blinders on a horse to make sure he had her full attention. "The Bible says every good and perfect gift is from above. I will treasure you like the gift you are, Paisley Therese."

Her eyes shimmered with unshed tears. "*Min skatt?*"

"*Min skatt.*"

The thing he'd learned about Christmas this year was that God had already given him everything. God was enough. Which meant Paisley was a cherry on top of the sundae. Or, more appropriately, the star that lighted his way.

The End

And Now . . . for the REST of the story . . .
and a few little things you might enjoy

Discussion Questions

1.) Though Paisley forgave her father, she still had to deal with believing lies about herself as a result of the abuse. What are some lies you've believed about yourself?

2.) Paisley is scared of getting hurt again, and in her efforts to protect herself, she teeters on the verge of treating Josh abusively. Have you ever hurt someone else as a result of your own pain?

3.) Paisley's pain is more than emotional. She has a physical ailment, as well. Why do you think God allows disease? Is there any good that can come from it?

4.) Josh is used to getting whatever he wants. How can this lead to manipulation in life?

5.) Josh doesn't know what he wants anymore while Paisley knows she won't ever have what she really wants. Have you ever fallen into either of these categories? How so?

6.) Sam gets stuck in the middle between Josh and Paisley. In such a situation, is it best to stay involved or remove yourself entirely? Would you have handled Sam's circumstances any differently?

7.) Dot and Annabel enjoy their lives despite the fact that they are living Plan B. When is a time that you've had to accept Plan B for your life? What did you learn through it?

8.) Annabel becomes a mentor to Paisley, using herself as an example of what not to do. Have you ever had to learn something the hard way but then were able to use your experience to help others?

9.) Josh had been looking for Paisley for a decade without realizing it. Do you think their love story would have been as powerful if it had all worked out from the beginning? Why or why not?

10.) The Star of Bethlehem played a role in bringing Josh and Paisley together. Have you ever looked back in your life to find that God had been leading you all along and that He knew exactly where you needed to end up from the very beginning? And/or have you ever missed God's direction for your life?

A Sneak Peek at Book Three—*Finding Love in Park City, Utah*
Releasing Spring of 2017

CHAPTER ONE

C.J. Lancaster checked her watch as she ran across the street of downtown Park City, Utah. If she weren't so rushed, she might enjoy the quaint storefronts that lined the valley between mountain peaks. Instead, she had to dart around tourists and hurdle snowbanks.

Thank goodness fur-trimmed boots were acceptable apparel for journalists at the Sundance Film Festival, though she was still freezing from the unfamiliar sting of icy air. Only one more block to go, according to the concierge at her hotel. Problem was, she was supposed to have been at the festival base camp fifteen minutes ago for her interview with actress Emily Van Arsdale.

C.J.'s breath fogged up her aviator glasses, and she whipped them off to wipe on her scarf. She squinted against the blinding reflection of sun on bright snow and continued her race down a walkway between two shops. Strands of leftover Christmas lights dangled from the wooden canopy overhead, and a couple of tourists stopped to pose for pictures with a bear sculpture on a bench. C.J.'s stomach churned at the sickening sweetness of it all. Was life really that perfect for some people?

A crossing guard in an orange vest raised a baton to keep her from crossing the next street. She stopped but bounced side to side with nervous energy. The bun she'd twisted on top of her head, in her frantic preparations for her flight out of L.A. that morning, tugged at her scalp with each hop. She didn't even want to think about how messy she looked.

The crossing guard lowered his baton and waved her through. "Have a great day, ma'am." Even the crossing guards were happy in this town.

She jabbed her sunglasses on and forced a smile to her lips. She could do this.

A couple of huge white tents welcomed her to her destination. She flashed her credentials hanging from a lanyard and entered the courtyard dotted with heaters and fire pits. There. The tent on the right. She fought the current of bodies flowing the opposite direction.

Oh no. Did that mean the Q&A was over? Had she missed her interview? All that work for nothing?

She spotted a bright orange jacket signifying a festival volunteer and rushed the woman's direction. "I'm here for my interview with Emily Van Arsdale."

The woman shrugged and pointed to another volunteer wearing a headset.

C.J. squeezed through the throng of bodies. She flashed her badge again. "I'm with Star News, and I'm a few minutes late for my interview with Emily Van Arsdale. Do you think she would still see me?"

The gentleman with silver hair shot her a grin. "I'm sure she would if she was here, but she left for the next film showing." His southern accent dragged out the words, making them almost sound charming. But they weren't.

C.J. groaned. Her head fell back, and she closed her eyes. Mac, her boss, wanted the article about Emily more than anything. But expecting her to catch a 7AM flight after waking her up at 3AM to let her know she was going to be filling in for a sick reporter was not the way to get it. Of course, Mac wouldn't take any of the responsibility. He'd say she'd failed to complete the task he'd hired her for. Should she even try to write another article that day, or should she simply head to her hotel room and let her aching body catch up on sleep?

The volunteer cleared his throat. "I bet you could talk to Emily at Redstone Cinema. You might even be able to watch her film. They reserve seats for the press."

Now those were charming words. C.J. lifted her head and stared at the man, hoping to gauge the validity of such a claim.

He looked away and spoke into his headset like one who held authority. When he looked back, there was a twinkle in his eyes. He obviously loved what he did. She might as well try to enjoy her job, as well.

"How do I get to Redstone?"

Sam Lake bit into his concession stand ice cream bar and surveyed the insanity that had become his brother's life since Tracen married Emily. Lines of people filled the theater lobby and wove through the maze of velvet ropes. There was a line for pass holders who'd paid thousands of dollars to be the first to get into any film they wanted. Then there was the line where ticket holders could wait up to two hours before the film began. Then there was the wait list line in case any seats were left after the pass holders and ticket holders had been seated.

All those people in all those lines stared and pointed and took pictures of Emily from where she hid out at the table behind a grouping of potted plants. No wonder Tracen always wanted to hurry home to his cabin in Sun Valley, Idaho.

In fact, at that moment Tracen was looking longingly through the glass doors toward blue sky and white mountain peaks where the Olympics had once been held. Sam knew the feeling of longing, but he refused to look. After falling off a ladder and breaking his ankle when removing Christmas lights a couple of weeks ago, he'd had been sentenced to surgery and a few months in a walking boot. There would be no more snowboarding for him that winter.

"Sam." Emily's tiny frame scooted beside him. She spoke quietly as if not wanting to be overheard by the mass of humanity. "Will you be my bodyguard so Tracen can go snowboarding?"

Bodyguard? Sam had been a soldier in the Army, a wildland firefighter, and a ranch hand in the past few years, but he'd never been a bodyguard. Might be kind of fun. "What do I have to do?"

"Not much. Just give Tracen reassurance I'll be safe. I mean, I know you'd rather be snowboarding, yourself, but . . ." Emily shrugged.

She was trying not to rub it in since his accident had shattered his pride even more than it shattered his ankle. Playing the role of bodyguard could make him feel useful again. "Sure, I'll be your bodyguard."

Her shoulders visibly relaxed. "Thank you so much. I think Tracen needs a break if he's going to make it through tonight's opening party."

Sam tossed his Popsicle stick into a nearby garbage can and licked the sweet, sticky remains of vanilla ice cream off his lips. He smiled at the image of his brother dressed up for a glitzy party. Tracen hadn't even worn a tuxedo to his own wedding. "That's a good idea."

Emily beamed and squeezed his bicep before stepping away to talk to Tracen. Sam was the only other Lake who'd arrived for the festival so far. His two oldest brothers and their families would be coming later in the week for future showings of the film and the awards ceremony. Mom and Dad were supposed to fly in that night. Then there was Sam's brother Josh and his fiancée, Paisley, who would be taking their parents back to Montana after the festival to help Paisley finish planning a Valentine's Day wedding.

Sam was happy for Josh, but not happy about being the only single Lake brother left. As the baby of the family, he'd probably get stuck at the kiddie table in the giant cabin they'd all be sharing for the next two weeks. Maybe he'd reenlist in the Army after Josh's wedding. That is, if the military would take him with the screws and plate in his ankle.

Tracen joined him and clamped a hand on his shoulder. "You sure you can handle her?" he asked.

Handle Emily? Emily could handle herself. Sam was only supposed to make sure Tracen didn't worry about not being there with her. "I'll keep the paparazzi away," he promised.

"You'll give them the boot?" Tracen joked.

Sam shook his head at the bad pun. "Too soon."

Tracen stepped backwards and rubbed his hands together. He didn't even look like he'd heard Sam's response. He was already mentally preparing to shred the mountain. "Thanks, man. I'll see you guys at dinner."

Sam nodded. It wouldn't be so bad. He'd get to know his sister-in-law better. He'd have great seats for the documentary about the athlete Emily helped her mother train for the Rio Olympics in the sport of trampoline. And heck, he might even be on the big screen himself as he'd lived with Tracen and Emily for a while. That kind of made him a celebrity, too, didn't it?

Sam took his position as sentinel and crossed his arms to look out at the crowd. Any of them could be celebrities. Or future celebrities. Maybe Tracen wouldn't be the only Lake brother to date an actress.

Except, Sam really shouldn't be dating if he was going to reenlist. Military and marriage hadn't mixed too well for his buddies. And Sam had yet to meet a woman he would be willing to give up his freedom for.

An argument erupted at the doors to Theater One where Sundance volunteers had begun "loading" for Emily's documentary. A skinny woman in fur boots and a navy blue scarf waved a badge at the ticket taker. The ticket taker shook her head then pointed Sam's way.

The woman turned. Removed her sunglasses. Focused past him to where Emily was conversing with her mom and the film director. Then the woman made eye contact with Sam.

Her expression faded long enough for him to see the wrinkles of weariness, but then it changed. Her eyes widened. Her chin lifted. Her shoulders squared. And her lips turned up as if in absolute delight.

He blinked in the brilliance of it. And he couldn't help smiling a little bit himself. Because she was headed his way. And he was going to get to play bodyguard after all.

C.J. wanted to throw a fit. She wanted to drop onto the ugly blue carpet of the cinema lobby, kick her feet, and wail at the unfairness of life. She didn't want to be here. She didn't want this job. She had so many more important things to do than interview the rich and famous to make them even more rich and famous.

But as she wasn't rich and famous herself, she had to work. She had to make her boss happy. And she'd come so close to achieving her goal that she wasn't going to stop now. If Emily Van Arsdale's tall bodyguard with the watching eyes and mischievous smile didn't let her charm her way past, she was ready to punch him in the gut. It might not help her get her story, but she'd at least feel better.

"Hey," he said in a deep voice that matched his muscles. His arms were crossed, but his expression was open. Maybe even curious.

C.J. took a deep breath of the nauseating, popcorn-scented air. "Hey."

She stopped in front of the man and tried to keep from peeking past to see what Emily Van Arsdale was doing. C.J. had also spotted a gray-haired woman. Could that be Emily's mother? They both had the same bright blue eyes.

The bodyguard's eyes were brown. Dark brown. And they studied her. What did they see? She could feel her bun drooping to the side. Definitely not professional. She reached up to pull out the pins and shake her hair loose. Her scalp ached. She massaged. That felt a little better but hadn't helped her get closer to Emily. Now what?

She'd ask a question. "Are you here to watch Emily Van Arsdale's documentary?" There. He'd have to talk about the actress now.

"Yes. Are you?" One of his eyebrows lifted in a challenge as if he knew she hadn't been allowed inside the theater.

She should kick him right there. Though playing the damsel in distress might get her farther. She dropped her head to one side and softened her voice. "I didn't get a ticket in time."

The man clicked his tongue and shook his head, but he seemed more entertained than sympathetic. "There will be other showings. You've got two weeks to try again."

She narrowed her eyes. Oops. She was supposed to make him want to rescue her. Make him want to impress her enough to introduce her to the actress. She turned her glare into an eyelash flutter. "Yes. There's always hope."

The man smirked. "Big Emily Lake fan, are you?"

Emily Lake? Oh yeah. The actress had gotten married and changed her name. C.J. would play along. "Yes. Big fan."

The man's gaze dropped down to her credentials for a second. Had he seen her media pass? "Are you sure? Because you didn't even know her last name."

Well, that route wasn't going to work. C.J. could knee him to get past to Emily, or . . . she could take advantage of that spark of interest she'd heard in his greeting. As long as his interest wasn't the kind of interest that caused traffic to rubberneck around a car accident. Her life had pretty much become a train wreck as of late, but hopefully her state of being wasn't so obvious.

She held up her hands. "You caught me. I was actually looking for an excuse to come over and talk to you."

His warm chuckle seared her frayed nerve endings. Her ego was already fragile enough without his mockery, but perhaps he wasn't mocking. Perhaps his laughter meant he was enjoying her attention. Not all men were like her ex-husband, were they?

Should she laugh along with him or blush and run? He wouldn't be able to catch her with the cast on. What kind of body guard wore a cast, anyway?

He held out his hand. "What's your name?"

Her heart tripped over the idea of touching him. But it was a hand shake. A formality. She slid her palm into his, and the heat of it soothed her nerves even more. Again, what kind of bodyguard was this guy? Shouldn't he be cold and intimidating?

She pulled her hand away and balled it in the pocket of her pea coat. "I'm C.J. Lancaster. And you are?"

"I'm Sam Lake."

Lake? Oh no. C.J.'s hand came out of her pocket to cover her mouth. She'd hit on Emily's husband. She was never going to get the interview now. She might even get blacklisted from the festival. Mac had warned her that could happen if she monopolized Q&A sessions, but he'd never mentioned this. This was too horrible to even imagine. C.J. would have been better off punching the guy.

Sam's perfect white teeth flashed as his crooked smile grew. "I'm Emily's brother-in-law."

"Oh . . ." She let out her breath in a whoosh. Her hand dropped from her mouth to his forearms still crossed in front of his chest. Shoot, she was touching him again. She pulled her hand away but checked for a wedding ring on his finger. None. She wasn't in danger of becoming "the other woman" after all. If she was ever going to date again, she'd have to make it a habit to check for wedding rings. Rookie mistake. "That's . . . that's good," she said.

Her gaze rose up to meet his. Did he know what she'd been thinking, or could she possibly salvage her plan to get past Sam to speak with his sister-in-law?

His eyes sparkled. "So, what does C.J. stand for? California Journalist?"

Warning bells rang in her head. Abort. Abort. "No. I . . . uh . . ."

"You're the reporter who missed your interview, aren't you?"

He knew. She had to humble herself and plead her case. Maybe he would understand. "Yes. Though I wasn't the reporter scheduled to be there. Gretchen got sick, and I found out at 4 a.m. that I had to fill in. I didn't make my flight, and since I got here I've been running all over town trying to find Emily. Now I've found her, and I'm begging you to let me talk to her. I'm sorry I pretended otherwise. My boss really wants this story, and I really need my job."

Sam ran his fingers through thick, dark hair, and she realized she was clutching his other arm. She dropped her hands to her sides and moved back. Clinging to him wasn't going to help her cause.

A woman in an orange jacket stepped next to them and waved to the people behind Sam. "Emily, we've got the theater loaded, and I'm here to escort you to your seat."

Oh no. C.J. wouldn't have time to talk to Emily now. Though maybe there was an extra seat for her, and they could talk after the show. Sam could make it happen if he wanted to.

Emily and the gray-haired woman stepped closer to walk past.

C.J. turned. If she reached out she could tap Emily on the back. She could plead her case to someone she hadn't already embarrassed herself in front of.

Sam's hands settled on her shoulders and slid down to her biceps to hold her in place. Her muscles tensed. If ever she was going to elbow him, this was the time.

But Emily's blue sky eyes looked C.J.'s way, and C.J. froze.

Emily smiled before glancing up at Sam. "No rush, Sam. I'll save your spot."

"Thanks, Em." His voice was so low. And so close to C.J.'s ear. It gave her shivers, which was silly considering their situation. Maybe she was cold.

C.J. watched Emily Lake walk away. She'd wasted a whole day. She should have gone back to her hotel room and crashed. She would now. There was the opening night party she could attend that evening, but it would be pointless if Sam was going to keep her away from the biggest star there.

Sam's hands dropped from her arms. "Do you have a card?"

She blinked at the request. He wanted a card? As in a business card? She spun to face him and scratched her head. "What?"

He lifted a shoulder. "My brother is pretty protective of Emily. He wouldn't want me to let just anybody interview her."

Her lips parted. Sam was still considering her request? She studied him now. He was handsome enough to be a movie star himself. Maybe he was. Maybe he'd been the one to introduce Emily to Tracen. C.J. knew nothing of this guy except that he could open the door she'd been trying to break down.

What was she waiting for? She gripped the slick plastic pocket at the end of her lanyard and dug for one of the business cards she'd stuffed behind her media credentials.

"I studied journalism at UCLA," she gushed. "And I had a job with the Times for a while." If only they'd had another position for her. She held out the card, hope bubbling in her chest. "I quit to pursue writing biographies, but . . . uh . . . that didn't work out. So now I'm with Star News."

Sam took the card. His eyes rose to meet hers.

Her heartbeat drummed louder. She babbled on to pretend her excitement was all about the story. "You can read my work online and decide if you think I'd write a good article about Emily or not. Then you can . . . call me." She was only there for the story. Only talking to Sam so she could do her job.

He nodded and pocketed the card. "I'll call you."

Her breath caught in her throat, which, if she was honest with herself, she would admit was a reaction that had nothing to do with a silly interview.

A Note from the Author

Dear Reader,

I hope you enjoyed Josh and Paisley's story as much as I did. It's a sequel to *Finding Love in Sun Valley, Idaho*, which I wrote eight years ago, and it was as absolute delight to get to hang out with the Lake brothers again. As I hadn't originally planned to write a sequel, I started by rereading *Finding Love in Sun Valley* to remind myself what kind of character Josh was. The things that stood out were his work in advertising and his history in rodeo. So I wrote a story that combined both worlds.

Setting the story at Christmas brought joy to my soul. I share a birthday with my mother five days before Christmas, and my daughter was born two days after Christmas, so it's a special time of year for me. But that also makes it easier to get drawn into the busyness of the season and miss the meaning. I wanted to dig deeper into the nativity story to bring it alive in a new way. Studying the history of the Star of Bethlehem made for a perfect example of how God leads us when we are looking for direction.

I haven't spent much time around horses, so I had writer's block trying to write about a ranch until my friend invited me out to her farm, which inspired me to research Fjord horses and include the Norwegian heritage. I also incorporated horse stories I'd heard before. The story of Josh asking Santa for a horse for Christmas and then finding one in his front yard Christmas morning really happened to my uncle.

Another real life influence for my novel were the ladies at my church who inspired the characters of Dot and Annabel. These two women, Leslie and Rosie, bring me joy every Sunday when I walk into the bathroom after the service to find them cleaning with their pink and zebra print rubber gloves. They are a blessing as they treat every church guest like a celebrity. Leslie really does have a tattoo on the back of her head, though Rosie doesn't wear pink cowgirl boots—she wears neon high tops.

I had fun with this story, but it broke my heart at parts, too. My daughter came home from school one day to find me crying in front of the computer. "What's wrong, Mom?" she asked. I sniffed. "Paisley can't have kids." She gave me a weird look. "You know that's your fault, right?" But I didn't stop there. I made it worse. I gave Paisley a fearful heart that believed the lies she'd been told in an abusive relationship. And that is really the point I wanted to make through the whole book because it's a lesson I'm still learning myself.

This book isn't about forgiveness. There's lots of books on that subject. This is about the work that has to be done even after we forgive. Because the emotional wounds are real. And if we don't find healing, we can get ourselves into more bad relationships or sabotage good relationships. If this is you, I recommend finding a Christian counselor and consider reading Leslie Vernick's book, *The Emotionally Destructive Relationship*. The book defines seven types of heart issues that will destroy relationships. Paisley had *"The Fearful Heart."* And just like she overcame it, you can overcome, too.

Warm wishes,
Angela

You can learn more about Angela here:

www.angelaruthstrong.com
www.facebook.com/groups/1557213161269220/
twitter.com/AngelaRStrong

Angela Ruth Strong's Books

Resort to Love Series
Finding Love in Big Sky, Montana
Finding Love in Sun Valley, Idaho
Finding Love in Park City, Utah

Suspense
Presumed Dead
Love on the Run (False Security)

Fun4Hire Series for Ages 8-12
The Pillow Fight Professional
The Food Fight Professional
The Snowball Fight Professional
The Water Fight Professional

Body and Soul Series
Lighten Up

www.ingramcontent.com/pod-product-compliance
Lightning Source LLC
Chambersburg PA
CBHW071008190525
26915CB00022B/252